I0547136

THE DEAD OF JERUSALEM RIDGE

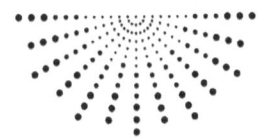

THE DEAD OF JERUSALEM RIDGE

A PIPER BLACKWELL MYSTERY

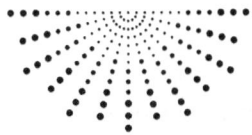

JEAN RABE

Boone Street Press

The Dead of Jerusalem Ridge
A Piper Blackwell Mystery
Jean Rabe

Boone Street Press

Boone Street Press
Illinois

Cover design by Juan Villar Padron

Interior design by John G. Hartness

Editing by Christine Verstraete and Janet Deaver-Pack

Boone Street Press

First Boone Street Press Edition: 2020

Name: Rabe, Jean, author

Title: The Dead of Jerusalem Ridge, a Piper Blackwell Mystery / Jean Rabe

Description: First Edition. Boone Street Press

Identifiers: ISBN 13: 978-1-7325267-2-3

LCCN: 2020908852

Printed in the United States of America

Praise for *The Dead of Winter*

Mystery just got a little less cozy in THE DEAD OF WINTER.
— *New York Times* and *USA Today* bestselling author Steven Savile

Jean Rabe delivers a suspenseful morsel that not only celebrates the Yuletide season, but also keeps you up at night with a well-crafted mystery. THE DEAD OF WINTER is chilling indeed!
— Raymond Benson, *New York Times* bestselling author

THE DEAD OF WINTER was a blast—lots of fun to read! Jean Rabe's characters come to life through the written word, and it takes a real writing talent to accomplish this feat.
— Denise Dietz, *USA Today* bestselling author

Praise for *The Dead of Night*

Jean Rabe always manages to surprise and never fails to deliver the goods! THE DEAD OF NIGHT has plenty of twists and turns. Highly recommended!
 — Jonathan Maberry, *New York Times* bestselling author

Jean Rabe writes the perfect mystery! I was kept guessing about *everything* to the very last word. Great characters. The girl can write!
 — *New York Times* bestselling author Faith Hunter, writing as Gwen Hunter

In THE DEAD OF NIGHT, Jean Rabe gives us another compelling Piper Blackwell mystery. After a clandestine meeting with a grizzled WWII veteran "Mark the Shark," also known as "Mr. Conspiracy," Piper stumbles, literally, over the bones of a child. Rabe weaves Piper's investigations of this long-cold case and the high-tech theft of an old man's earnings into a thoroughly satisfying and complex novel with deeply realized characters and beautifully vivid writing.
 — Jaden Terrell, Shamus Award nominee and internationally published author of the Jared McKean Mysteries

Praise for *The Dead of Summer*

Just when you think you've read the best from author Jean Rabe, she throws the thrill ride of a lifetime into her latest mystery. THE DEAD OF SUMMER starts with a bang, a scrunch, a twist, and screams... lots and lots of screams. The book hooks you from the start.
— Mary Cunningham, author of the Andi Anna Jones Mysteries

Jean Rabe immerses you in the sights, sounds, and smells of summer in rural Indiana, as she subtly weaves characters, clues, and high-speed action into a satisfying criminal confection worthy of a blue ribbon as Best Summer Mystery. Not quite a cozy, but a helluva whodunnit.
— Donald J. Bingle, author of the Dick Thornby Spy Thriller series

Sheriff Piper Blackwell's third outing has her getting on the wrong side of some very bad dudes in a murder investigation. The best thing about Rabe's series is not only her ability to spin a good yarn, but to write such believable and interesting characters that her books are like visiting old friends. They're all back in this newest one, and it'll keep you turning the pages far past your bedtime. Don't miss it.
— Michael A. Black, author of *Blood Trails*, *Legends of the West*, and *Dying Art* and *Stealth Assassins* in the Executioner series (as Don Pendleton)

For the Marys
Zalapi
Konczyk
Bamford

CHAPTER ONE

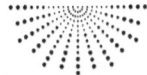

3 P.M. SATURDAY, SEPTEMBER 5TH

The rain felt good, but it complicated things by erasing the tracks she'd been following. Coming down in a syncopated pat-a-pat-a-pat, soaking through to her skin, it pleasantly cooled her. The temperature was in the low nineties, and before this deluge blossomed she'd been sweating under all her gear.

Piper crawled through the spurge, coming to a swath of mud that stretched toward a row of beech trees with silver-gray bark that matched the color of the sky.

Pat-a-pat-a-pat-a-pat.

Shit, Piper thought. She'd have to risk cutting across open ground, making herself a visible target. *Shit and two is four and four is eight.*

She sucked in a breath, the fragrance of goldenrod making her stifle a sneeze. The raindrops were large, dimpling the mud in front of her.

Listening.

Nothing but the rain and the shush of small branches rubbing together in the wind.

One more breath and she skittered forward, staying low, the mud plastering the front of her khakis and long-sleeved tee, feeling the

1

ooze slip past the collars of her favorite L.L. Bean hiking boots to invade her socks.

The tunnel of beech leaves on the other side welcomed her.

Listening.

She thought she heard something—a heavy footfall maybe, a splash. Her imagination? She pictured the map nestled in plastic in her backpack, recalled its details. There was a creek nearby. How close? Something, some*one* had splashed in the creek. Her quarry?

A rifle rode on top of her pack, its stock touching the back of her neck. Piper reached for it, and then froze, listening more intently.

A Hercules beetle crawled across the back of her hand. Green and tan with black spots, an ugly long thing she wanted to fling away, but she didn't dare move.

Listening.

There! Another splash. Definitely someone in the creek. Followed by the sound of something bumping against something else.

Was her quarry careless? Or was he deliberately making noise to lure her in?

The beetle moved on and disappeared in a patch of moss. Smaller beetles scurried nearby and black ants worried at a rotting piece of bark, mindless of the weather. Gnats formed a miniature cloud under an umbrella leaf. The mosquitoes had vanished with the rain ... a good thing, she noted, as she'd not brought repellent. The scent of the loam was heavy here.

Piper held her breath and inched forward.

To her right she spotted an empty can, old and rusty, discarded a long while ago. Shame to leave trash in the woods. Just beyond it was a heel impression in the mud; the rain hadn't quite taken it. Recent and deep, from a big man. Piper saw another print and crawled faster as she unslung the rifle, rose to her knees, and peered through a break in the ferns.

Pat-a-pat-a-pat-a-pat-a-pat.

The creek was just past the tree line and down a short rise, a wide gray ribbon cut by rocks. Piper watched the rain attack its surface, spitting water back up, the near bank a smooth band of mud disturbed by fresh boot prints.

Her heart thumped. He had to be on the other side of the creek, probably hunkering down behind the foliage, waiting for her. The landscape was a smear of greens and browns shadowed by the dome of clouds and the storm. She couldn't see him.

But if he was indeed on the other side, he'd see her if she broke for the creek.

Shit, she thought. *No good option. No good way to circle around.*

Piper could wait it out right here, a reasonable spot, concealed by tall sawgrass and trumpet honeysuckle. The rain swirled the colors, darkened what had started out as a bright day, made it difficult to peer through with all the water running in her eyes. *I should've worn a hat, something with a brim*, she thought. *Should've taken that precaution.* Maybe her quarry had a hat. At least the downpour kept her cool, gave her patience. If she was lucky her quarry wouldn't be as patient. Maybe he'd—

A silhouette separated from the miasma of green on the other side of the creek. An expert shot, Piper could get him, but her maximum range was one hundred feet, and the target was beyond that. Too, the rain and wind would alter the trajectory.

She needed to be closer.

Piper's index finger teased the trigger.

Her walkie-talkie crackled softly; she'd turned the volume down as low as it would go. A voice came through the earbud: "Christmas! What's your position?"

She didn't know her position, not exactly. The map in plastic was out of reach. The area was wholly unfamiliar to her.

"Near the creek," she whispered. "Target on the other side."

"Only one target, Christmas?"

"Roger, Spaceman, just one. Eyes on him now."

"Me and Renegade are following two, and that leaves one unaccounted for. Hemi is—"

"On the fourth," came another voice. Hemi, Piper recognized his rasp. "I'm dogging him. I'm near the creek, too. All the mud. What an

3

awesome day we picked for this." A pause: "Where near the creek are you, Christmas?"

I don't know, Piper thought. *Somewhere along the damn creek.*

"My target's moving," she whispered. "I'm following to get in range."

She thumbed off the walkie-talkie, not needing the distraction of her teammates' chatter, and shimmied out of the brush, sliding on her belly down the rise, and jumping to her feet at the edge of the creek. The silhouette had moved farther away, hopefully didn't know where she was. The hint of success tugged at her thoughts.

Couldn't tell how deep the water was, not clear enough to see the bottom. But she spotted what was left of his boot prints in the mud at the edge. If he'd crossed here, so could she. Piper stepped in, then slogged across carefully, the water above her knees at the deepest part, the bed slippery and threatening her balance. On the other side she let out the breath she'd been holding and searched for his tracks. The mud had been disturbed here by something. Maybe an animal, or ... there, another heel imprint and a partial indent from the tread. A wide foot. And a dropped candy bar wrapper. She snapped it up and stuck it in her pocket, hated seeing garbage in the woods.

There were winterberry shrubs and milkweed on this rise, and she scrambled up the rocky ground and stayed low behind the bushes, turned on the walkie-talkie again and heard Spaceman arguing with Renegade, clicked it off once more and edged around the thickest clump.

Pat-a-pat-a-pat-a-pat.

No sign of the shape, just the dizzying blotches of greens and browns and more rain.

Shit and two is four.

"Christmas!" The shout came from behind her, Hemi. "Look out!"

Piper spied movement to her right, and she spun, nearly skidding back down the rise. Digging in her heels, she brought up the rifle and squeezed off four shots—three misses, but one nailed him dead center.

"Argh!" her target hollered, his own weapon falling as he dropped to his knees and slipped down the bank, landing splayed on his back at the edge of the creek, the blossom of dayglow yellow paint on his chest instantly diluted by rain.

Then a shot came her way, and a second. Both were near misses, the blobs of blue paint sailing over her head and bursting against a trunk. She turned toward the new source and lunged, leading with her gun, firing without really aiming, balls of yellow paint racing out of the barrel of her Splatterking.

Other guns opened up around her, the sound not unlike real weapon fire. The blue and yellow paintballs came from different angles, and Piper tried to mentally triangulate them. The blue paint was from the enemy. Someone was firing from behind an oak, and another—one of her comrades—was directly to the north under cover of some winterberries. Three rounds came at her from the west, one striking her leg and turning the muddy khaki a bright royal blue. The other shots missed and she stepped into a bush, ignoring the jabs of the branches, wanting the concealment it offered.

"Christmas! I'm hit." Hemi made a gurgling sound and through a gap in the leaves she watched him theatrically flop into the creek. Must have been a kill shot he'd suffered.

One down on her side, one down on theirs. Three more on each side remaining. She flicked on her walkie-talkie. "Spaceman," she whispered. "Renegade. Where are—" She didn't get the rest of the words out, interrupted by crashing, rustling, feet slapping the mud.

Piper stood and fired in that direction, two balls striking her target in the chest—both kill shots, but leaving herself open. She felt the impact of paintballs slamming into her back. One. Two. Three.

Kill shots in return, all of them.

Piper let the Splatterking drop, then she fell to the ground, a confirmed loss.

"I shot the sheriff," someone started singing loudly and off-key.

5

CHAPTER TWO

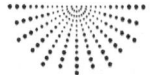

4 P.M. SATURDAY

Chief Deputy Oren Rosenberg was thinking about roast beef as he drove. His wife had put one in the crockpot this morning, a nice big sirloin tip, set it on low, and threw in carrots and a packet of onion soup mix. She would make the juice into gravy for mashed potatoes, and it would be ready at five-thirty. Oren was fond of roast, and when his wife cooked one it barely fit in the pot, even though it was for just the two of them. She said that way there would be plenty of leftovers for lunches the following week. His stomach rumbled in anticipation.

Oren got off work in an hour. Maybe they'd have a glass of wine with dinner, watch a movie on that big screen television—sixty-five-inch flat panel ultra HD—they'd bought on sale at the Owensboro Walmart a week ago. Then he'd work on one of his jigsaw puzzles in the den while she read a few chapters of a romance book before they turned in. Saturday evening was not exciting for the Rosenbergs, but it was a comfortable routine he looked forward to. Couldn't stay up late as he had to work tomorrow, too—his one weekend on this month.

Oren would turn sixty-six next week.

His wife had reminded him of that upcoming milestone over

breakfast. He didn't need the reminder; he damn well knew his own age. One year older than her. They'd attended high school together, but he was in the class ahead and he hadn't known her back then. They'd met after his military stint, set up on a blind date by a friend. They clicked, going out only four months before getting married. He kept a small photograph from their wedding in his wallet, not a touch of gray in their hair then, and no hint of wrinkles.

He was still taller than six feet. And now with a curly mass of steely hair and skin weathered by his time outdoors, Oren considered himself a young senior citizen, fit, and in better shape than a few of the deputies more than a decade younger. Hell, he even jogged once a week.

She'd probably mention retirement again at dinner.

Or if not tonight, then on his birthday. He hoped she wasn't planning a party with a big cake. He didn't want a fuss made.

She'd retired two years ago—too early in his opinion—and filled her days with trips to the library to pick up stacks of magazines and romances, fretting over various craft projects and completing about half of them, and baking things from recipes she spotted on the internet. Seemed boring and with little good purpose. At least she was happy. He loved her, truly, but he didn't want to spend more time with her and get sucked into her hobbies ... which is exactly what she wanted. What Oren wanted was to remain with the sheriff's office, even though he'd lost the election for the top spot last year and had to serve as chief deputy to a twenty-three-year-old. The sheriff was a year younger than his granddaughter.

Being in law enforcement gave Oren drive and kept him active. Twenty years with the Rockport Police, twenty-two with the sheriff's department here in Spencer County. He didn't want to do anything other than this. And he was good at it. He *should* have been sheriff, and he'd be sixty-nine when the next election rolled around. He wouldn't run again. No one would vote for a sixty-nine-year-old candidate. For governor or president, sure, geezers could run for those offices, but not for sheriff.

Maybe he'd retire at seventy. Tom Selleck was seventy-five, and he

7

played a police chief on television. Selleck looked good, active. Oren found some similarities between himself and the actor's *Blue Bloods* character. But Selleck had a lot more money than Oren. Not more handsome though, he thought.

Oren turned off the county road and pulled onto a long blacktop driveway, sat at the end a moment, studying his eyes in the rearview mirror. There were little lines all along the edges, creases in his forehead. No age spots. Tom Selleck probably had age spots that he covered up with makeup. Oren adjusted the collar of his shirt, radioed Teegan, the goth dispatcher, regarding his position, and edged his Explorer forward until he was even with the house. He got out and stretched, turned, and stared down the driveway directly across the road to a big white saltbox. There was a wooden sign in the front yard, also white, hanging from a post like a fancy realtor's notice. Oren guessed it was roughly three feet square and hand-painted, as a couple of the letters were crooked. It read: BUDDHIST CULTURAL CENTER. Two men in green overalls tended a garden in the side yard.

It was why he'd been called out to tiny Fulda ... that Cultural Center.

Oren stared at the saltbox a moment longer, nodded when one of the men in overalls waved to him, then he thrust his hands in his pants pockets, pivoted, and strolled up the sidewalk to the two-story house on this side of the road, a tan colonial with red trim and a small front porch with a canvas awning over it. He glanced up, the sky cloudy. It had rained a couple of hours ago, but thankfully the storm system had moved south. The awning sagged with the weight of water caught in it.

"Let's get this over with," he muttered.

Oren knocked on the door and wasn't surprised that it opened immediately. Chris Hagee had probably been watching for his Explorer to turn onto the driveway.

"Afternoon, Chris," Oren said.

"Oren." Chris stayed square in the doorframe, made no motion to invite Oren in. He let out a huffing breath. "Good to see you, Oren.

But I wanted to talk to Sheriff Blackwell. I specifically asked for the sheriff to stop by." A pause: "No offense."

Chris was younger than Oren by maybe ten years. He appeared almost frail next to the chief deputy, reed-thin with a shirt that was a size or two overlarge, dark circles under his eyes, pale complexion. Chris called himself a farmer, and he had been for many years. Now Chris rented out his land and let someone else work it. Looking at Chris made Oren double down on the notion of continuing with the sheriff's department; he didn't want to shrivel in retirement. Too, Chris drank. The scuttle was he always drank too much. Oren thought he could smell beer on the man's breath. But Chris was talking plainly, nothing slurred.

"Sheriff is gone for the three-day weekend," Oren said. "Went down into Kentucky."

Chris snorted. "Vacation? She took a vacation? She ain't been in office for more than ... what ... eight months?"

"Yeah, eight months, five days," Oren said.

"She ain't been in office long enough to take a vacation."

"Three-day weekend. Labor Day holiday Monday."

"I 's'pose." A muscle in Chris' jaw twitched. "Kentucky, eh?"

"She's with friends from her old Fort Campbell Army unit, some sort of reunion." Oren didn't need to offer any explanation, but the man was a real *kokhlefl*, and so he provided that little tidbit for Chris' gossip collection.

"I wanted to talk to Sheriff Blackwell," Chris whined.

"She'll be back in the county Tuesday. You can call the department then."

"Piss." Chris ground the ball of his foot against the threshold. "I don't want to wait until Tuesday, Oren. I waited long enough. Too long. I waited too damn long." He gestured across the street to the white saltbox. "Ain't right, a Buddha temple on my road."

"It's a center for the *Buddhist* culture," Oren gently corrected. "Like a retreat, I guess. They're within the county zoning laws. It's legal."

"Well, it's immoral. It shouldn't be there."

"Chris, you need—"

9

"I need for it to be gone. For *them* to be gone. I've been complaining about it ever since Anthony moved in there and hung up that sign. Six months going on seven. I've been bringing it to the county's attention for near seven months now. Wasn't so egregious at first, that temple." Chris made a fist, squeezing his hand so tight the knuckles turned snow white.

Oren was surprised Chris had the word egregious in his vocabulary.

"There wasn't no one come around the place at first," Chris continued. "There wasn't a sign at the beginning. It was just Anthony. All through the winter it was just him. And I liked him, Oren, back when he was a kid and lived there with his dad. Back before he went all weird after high school and moved to Thailand to be a Buddha. But lately, since … oh, say … the first part of May, maybe it started in April, yeah April … there's been up to a dozen people there. Some visiting for the day, some staying for longer. Looks like a couple of them are living there permanent. All men. Who knows what they're doing over there? Lighting incense, praying to a fat statue. Who knows what they're doing? Just men. I know it ain't right."

Oren shifted back and forth from his heels to the balls of his feet. He thought about the roast he'd be sitting down to in a little more than an hour. Definitely going to have a glass of wine with it—or two. When they'd made the trip to Walmart for the big TV they bought a few bottles of a Cabernet Sauvignon. Time to open one.

"They've not hurt anyone, Chris. Not that I can tell. The department hasn't gotten complaints from anyone else about them. Just from you."

"Well, I ain't letting it drop. And I ain't the only one who's upset. Maybe they ain't complaining to you, the other folks from Fulda, but they're complaining. I been talking to a lot of people in the county about it, and not just the ones that live along this stretch of road. I ain't the only one who's upset, I say again. Even my wife—"

"Is Joan complaining too?" Oren wondered. Chris' wife was a reasonable soul. Maybe he could talk to her and that would help calm Chris. "Can I speak with—"

"My Joanie ain't here." Chris' eyes grew dark and his jaw clenched. "She's at her sister's in Owensboro. Staying there. Been there a few weeks. She's not coming back until the Buddhas are gone."

Oren shook his head. "I'm sorry about that, Chris. You—"

"—could get the sheriff to do something about *them*." Chris gestured again at the saltbox. "That's what you're getting paid for, why you're with the department, to take care of problems in this county. That's a problem. A big ass problem. I had a good life here until they showed up. I'll get that good life back when they leave. You should've won the election, Oren. If you'd won, them Buddhas would be gone right now. Hell, they wouldn't've even set up shop."

"They're not breaking any laws, Chris."

"Oren." The word came out as a plea. "I offered to buy the place. Give Anthony a good, fair price for it so he can move back to Thailand where he belongs. He won't sell. You could make him sell. You could make them leave."

"Can't do that, Chris."

"Sheriff Blackwell. She could—"

"She's not going to tell you anything different, Chris. But she'll be back Tuesday, and I'll leave a message for her."

"Wait here." Chris left the doorway, and Oren stood there, listening to him rummage around, hearing papers shuffling, a thump, and a drawer being slammed. He glanced up at the underside of the awning, heavy with rainwater it had collected. The awning should be fixed so the rain ran off rather than gathered. "Just a minute!" Chris called from somewhere in the house. Oren looked into the living room. Newspapers, magazines, and half-crushed beer cans crowding the coffee table—evidence Joan was indeed gone.

Chris was back a few minutes later, waving a spiral notebook, the kind like kids used in school. "It's in here. All of it." He opened it and showed Oren a page. It was set up like a ledger, with times and dates running down one side, hand-drawn columns that noted comings and goings from the place across the street, descriptions of the men, scattered names denoting people Chris knew. "See, I been keeping track."

Chris snapped the notebook shut and stuffed it under his arm.

11

"Looks like you've been busy," Oren said. More like Chris had become obsessed.

"I been recording what's going on over there, and it's not pretty, Oren."

Oren held out a hand. "Let me take a closer look at your notes, Chris. Maybe I can—"

"Nope. I'll show it to Sheriff Blackwell Tuesday. The sheriff, not her chief deputy. No offense, Oren. And that's if I can wait until Tuesday. I already waited a long time. I want Joanie to come home, I want my old life back, and so they have to go. Tuesday. Maybe I can wait that long. Maybe I can't. We'll see."

"Chris, be careful."

"I'm just saying, Oren."

"You and I go back quite a ways, Chris."

"Yeah, I know. I got no trouble with you, Oren. I ain't prejudiced about race or religion. Ain't prejudiced. But that monk across the street, Anthony Delaney. His religion might be fine and all, but it'd be better practiced somewhere else, over in China. Back in Thailand. Korea. You know his father died New Year's."

Oren knew. He had investigated the elder Delaney's death.

"I found the body, Oren. Out there in the front yard. My Joanie, she called your department." Chris stabbed a finger at the air. "That's when Anthony came back from Thailand and inherited the house, after his father died. Maybe Anthony'll die too. You never know about things."

"Chris, if you're threatening—"

"I ain't threatening anyone, Oren. Just saying you never know about things. You never know. Tuesday. I guess I'll have to wait. See what Sheriff Blackwell can do." Chris stepped back and slammed the door. Softer, behind the wood, Oren heard him say: "See what the sheriff can do, 'cause you apparently can't do nothing about it Chief Deputy Rosenberg."

CHAPTER THREE

6 P.M. SATURDAY

The cabin had belonged to Spaceman's grandfather, who'd had surgery to put rods in his back and didn't consider himself limber enough to come out here anymore. The old man recently turned over the deed for it, plus the ninety-nine thickly wooded acres it sat on in Ohio County, Kentucky, to Spaceman—Piper's Army friend Tom Carpenter.

Three vehicles were parked about fifty feet away behind a line of hickory trees, two small SUVs that the seven other paintballers had crammed themselves and their gear into, and Piper's tiny red Smart-Fortwo that had barely made it through the ruts and over the rises, and which she figured had suffered some undercarriage damage doing so. She hoped it would make it back out to the county road when it was time to go home Monday night.

The cabin was large, with three bedrooms, an eat-in kitchen, a living room, and a study. More than a hundred years old, it desperately needed furniture, indoor plumbing, and some maintenance, which Spaceman said he intended to get to after the first of the year. That would coincide with him waltzing away from the Army and into a desk job at Carpenter's Pre-Owned Autos and Trucks in nearby Hartford. His grandfather was giving him the car dealership too.

13

Spaceman said he'd put a down payment on a little two-story house in neighboring Horse Branch, but if he got this cabin fixed up the way he wanted, he might live here instead.

Half of the roof over the porch was intact, and Piper sat underneath a good spot on a rickety bench next to Hemi. She watched the storm continue to muddy the landscape. The air smelled good and sweet, not a trace of civilization sullying it. No wi-fi out here, no cell reception, no way to check in and make sure things were running smoothly. But with her chief deputy having nearly as many years in the sheriff's department as she'd been alive, she didn't worry. And her detective was an experienced veteran from the Chicago Police Department; neither of them needed her help. Spencer County was in excellent hands.

"You're going to be hurtin' come tomorrow, Christmas," Hemi said, giving her a once-over. "Not wearing a vest."

"Spaceman didn't tell me I needed a vest. Just told me I needed to buy a paint gun."

Piper was already aching from the impact of the paintballs, suspecting she had a trio of bruises purpling her back, and a smaller one to match on her leg. She was barefoot and dressed in lounge pants and an Aerosmith t-shirt, having changed after washing off in the rain.

"Yeah, that's bad on us. We should have told you to buy a vest." Hemi shook his head. "And knee pads, too."

"I'll manage," Piper returned. "Doesn't hurt as much as real bullets."

"True, Christmas. So true."

"Besides, I don't want to invest in this as a hobby until I know if I like it."

"Today was your first time, Christmas? I know you didn't play with us at Campbell, but I figured damn near everybody has paintballed before."

"My first time at paintball. At crawling through the mud and shooting people? Hell no. I've done that before."

He laughed, a friendly warm sound. "I've missed you, Christmas. Missed you very much."

Christmas was a nickname she'd picked up on her first tour in Iraq. The soldiers in her unit had tried out various holiday designations on her because she was from Spencer County, known for all things merry-related: Eleven for eleven pipers piping, Stocking, Saint Nick, Prancer, Snowflake, and they finally settled on Christmas—Hemi's suggestion.

"You did great for a first-timer. You had two kills."

"And got killed."

"Me too. Everybody dies eventually. For real."

Hemi was derived from Daniel Hemisford, and it fit him well because he was large, loud, and indefatigable, like the engine. He and Piper had gone through basic together at Fort Campbell and were assigned to the same overseas unit, she with MP training, and Hemi concentrating on explosive ordnance disposal. Back then he had a buzz-cut, his black hair looking like a fuzzy shadow. Now his head was wholly shaved. She figured Hemi'd stay in to get his twenty, which was what she had originally planned to do.

Piper had enlisted right out of high school and put in four years—making sergeant in two-and-a-half, earning a Purple Heart when she was wounded saving her commanding officer and four others. She was in the process of re-upping when her father was diagnosed with cancer a second time—non-Hodgkin's Lymphoma. She pulled her papers just as she was due for another promotion, and went home to Spencer County to help him. During the course of his treatment he managed to talk her into running for sheriff, a post he'd vacated when he became too ill to hold it. She ran to appease him and for something to do, was surprised she won, and had just started her ninth month in the office. More, she was surprised how much she liked it.

"So, what's next for you, Hemi?"

"After the bluegrass festival Monday—you are joining us for that, right?"

She nodded.

"Me, Spaceman, and Renegade are going to Bardstown. An hour from here, I think, maybe a little more. There's a bar on my bucket list called The Old Talbott Tavern. Been open since 1779, two-foot-thick

15

stone walls. Not kidding. Oldest stagecoach stop west of the Allegheny Mountains. Abraham Lincoln, Jesse James, George Patton, Daniel Boone—those are just some of the long-dead souls who drank there. I'm gonna drink there too. There's a sketchy motel nearby where we're gonna get a couple of rooms and crash, drive back to Campbell sometime Wednesday. I gotta report back Thursday. I think Spaceman and Renegade'are free through the weekend ... just in time for them to ship out again. You should join us at Old Talbott, only cost you two more days off."

"Sounds ... interesting," Piper said. An evening of drinking in a more than two hundred-year-old tavern didn't exactly sound like fun. "I have to be back to work Tuesday. Only have these three days."

"Oh."

"But that's not what I meant, Hemi. Not what you're doing right after this weekend. After that."

"Oh. *After* after. Not much on the paintball front for a while. I had signed up for the Winter Classic three-man tourney, serious money up for grabs in the south in January. But I can't go."

She raised an eyebrow.

"The Winter Classic. It's competitive paintball. I'm giving my slot to Spaceman since I won't be in the States. But I should be back in time for the Sunshine State Open next summer. Already got my registration in." He leaned back and the bench creaked ominously. "I made buck sergeant last week—E-Five."

"Wow. Congrats."

"And a new assignment. I've got two more weeks at Campbell before I ship out for Camp Arifjan in Kuwait. If I was getting posted overseas, I wanted Germany, but that didn't happen." He shrugged. "But I figure Germany will happen eventually, right? Can't see me doing anything else except the Army."

She returned his shrug.

"What about you?" he shot back. "What's next for you? After after?"

"No plans for competitive paintball. But in my day job, get the number of DUIs down in the county, and make a narrow-minded farmer play nice with his Buddhist neighbors. I'll probably have more luck with the DUI thing than with the farmer. Finish my term. Maybe run for a second."

"Wow. Sheriff Christmas. You like it."

She nodded. "I do indeed, Sergeant Hemi."

"So, you're not going to come back to us." He didn't phrase it as a question.

She hesitated before shaking her head. There was the chance she wouldn't be reelected. Maybe the Army would be an option then. Or maybe she'd find something else to do. "I own a house," she said. "A nice one. And cars and motorcycles. I have a dog and a cat." *And a significant other.* "I've put down some roots."

"That's too bad, Christmas. Always figured you in for the duration."

"I'd figured me for a lifer too … or a twenty-year run, at least. I liked it, you know, Army life. A schedule, routine, assignments. It made me feel significant, doing something that mattered. But being a sheriff is significant. I'm still doing something that matters, that hopefully makes a difference for me and others."

"Philosophical on me, Christmas. All Hallmark Channel and unicorns and rainbows." He paused. "They give you any shit 'cause you're little?"

A smile teased at the corner of her lip. "Some folks in the county give me shit because I'm twenty-three. But that'll change soon."

"When you hit the big twenty-four?" Hemi laughed, a deep, sonorous rumble that was answered by thunder she felt tickle the soles of her feet through the porch boards.

"Yeah, when I hit the big twenty-four."

"Maybe I'll buy you a better paint gun for your birthday, order it from Amazon and have it delivered all nice and wrapped. Something with a better range than what you brought with you. And some better balls."

"What's wrong with my balls?"

He laughed louder. "You went the cheap route. I saw what you loaded. You probably think paint is paint, and it's not. Well, paint *is* paint, but the more you spend, typically the brighter and thicker the

17

fill. High-end paintballs, tournament paintballs, what I'm using this weekend, are the brightest. The shells are brittle and designed to shoot through a low-pressure tournament-grade gun. They're more likely fresher, too, which means they have a better fill. I'd have you try some of mine, but you got a cheap gun. My high-grade balls would be lost on that. But next time we'll get you outfitted right, and when we all come out here again you can—"

"Cheap gun? Hey, don't insult my Splatterking! I paid almost fifty bucks for it." It was royal blue with a shiny silver stripe down the barrel, and she wondered if she should have paid a little more for another model that came in camo or some dark color that might not give her away in the woods. And paint? Yeah, she bought the cheapest case she found online.

"Fifty bucks? Really? You bought a paintball gun for fifty bucks?" The voice came from the doorway—Spaceman. He was the oldest in the group at thirty, nearly finished with his second four-year hitch. Prior to that he'd attended college, getting some sort of degree in business and marrying midway through. He never talked much about college or his wife other than to say both were behind him. He had the broad shoulders of a swimmer and the graceful stride of a cat. He was the one who'd invited Piper to this weekend.

She'd accepted immediately, even though Spaceman admitted she was a fill-in for Zombie, the regular fourth on their paintball team. Zombie was going to be walking down the aisle in a few weeks and was spending his remaining bachelor days on the final details.

"A Splatterking," Spaceman laughed. "Okay, it's not awful, Christmas. I had one until I got into the competitive stuff a few years ago. But a Splatterking has a sucky range."

Piper turned so she could see him.

"You'd do better with something like this." Spaceman passed her his rifle. "Stryker Elite, fully electro-pneumatic marker with four firing modes. Adjustable telescope shoulder stock, barrel has a shroud, programmable board, fires twice as far and lots more accurate."

Piper carefully handled the gun. It was at least double the weight of her fifty-dollar special.

18

Spaceman continued. "Got an LED visual setting indicator and a rip clip loader. Paid about four hundred for it, counting a couple of aftermarket accessories I had fitted."

Piper whistled. "That's a lot of money to shoot paint."

"Not if you're into the competitions," Hemi cut in. "I spent about three hundred on mine at a blow-out sale. Sweet magnetic response trigger, external velocity adjuster, only uses a nine-volt battery."

Renegade slipped around Spaceman and gave him a playful thump on the chest. She was smoking a joint and looking directly at Piper.

"What?" Renegade taunted.

Piper smiled. "I didn't say anything."

"But you were thinking it. There was a lecture forming on your pretty lips. You gonna arrest me, Sheriff Christmas? And what about Harold? He's smoking too."

Harold was on the other team, all of them inside supposedly discussing strategy for tomorrow.

"This isn't her jurisdiction, Rene," Hemi said.

"Doesn't mean she can't do a citizen's arrest or something," Spaceman said. To Renegade: "Pot's illegal in Kentucky. You damn well don't have a medical prescription for it."

"And you do, Space?" she taunted.

"Take it inside, Rene. Don't start something."

Renegade, Rene Marlor, was the only other woman on the weekend outing. She'd been in Piper's MP class, and they'd shared a cruiser on base on several occasions. They got along well enough then, but things got itchy when Piper got promoted and Rene didn't. They were friends—but not very good ones.

"Don't start something," Renegade parroted. She swung around and went back in the cabin. "Don't start something. Hey, Harold, Sheriff Christmas isn't going to arrest us. Light up another."

"Got about an hour before twilight," Spaceman said. "And I got some hamburgers and beans on the stove. Coffee and beer. A couple bags of cookies."

"I can smell 'em, those burgers. I'm hungry. Real. Hope you got cheese for 'em." Hemi stood and the bench shifted. "How can you have electricity out here and no plumbing, Spaceman? How come I gotta be like a bear and go out into the woods to take a—"

"Got a generator, got solar. And we got rain. Lots of rain today. That's plenty of running water, don'tcha think? I'll get some real plumbing after the first of the year, after my ETS." Piper knew that stood for end of time in the service.

She got up and followed Spaceman inside, pausing in the doorway. She thought she heard something out in the woods, something moving through the brush. A burst of chatter from inside the cabin drowned everything else out.

Still, Piper stood motionless for a while, listening.

CHAPTER FOUR

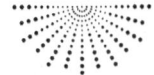

7 P.M. SATURDAY

Teegan wore a purple long-sleeved blouse over a pair of bleached skinny jeans, belted with a paisley scarf of myriad jewel tones. It was too warm today for long sleeves, but she'd gotten a new tattoo this morning, a pretty vine that ran from her shoulder to her wrist ... the flowers and goat weed butterflies would be applied on her next trip.

Oren worked this weekend, and so she didn't want him to see her new ink—not all unfinished and her skin red from the work-in-progress. More, she didn't want to deal with him saying something about it. Her body was her business—not his—how many tats and piercings she got, how goth or average she decided to look on a given day, her call. She'd show off the new tat in all its glory when it was finished; let him grumble about it then.

She had three necklaces of varying lengths, a simple gold chain with a turtle charm on it, a string of polished agate chips with silver bead spacers, and a wire-wrapped chunk of glass she'd fused in her kiln and that dangled from a braided leather cord. She had amethyst hearts in her ears, a small hoop in her nose, and a brass ball stud beneath her lip that matched the one in her tongue. Normally she also

21

wore a little barbell in her eyebrow, but the spot was itchy, and so she'd left it empty.

Teegan's hair had been freshly dyed—violet black, a sassy shade, and she wore it long and straight. She considered herself part of the goth subculture, but the hair was the only goth-thing she had going today. She'd wanted to look more ... what? Ordinary? That wasn't quite the vibe she was going for. Workplace edgy. Better. She liked that—workplace edgy today. She paired her outfit with three-week-old Birkenstock Arizona sandals with blue suede straps, and she had an ankle chain with skulls and daggers on it to complete the look ... okay, two goth things going, but the ankle chain was difficult to notice.

Oren hadn't said anything to her when he'd stopped at her desk and left around five, other than: "Hey, Teegan." No "you look nice today," or "you look almost normal today," which he sometimes offered. No disparaging comments on her piercings. He'd seemed in a surly mood, probably because of Chris Hagee. But he could have at least said "happy birthday."

Teegan was forty-five today.

Teegan didn't mind working the weekends, always interesting. Saturday nights were usually drunks, sometimes driving farm equipment or lawn mowers, and once in a while a juicy domestic skirmish or two was thrown in. But this Saturday—her friggin' birthday—had been achingly slow so far. One fender bender south of Santa Claus involving a pontoon boat on a trailer. The drunks weren't out yet.

"Happy birthday to me," she said, twirling a strand of hair around her index finger. She'd dressed like this today because ... because she thought maybe someone would stop in to see her, bring her flowers or chocolates or at least a card. She'd thought someone might make a fuss, give her a surprise party in the break room. The mail was delivered before she came on shift ... nothing for her. Two birthday cards had been sent to her home ... one from her car insurance company and the other from her dentist.

She'd not telegraphed that it was her birthday, though anyone who looked at her Facebook page could have seen the notice. At least Facebook cared. Maybe she should have dropped hints. Maybe she should have ordered her own damn flowers and set them on the corner of her desk. People coming into the office, even Oren, would notice a bouquet and ask about the occasion.

"Happy happy birthday," she half-sang.

Teegan had thought about taking today off, doing something special. But she wasn't seeing anyone right now, there were no geek-related conventions scheduled within reasonable driving distance, and what would be the point of spending her birthday alone anyway? Better that she was in here at her post and had something to occupy her.

Forty-five.

Crap. In five years she'd qualify for AARP membership and be eligible for a pension.

Another five years past that and she could ask for senior discounts at restaurants.

Forty-friggin'-five. And no one noticed. If she had only—

Teegan surfaced from her melancholia and answered a 9-1-1 call about a green Camry weaving on 162. She dispatched a deputy to investigate and alerted Santa Claus police in case the Camry made it into their town limits. Probably the first drunk of the night, she thought. DUIs were the number one ticketed offense in the county.

Teegan would get off at eleven; maybe she'd stop at one of the bars on the way home and treat herself to a celebratory birthday daiquiri. Or two. Strawberry.

"With an umbrella in it," she said.

A call came in on the non-emergency line. Teegan's eyebrows rose when she saw the ID.

"Spencer County Sheriff," she answered. "How are you doing, Nang?" Nang ran the only gas station in the tiny town of Fulda, about a half hour's drive from the department. The place also served as a little grocery store and Vietnamese restaurant. It was well known that Nang was Sheriff Blackwell's significant other. Did Nang not know that Piper was away for the long weekend playing soldier with her Army buddies? Was he calling here looking for her?

Maybe, Teegan thought with a spark of hope, he'd called to wish her a happy birthday.

"A drive off," he said almost breathlessly. "A damn drive off."

"Oh." She called up a file and started typing. "Let me get the info and I'll put it out."

"It's not a fortune," he fumed. "It's the principal. It's not right that someone steals from me. Thirty gallons of gas, seventy-eight dollars. Not right."

She'd seldom heard Nang upset. "Can you tell me anything about the—"

"SUV, GMC Denali Yukon, metallic blue, bumper sticker on the back right said 'my son is an honor student.' Couldn't tell whether it was an eight or a B on the Tennessee license plate." He rattled off a description of the driver. "A bumper sticker on the left said 'Nashville Music City' inside a guitar."

"Hang on." Teegan put him on hold and connected to the mutual aid channel for police, state police, and sheriff deputies on patrol, issuing a BOLO—be on the lookout—and repeating the information Nang had given her. "Last seen on five-forty-five heading south."

"I have a surveillance camera," Nang said when she came back to him. "Almost a month old. Piper talked me into putting one up after I had a few drive offs in August. I have video of the thief. Not right, Teegan. Not a lot of money, but it's not right. It's theft. I watched him pull in, gas up his SUV, and then get back in and drive off. I tried to run after him, that's when I saw the bumper stickers. He put his hand out the window and flipped me off."

"Rude," Teegan said.

"Brazen, Teegan. That asshole ... excuse my language ... was brazen."

"A lot more reports of this sort of thing lately," Teegan returned. "Some of the guys are good at it, real pros. And SUVs swallow a lot more gas. Self-serve rural station like you have, probably didn't know you have surveillance."

"It's not right," Nang repeated.

Teegan liked Nang, and certainly liked his cooking. "I'm going to dispatch Diego. He's on second shift this weekend. He'll get a copy of your footage and—"

"And then what?"

"We'll figure out who the thief is. If someone doesn't nab him along the road, using the car information and video, we'll take it before a judge, submit it, and get an arrest warrant." She typed in a few more notes. "And why are you still at your store on a Saturday night?"

Nang made a huffing sound reminiscent of sand blowing. "Piper's in Kentucky with old friends," he said. "And my night manager called in sick. Good combination, eh? I am stuck here."

"Not a fun weekend," Teegan returned, thinking of her own situation.

"Tomorrow will be better. Piper's dad is coming over for dinner, bringing his dog Wrinkles, so I will make extra. The pug eats a lot. No onions because Wrinkles shouldn't have onions. I think I'd like to get a pug for myself. I'm watching the postings on rescue sites."

"You'd spoil it with your cooking. What are you fixing tomorrow?"

"I'm going to make *nom hoa chuoi* and *banh xeo* with rice paper. For dessert, *xoi la dua*."

"Sounds tasty." Teegan had no idea what the dishes were, but everything she'd had from Phan's Quick Stop—Phan was Nang's family name—had been delicious. Teegan thought about the banana and peanut butter sandwich in her desk drawer. She reached for it, scrunched her nose, and dropped it in the wastebasket. Not a suitable birthday dinner. "We'll get him, Nang, your drive-off." Though she couldn't guarantee that.

"Hey, Teegan, do you work tomorrow?"

"No."

"Then join us for dinner. Yes?"

"Yes. Thanks. What time?" She'd bring a bottle of wine.

"Six."

The next call was a fender-bender north of Rockport. Exciting night, she thought.

It was a few minutes past nine when the door jangled and a pizza delivery man came in toting a large cardboard box and a two-liter bottle of Mountain Dew.

"Delivery for Theresa Gander," he announced. He looked to be barely out of high school and pencil thin, with a shock of blond curly hair that hung down to his shoulders. "You Theresa Gander?"

"Yeah," Teegan said. Everybody called her Teegan, but her full name was Theresa Elizabeth Gander. She preferred Teegan.

"Happy birthday!" the delivery man said. His name tag read: Morris P. "One extra-large deep dish sausage and mushroom." He placed it on the edge of her desk, sat the soda next to it, and stood waiting.

"Who sent me a—"

"I don't know who ordered it," Morris said. "But it's been paid for. Don't you want it?"

"Yes, I want it."

He stood waiting.

A tip, she thought. *He expects a tip.* She fished in her pocket and handed him a five.

Nodding, he swung around and headed out.

Teegan opened the box and inhaled the aroma. Oh, glorious with its big pieces of sausage and mushrooms, lots of cheese. She grabbed a piece and chewed appreciatively. She was all the way to the crust when she thought that maybe it wasn't the safest thing in the world to chow down on a mystery meal from an unknown source.

She saw a phone number on the box, punched it in, and as she reached for a second piece demanded that the person on the other end tell her who ordered this pizza.

"Zeke," she repeated back to them. "Zeke the Geek."

The first-shift dispatcher had remembered her birthday.

The day wasn't a complete loss. Someone had made a fuss, was thoughtful. She'd get three meals easy out of this. And dinner at Nang's tomorrow night.

"So good," she gushed. "This is so very good." She'd email Zeke a thank you note as soon as she was stuffed. He was staying at Piper's house for the weekend, pet-sitting.

Another call came in on the non-emergency line.

The third-shift dispatcher was reporting in sick. Really? A little more than an hour until he was supposed to come on duty. Couldn't he have called in earlier to say that he was heaving his guts out? A Saturday night, holiday weekend, no way would Teegan get someone in here to take his shift.

That meant she was pulling a double.

"Crap," she said. "Happy birthday to me." At least she had pizza.

CHAPTER FIVE

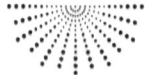

11:30 P.M. SATURDAY

The Explorer made her feel like she was encased in a tank. It maneuvered well enough, took potholes almost effortlessly, and overall was a smooth ride. The driver's seat was seriously comfortable. It was just … huge. Millie knew it was the same complaint her boss—Sheriff Piper Blackwell—had about the vehicle. Didn't matter that she'd been driving one on third shift for the past four months since she'd been hired as a deputy, Millie knew it was always going to feel overly large.

But it had plenty of room behind the grid to sit a couple of hefty drunks, which had been her main call-outs; third shift was prime time for DUIs.

"Why am I talking to you, Teegan?" Millie asked after keying the radio. "You're pulling a double tonight?"

"My luck," Teegan answered. "And your luck that you get to deal with Chris Hagee. He's at G's Bar in Fulda, called in a complaint about something illegal going down there. He won't be more specific, and though I'd love to ignore him—"

"I got you. I'm on my way. I'll be there in ten minutes."

"I'll let him know," Teegan continued. "No lights or sirens. It's likely nothing. Maybe Hagee's just being a nuisance. Oren had a call-

28

out to his house this afternoon, Hagee griping about his neighbors. Maybe you can arrest him for harassment or something, toss him in jail overnight for drunk and disorderly. But he sounded pretty lucid on the call. Let me know what's up."

"Sure." Millie was familiar with Fulda, one of the unincorporated specks on the map that made up Spencer County. She regularly ate at Nang's place in Fulda—sometimes with her grandfather Chief Deputy Oren Rosenberg. And before she'd gone away to college, she was a regular at the World War II veterans' memorial in the woods nearby where a shooting match was always held the first weekend in October. She'd won it twice and might enter again this year. The hint of a town dated back to 1840, built up by immigrants who named the place after a city in Germany that many of them had come from. St. Boniface Catholic Church was listed on the National Register of Historic Places. It had boasted a post office for nearly one hundred and fifty years, but that shut down in 1995. Now Fulda was basically a snooze.

And it was home to G's Bar, opened in mid-June by just-retired high school literature teacher Gretta Mueller, who wanted to keep busy. Millie had driven by the place, but had not yet been officially called to stop there. She counted a dozen cars in the lot across the road and out front, a booming business for this itty-bitty speck. She parked, turned on her body cam, and went in.

G's was an old building that a few decades past had been a flower shop when Fulda had a business district. Rundown on the outside, because maybe Gretta hadn't gotten to exterior remodeling yet, it was shiny and new on the inside with a hint of rustic style. The bar was dark polished wood with brass trim, and the stools looked leather-covered. There was a jukebox, the old-fashioned kind with real 45s in it, but it wasn't playing anything; maybe it was just for show. Two pool tables in the front had Coca Cola lights hanging over them, and several round dining tables spread out over a pitted, impressive hardwood floor were filled with customers, who paused their conversations to regard Millie.

She was twenty-four and in full deputy regalia, including her hat.

The rest of the occupants—all men, save a bartender—were in jeans and t-shirts and in their forties to seventies, looking rough around the edges and relaxed.

Millie counted twenty-three seated patrons, three of them at the bar. A man and a woman, both in their mid-sixties and similar in height and appearance, tended bar; the woman no doubt Gretta Mueller. The man was maybe her husband or brother. Millie spotted Chris Hagee, sitting alone at a table in the back, waving at her.

She walked toward him, studying the room as she went and not seeing anything illegal going down like Chris had complained to Teegan about. But she was recording all of this on her cam so she could review the footage later. She stood opposite Chris, observing the half-full glass of beer and a bowl of peanuts beside a napkin with scribbled notes on it. Near at hand sat a cell phone with the screen showing a cat video.

"You're Oren's granddaughter, right?"

She nodded and sat when he gestured at a chair.

"You don't look anything like him, but I heard his granddaughter got hired. Figured that was you. Figured if Oren was on days, his granddaughter would have nights."

"What's this about, Mr. Hagee? The dispatcher said you'd noted illegal activities."

"*Activity*," he corrected. "One activity." He ran a thumb around the top of his beer glass and peered at the surface as if he saw something interesting in the reflection. "Just one illegal activity, and ain't it a doozy. I need you to arrest the owner of this bar, Gretta Mueller. I want her pudgy ass thrown in jail." He nodded his head in the barkeep's direction. "Not her twin brother Gunther. That's Gunther working the place with her. It's just her that needs to be locked up."

"Mr. Hagee—"

"It's illegal for a bartender to give away beer."

A one-page laminated menu lay flat on the center of the table. Millie glanced at it, seeing listings of foreign, domestic, and craft brews, house mixed drinks, and a limited selection of sandwiches and appetizers. This place meant Nang had a little competition in the food department in Fulda.

Chris sat back and squared his shoulders. Millie thought he looked tired and resigned, definitely unhappy. Maybe he'd been drinking too much, though his speech didn't sound slurred. Millie had become good at detecting drunk-talk.

"How long have you been here tonight, Mr. Hagee?" She noted that the patrons had lost interest in her and had gone back to their conversations. A man with a cane got up and went to the jukebox, dropped in some coins, and pushed a button. Tracy Lawrence started singing *Paint Me a Birmingham*. The machine worked, it wasn't just a decoration. Two men started playing pool.

"A while." He tipped his head toward the bar again. "I'll leave when I see you arrest her."

"What is it you think she's—"

"I don't *think*. I *know*. I watched her. I told you, she gave away beer. Wrote it down when she did it. First glass was at 10:30, then a half hour after that, and the third time … that's going on right now. You take a look. I been studying the law in my spare time. Indiana law."

Millie watched the bartender hand over a glass of beer. She studied the law, too. She was enrolled in online law classes. She already had a bachelor's and master's, and she intended to eventually get her law degree and open a practice.

"You just saw a Class B misdemeanor," Chris said, wrapping his fingers around his beer glass. "I paid three bucks for this. It's three-dollar draft beer night. See? Says so in the menu. Everybody in here needs to pay three bucks a glass. Gretta? She's been giving free beer to Henry Tucker. The guy in the gray t-shirt at the bar. They're more than friends if you get my drift. You saw her do it, give him a beer. G's doesn't allow tabs. You order a drink, you pay for it right away."

Millie watched as a man at the middle of the bar handed over a five-dollar bill in exchange for a small mixed drink.

Chris pushed the napkin toward Millie. He'd just scrawled 11:50 on it.

"Those are the three times she gave old Henry a free drink. Now,

31

Indiana law says bartenders can be found guilty of a Class B misdemeanor if they provide a drink on the house. Indiana law states that sellers of alcohol ain't allowed to discriminate between customers by offering drinks at different prices or free. Penalty is jail time and up to a fifteen hundred dollar fine."

Millie watched Henry Tucker take his free beer back to a table.

"Now, it ain't illegal for Henry to drink that free beer," Chris continued. "And I ain't noticed her give a free beer to anyone else." He tapped a few keys on his phone and the screen shifted to an Indiana legal website where he'd highlighted the state code, chapter, and section. He pushed this at her, too. "But G? She just broke the law with that on-the-house draft."

Millie squeezed her hands into fists under the table. Who cared if the owner gave a couple of free drinks to a friend? Her bar, her beer, she couldn't see the harm. But she glanced at the cell phone screen and suspected the odd law was really on the books. She retrieved her phone and connected to one of the law sites she was familiar with, noting that Chris watched her. A little scrolling and she came to the same law. Yeah, it was a real thing. She hid a sigh.

What was Chris Hagee getting out of this? Hassling the only bar in Fulda? Or was he instead toying with the sheriff's department?

"Mr. Hagee, I don't think a few beers are cause to—"

"So, you ain't going to enforce the law?" He took a sip of his beer, pulled back his napkin, and made another note on it. He kept it close; Millie couldn't see what he'd just written.

"Maybe she owes Henry Tucker something," Millie suggested. "And the beer is paying him back. Or—"

"Henry Tucker is an asshole who lives down the road from me," Chris said. "I think he's friends with the Buddha monk across the street. Anyway, Henry goes over to their temple once in a while, probably once a week. Maybe he's switching to their religion, tired of being Baptist. Won't sign my petition to get them Buddhas to leave." The last he said with a growl. Chris finished his beer. "And while I might take issue with Henry Tucker's politics, I ain't asking you to

32

arrest him. He didn't break the law. I'm asking you to do your duty and arrest Gretta. Class B misdemeanor."

Could she arrest the bartender? Millie relaxed her hands and took a deep breath. Short answer: yes, she probably could arrest Gretta Mueller. Medium answer: she could decide not to intervene. If officers with radar on the side of a highway clock cars going over the speed limit and don't stop them ... that's what this reminded her of. The officers make the determination *when* to intervene, when the speed is too excessive and a ticket is warranted. Long answer: in this particular situation, knowing Hagee's tendency to complain, she'd have to take some sort of action.

"Here's what I'll do, Mr. Hagee," Millie said, as she pulled out a notebook and started writing. "I'll interview you and some of the other people here, put together a report, and send it to the county prosecutor to make a decision on charges. Ultimately, it's up to the district attorney whether to prosecute. I'll issue the bartender, Gretta Mueller, a notice to appear."

"Like you writing someone a traffic ticket?"

"Yes, like that," she replied. "Still, it's up to District Attorney Scales whether to file formal charges and prosecute. I'll even stop in his office Tuesday. The courthouse is closed Monday for the holiday. I'll stop in and talk to him about this." What she didn't say was that she'd tell the DA to take her report with more than a grain of salt and that Chris Hagee was a certified nutjob. In the end, she'd be passing the proverbial buck to the district attorney and letting him take the heat from Chris.

"And I suspect it'll be in the local paper."

"Likely," Millie returned.

Chris smiled at that. "I'll stop in the DA's office Tuesday, too." He folded the napkin and put it in his pocket. "Thanks for coming out, deputy."

CHAPTER SIX

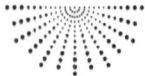

8 A.M. SUNDAY, SEPTEMBER 6TH

Piper read the spines visible through the dusty glass in the barrister's bookcase. There didn't appear to be a single murder mystery in the lot. *The Journal of John Swift, The Journal of Jonathan Swift, The Hunchback of Notre-Dame, Nicholas Nickleby, Ivanhoe*—she'd read that one, *Captains Courageous, The Pickwick Papers, A Christmas Carol*—who hadn't read it?, *A Hero of Our Time, Romeo and Juliet, The Tempest, The Count of Monte Cristo*—she'd read that also, *Dead Souls*, and *The Cottagers of Glenburnie*. Most of the books didn't have titles on the spines. All of them looked truly old and worn.

"Spaceman!" Piper raised her voice so he could hear her. "Interesting reading. These can't be yours. Not a Stephen King or a Peter Straub in the bunch."

"My grandfather's collection," he answered. "Or more likely his grandfather's. A lot of those books are more than two hundred years old. Not really worth anything, though, I looked them up on eBay. You got to have a first printing and in good shape apparently."

"Read any of them?"

"*The Count of Monte Cristo*. That one a long time ago. Hey, don't

34

take the books out, please. I need to ask my grandfather if he wants any of them. Breakfast in a few!"

Piper took a last look at the books, thought about the new Harry Bosch novel waiting for her at home, and joined Hemi at the table.

"Coffee." Piper held her nose over the mug. She'd been spoiled by the Dark Italian Roast stocked at the sheriff's department and the fancy coffee maker there. This sludge had been brewed in one of those old glass pots like they had in the diners on television shows. Still, it was hot and full of blessed caffeine, and she drank it down fast and poured a second. She hadn't slept great last night, stretched out in a sleeping bag on the floor in one of the bedrooms, listening to the rain patter against the roof and into buckets set under leaky spots. Plus, Renegade snored like she was cutting down redwoods. Piper thought the caffeine would give her the needed rush to make it through a day of paintball. The acrid taste on her tongue should help keep her alert.

She'd enjoyed playing yesterday, despite the mud. It might be a hobby she could embrace and lure Nang to try, though she wouldn't spend hundreds on one of the fancy guns. And she doubted she'd ever get into competition paintball. But she hoped to come out here again with her old friends, especially reconnecting with Hemi, who was like a big brother. Too, it was just nice being in the woods, secluded, away from technology and the worries of work. She wondered if Spencer County was staying quiet this weekend. If something wholly awful happened they knew where she was, as she'd given them GPS coordinates. It was a little less than an hour's drive from the department.

"Stopped raining," Hemi said. He poured a cup of coffee and downed it in one swallow. "That's pretty awful. Sludge." He refilled his cup. "When's breakfast?"

"Ten minutes," Spaceman replied. "Sit and wait for it." Renegade was helping him in what passed for the kitchen.

Piper smelled bacon, glorious bacon.

Spaceman had fed the other four paintballers an hour ago. They comprised Team Alpha—Gonzo, Brick, Hot Sauce, and Harold—who were out in the woods setting up ambush sites.

"I've been reading about Sybil Ludington," Hemi said.

Piper drank some coffee. "Was she at Campbell?" Piper had never heard of the woman.

"Hardly," Hemi continued. "I take an online American history course through a university in Arizona. Sybil was born in 1761, the youngest of twelve children."

Piper waited for him to go on with his story. Hemi loved to tell stories.

"Did you know she was as big a deal as Paul Revere? Bigger, actually, history just didn't take proper notice."

"I did not know that," Spaceman called from the kitchen over cooking noises.

"The Ludington farm was vulnerable to British attack and was a strategic spot between Long Island and Connecticut. Dad Ludington was worried about the Tories. Well, he had a right to be. The Brits attacked Danbury, roughly a dozen miles from Ludington's land, with about two thousand men. The Brits were trying to capture a stockpile of weapons in the city. Anyway, someone rode to Ludington's place, trying to spread the word and get a militia ready for an assault. But the rider's horse was too exhausted to go beyond the Ludington farm."

"Enter Sybil," Piper said.

"Yep. Sybil was sixteen that year ... 1777 ... her dad volunteered her. She knew the land and was a good rider, history says. Sybil was friends with all the farmers and could get to them and pull them together as a militia. The night was black as pitch, the roads were bad, and she had to evade bandits. She supposedly rode forty miles that night, no weapons but a stick that she fought off a bandit with. She got the militia organized, and her dad commanded them and led them to Ridgefield in Connecticut, drove the Brits back to Long Island Sound. The Brits had burned most of Danbury, but it could've been a whole lot worse if the militia hadn't come through. The Brits would've attacked all along the coastline. Sybil rode twice as far as Paul Revere, avoided capture, and did it alone. Revere had two other riders working with him to spread the word. I find it interesting that they teach kids about Paul Revere and his midnight ride, but there's no mention of Sybil. History is too male-centric, don't you think? I mean, you can find out about her, she's written up in some books, but not much, not what she deserved. And you have to go looking for it, do some digging. There's no 'Listen my children and you shall hear' like Longfellow wrote about Paul Revere. Way the hell too male-centric."

"Women in the military never get enough credit," Renegade put in. "I'm not a hot runner like Sheriff Christmas was, but I've got my eyes set on making General. I'll do it. I'm going to make noise about it when I get the star. And today … I'm going to get a couple of kills and make it to the top of the hill first."

"So, we capture *this* hill, right? For our first scenario?" Piper had her copy of the map on the table, smoothing out the curl and leaning close to better read it. The map was a copy, shrunk down from an original 1820 poster-sized version Spaceman said he got at the library. The hill was one of several in the eastern section. Spaceman's property, marked in red, stopped at the south where the hills started. It wasn't easy to read the print. He said he couldn't find a recent map with this much detail.

"Are we going to be trespassing if we go on the ridge?" Piper was ever mindful of legalities.

"Nope," Spaceman replied. "Public property. County property, the ridge and five acres on the other side. I go up there once in a while just for the view. People camp on it. An old bluegrass musician was raised somewhere over there in a restored house. Nice little museum nearby. Sells souvenirs."

"Not into museums." Hemi took a look at the map. "But I like bluegrass. Okay, *that* hill. If one of us makes it to the top without dying, we win. Team Alpha has to hold the ground. Brick's the only one I'm worried about."

"And if we lose, we have to buy dinner for Alpha tomorrow," Renegade called from in front of the stove.

"We won't lose," Spaceman said. "They'll be buying dinner for us. We capture that hill, come back here for lunch … beer and smoked sausages. Then we go out for round two, where the stakes are even

37

higher. We have the advantage. I've been traipsing this land since I was a kid. I know every inch. If you go past the ridge, you've gone too far, blown the objective. So don't go farther than the ridge. We need to win today."

Renegade brought plates to the table, the heavy-duty paper kind, and plastic forks. "I do not want to be on the losing side, Christmas," she said staring at Piper. "You damn well better aim righteously with that cheap gun of yours. I want a free steak dinner with all the trimmings."

"I want smoked salmon." Spaceman presented a platter of bacon and a bowl of scrambled eggs dotted with cheese and green peppers. Biscuits and homemade maple butter were already on the table.

"Christmas, yesterday was just to get you the basics. Took you to school so to speak. Today we're using competitive paintball rules. A lot of it is objective-based—capture the hill this morning. A single kill-shot—head or center of the chest—takes you out of the game, or takes the enemy out if you're the one who fired it. Three wound shots anywhere else equal a kill shot. We shoot yellow again. They shoot blue. Got it?"

Piper nodded and speared a mound of eggs.

Spaceman continued. "We use walkie-talkies, not the same channel as Alpha, set off in pairs—me and you, Hemi and Renegade."

"Got it," Piper said. The eggs were warm and as tasty as anything she'd had at a restaurant. She detected among the scattering of peppers and cheddar a hint of cream cheese. She'd ask Spaceman later for his ingredients and pass them along to Nang. She wondered what Nang was doing this weekend, and wished there was cell reception so she could call him.

"How long did she live?" Renegade asked.

"Huh?" Hemi paused in mid-bite.

"Sybil," Renegade replied. "What did your history class teach you about her end?"

"It's always the end with you, isn't it?" Hemi took a slug of coffee. "Seventy-seven. She was a little over seventy-seven, a long life for back then. There are a few statues of her, I think in New York. Her grave's a little thing, though, no monument or nothing … and there should have been one. The Revolution might have turned out different if it wasn't for her."

Thirty minutes later Piper strapped the Splatterking to her back, consulted the map one more time, and followed Spaceman into the woods.

"I figure if Hemi and Renegade come in from the north, and we head straight in from the west, we have a better chance. Divide and conquer. Only one of us has to make it to the top."

Piper preferred a unified assault, but agreed this could be stealthier. Alpha probably set ambush points along more than one trail.

"Straight in," Spaceman continued, "we ought to have some luck. Who's gonna expect us to head straight in on the target?"

Brick, Piper thought. Brick would expect a direct attack. She'd been stationed with him during one of her tours. On one night assignment Brick thwarted an ambush, killed five, and subsequently picked up a Silver Star. Brick was the leader of Alpha and in her opinion the one to be most wary about. Fortunately, he was firing paint today, and a paint gun lacked the range of the real thing, the accuracy too.

"Do you like bluegrass, Christmas?"

Spaceman was out front, better from Piper's perspective since he knew the territory. She glanced from right to left, then spun and looked behind her. The greens were vibrant from yesterday's deluge, the ground soft underfoot and springy in places along the narrow game trail. The air was clean and touched with the scent of wildflowers. Bird song and chirping filled the silence. She'd not noticed tracks, but Alpha could have covered them up if they came this way.

"Some," she answered. "A little. I like modern country music better. Saw a great concert this summer—Clint Holster played at the county fair."

"Big Nashville singer," Spaceman said over his shoulder. "I've heard him. Didn't figure him for county fairs."

"I didn't figure you for running a used car dealership."

"Life takes strange turns, eh? Hope I like it. I didn't figure you for a sheriff."

"Life takes strange turns," she agreed.

"Hell!"

Piper heard a whizzing a second before Spaceman yelled. She watched him drop to a crouch. She followed the move and shoved her back up against an oak. They shouldn't have been chattering, should have been quiet and stealthy.

Spaceman had been hit in the shoulder; the blue paint bright. They'd probably tried for a head shot, and they'd come close.

Listening.

The birds had stopped singing.

Something moved to the southwest, but she couldn't see through the tangle of undergrowth. Spaceman skittered behind a bush. Her walkie-talkie was silent; nothing from Hemi or Renegade.

Listening.

There, definitely to the south, and close, something moving parallel to her. She bolted up and sidestepped. A blob of paint whizzed past, missing her by inches at eye-height. She brought her Splatterking up, fired, ducked, rose again, sidestepped, and fired once more. Her first shot nailed a dead tree; the yellow paint blossomed against the ash gray trunk. Her second smacked into a helmet. A kill shot!

Ahead, Spaceman was on his feet, popping twin shots into the same target—one in the chest, one lower.

"My kill!" Piper yelled. Then she dropped and rolled across the narrow trail to the other side, coming up in a jumble of tall grasses. Her hair got caught on a low-hanging branch and she tugged free, checked her gun, and crawled farther southeast.

"Ya got me!" the kill confirmed. It was Harold, the only member of Alpha without a nickname. She'd met him at Campbell five years ago, a serious soul who hadn't cut it in culinary school and so enlisted, and reenlisted; he'd refused all nicknames they'd tried to apply. "How about you come out and take my picture, Spaceman? Christmas?"

Not a chance, old friend.

Harold might have a partner hiding, waiting to snipe. It wouldn't be Brick ... maybe Gonzo, the two were fast friends. Gonzo was a good soldier, seemingly indefatigable, but he was also a little clumsy and kind of strange.

"Yeah, I'll come get your picture," Spaceman returned. "You and whoever's with you."

Piper peered through a bush and watched Spaceman jackknife up, grab a thick branch, and swing into a tree, a hiss followed by a streak whizzing past, the paint missing and connecting with the foliage. In the next moment, Spaceman somersaulted down, making a racket and firing a series of shots into the brush yards ahead.

Hiss whizz, hiss whizz, phew, phew. It sounded almost like real gunfire, she thought, but it lacked the harsh punctuation.

She remained low and crawled in the same direction, and then had to stand when a clump of spindly maples blocked her. She stopped and listened, hearing Spaceman tromping through the underbrush, mumbling "I'll take your damn picture," hearing leaves overhead rustling, then hearing the cry of some bird. Piper looked up, seeing a hawk streak away.

Beautiful bird.

In fact, these woods, this day, all of it was beautiful. She was having fun.

Schwathup! Schwathup! Schwathup!

"Ah, crap!" It was Spaceman. "I'm out!"

Harold laughed. "Come get our picture, Christmas."

Piper crept forward, cautious, knowing there was at least one more enemy out there. Then she moved a branch and saw Harold.

He sat on a flat-topped rock; the three kill shots evident. He'd taken his helmet off. Her yellow paint was not as bright as the yellow blobs from Spaceman's gun—truth to Hemi's word about paint quality. Harold was in the process of removing his kneepads when he noticed her. "It's okay, Christmas, Gonzo hightailed it after he took a hit to his right arm. He's skittish as a rabbit today. Just me here. Honest."

41

She relaxed, but only a little. Spaceman tromped into the clearing. He was covered with blue paint, a bright smear from his chest and down his legs; only the goggles on his helmet were paint free. He took off the helmet and goggles and gave her a sheepish grin.

"Got too cocky. Hell, I should've known better. Should've known there'd be a trap around here."

Piper looked between the men, listening. She wasn't sure that Gonzo had indeed hightailed it.

"Paint grenade," Spaceman continued.

The *schwathup!* Piper realized.

"Three grenades, actually," Harold countered.

"I tripped a wire," Spaceman said. He looked to Harold. "But I'm not *your* kill. You were already dead."

"I'll let Gonzo take the credit for you then."

Spaceman extended a hand and helped Harold up.

Piper remained wary, listening.

"Hey, Christmas, we're going back to the cabin. Have a second breakfast. I'll let you use my gun if you're careful."

"Not fair," Harold said. "Your gun's too good for a rookie."

Piper shook her head, still listening between the gaps in the conversation. "I'm kinda partial to mine." She patted the stock of her Splatterking. Honestly, she would have loved to try Spaceman's fancy paint gun. But he'd mentioned four hundred dollars, and she didn't want to risk it. "Now, if you two corpses will excuse me, I've a mission to complete." She tipped her head and retreated back the way she'd come, hearing their friendly banter behind her.

"She'll be dead within the hour," Harold said.

Spaceman made a tsking sound. "I don't think so. I'm counting on her to win this for my team."

Piper hoped Spaceman was right.

She was less confident on her own. Not that she needed a partner, but Spaceman said he had been coming to this land since he was a kid. She'd never been here before this weekend, and the map for reference was two hundred years old. Too, the enemy had better paint guns.

Piper envied Spaceman a little—having this big chunk of

unspoiled woods to ramble through and appreciate. He'd have more time to enjoy it, settling down in nearby Horse Branch and working a car dealership. No more jaunts away to this country or that country, which most likely would've continued to be in the Middle East because he was fluent in Arabic and also knew a smattering of Russian and Turkish. She'd come back here, if he invited her. And next time she'd bring a vest and kneepads, and maybe Nang. But she wouldn't spend more money on another gun.

A sound over her shoulder.

She dropped and rolled into a bush, led with her rifle, and watched a deer slowly cross the game trail. She noticed a splotch of blue paint on its rump ... someone from Alpha had shot it. Rain would wash it off.

Her walkie-talkie softly crackled.

"Spaceman?" It was Hemi.

"Killed," Piper whispered. "Harold's down, too." No sign of the rest of Alpha, but she kept her voice low. Gonzo, Brick, and Hot Sauce were still out there.

"Christmas?"

"Yeah, Hemi."

"You breathing?"

"No hits, but it was close. I got the kill shot on Harold, before a tripwire set with paint grenades took out Spaceman. You guys didn't warn me about paint grenades."

"You're not carrying any?"

"No, Hemi. I'm not carrying any paint grenades. I didn't know there were such things."

"Ooops." Hemi sighed audibly. "My bad. Head's up. Hot Sauce is carrying a 40 Mike-Mike."

A grenade launcher, Piper translated. He had a friggin' paintball grenade launcher? Maybe her friends had all turned into geardos, soldiers who spent too much money on gear that really wasn't necessary. She was not going to be in that league. What was wrong with just using simple paint guns? She'd even balked at the fifty bucks for the Splatterking.

43

"You guys only told me to buy a paint gun," Piper reminded Hemi. "Just a paint gun. Didn't mention grenades or grenade launchers. Didn't—"

"Yeah, well. Sorry. Too bad we lost Spaceman. We still can win this, you know. We can do it without our fearless leader." There was a pause, a soft crackling of static, and Piper slipped carefully from tree to tree, listening for branches moving and finally hearing Hemi again. "Christmas, we're closing in on the hills. Me and Renegade are taking the closest one first. It's higher ground. Gonna get a better look at our objective in the middle before going in. Hang back until we report."

"Roger," Piper replied. But she wouldn't hang back, not wholly, as she wanted in on the action. She reached for the map. She was good at memorizing features and coordinates, had a compass with her, but even in the bright sun the light print of the photocopy vexed her. "Shit and two is four," she said, wishing Spaceman hadn't "died" on the tripwire.

She also wished it wasn't so hot.

Piper had survived tours in Iraq where the temperatures were brutal ... but it was her job and she had no choice. This was just for fun, and she was sweating like a proverbial pig. Another item on her "should've" list: she should have brought a terrycloth headband to keep the sweat out of her eyes. She often used one when she ran in the morning. It was probably ninety degrees already. Hat with a brim, mosquito repellent, and a terrycloth headband—provided she decided to do this again with her old friends. And grenades. She would buy paint grenades. A lot of them.

Minutes later she saw the ridge in the distance through a gap in the trees. She'd not run into any Alpha members, and wondered if one of them was trailing, just waiting for her to get close to the goal before pummeling her with paint. She had spotted one tripwire, disarmed it, and pocketed three paint grenades. She hoped for the chance to use them, even though they were the wrong color.

The game trail she'd been following ended, and she cut through thick, tangled undergrowth, spooking a pair of rabbits and seeing another hawk launch from high in a tree. She found a less overgrown section and pressed on from there, pausing only when she heard more paintball shots and wondering if her side or Alpha was prevailing. Then it was quiet again. She moved on.

Piper figured she should have heard from Hemi or Renegade by now. Maybe they weren't to the top of the nearest hill yet, or worse—maybe they were kills from the fire she'd heard. A confirmed kill was not supposed to talk on a walkie-talkie, though they could listen in. Or maybe they were just trying to be quiet, not risking even a whispered conversation.

She keyed her walkie-talkie anyway, kept her voice low: "Hemi."

Piper waited. Nothing.

"Renegade?"

Nothing again. Not even static.

If they'd both been taken out by Alpha, she'd have to risk King of the Hill alone ... with her fifty-dollar gun.

She clutched one of the paint grenades in her right hand and did a low crawl toward the closest hill. It was a good distance to cover this way, but if she kept her head down she wouldn't be visible to someone on the slope, and she wanted that advantage.

A little closer ... then she froze in disbelief when she heard more gunfire, louder this time. Real? Paint?

Another burst and she knew it was the real thing. Piper discarded her grenade, leaping up, and reaching down the back of her shirt for her pistol. A sheriff twenty-four-seven, Piper always carried her gun and badge.

Who the hell was using a real gun?

She heard two more shots, keyed her walkie-talkie, and rushed in the direction of the sound. Staying close to the trees, weaving through bushes, and leaping over a fallen trunk that had seemingly appeared out of nowhere, she kept her voice low, but clear.

"Spaceman, if you're listening in, someone has a real gun out here."

More gunfire—more *real* fire, and she called for Spaceman again, then Hemi and Renegade.

She needed to find Brick's frequency, and ask what the hell was going on.

"Spaceman," she tried again, voice still hushed. "Hemi. Renegade."

The greens blurred as she churned over the uneven terrain, bursting out of a tree line and heading straight toward the ridge.

"Christmas! Christmas, get down!" That was Brick, his voice unmistakable and cutting through the air, not over the walkie-talkie. Sounded like he was higher, maybe in a tree where a sniper might likely perch. He was somewhere ahead of her. "Real shooter, live rounds! Get the hell down!"

"I know!" Piper kept going, but not in a straight line. An erratically moving quarry was more difficult to hit.

Maybe there was a hunter on the property. She pictured the deer with paint on its rump. It was a few days before bow season in this part of the state. Gun season was two months off. That didn't mean someone wasn't out here hunting illegally.

"Christmas!" Brick hollered. He sounded closer now. "Stay the hell down."

Her walkie-talkie crackled, and through her earbud she heard Spaceman.

"What's going on? Christmas? Hemi? Renegade?"

She dropped down behind a stand of tall sawgrass near the base of nearest hill. Piper hadn't heard any more shots. Maybe the shooter nailed a deer and was done for the day. But the hair prickled on the back of her neck and she waited, listening, risking a moment to key her walkie-talkie.

"Spaceman," she whispered. "You at the cabin?"

"Yeah, second breakfast. Just gonna put it on the stove. But I'm listening in. I think I heard—"

"*Real* gunfire," Piper cut him off. "You heard real fire. Might be done now. Might be over, I hope. I swear it was real."

"Where are—"

"Near our objective, the hills. Brick's nearby."

"Jerusalem Ridge," Spaceman said. "It's called Jerusalem Ridge."

"I'm moving closer. I don't like it. I think Brick's in a tree, but I don't see him. Somewhere near me, I think. What's his channel? Harold still with you? Ask Harold for Brick's channel. I can't raise

46

Hemi." She looked ahead to see more choked grasses ringing the base of the hills. Another low crawl then, a move they'd taught her in basic. She was fast at it.

"Channel three," Spaceman came back. "Brick's team is channel three. You think the shooter's still out there? On my land? Or on the ridge? County property?"

"Get in your car, Spaceman. Drive until you have cell reception. Call the sheriff as a precaution."

She clicked the walkie-talkie over to channel three just as she heard Spaceman reach out to Hemi and Renegade. She heard Harold talking in the background.

Piper bumped over rocks and her elbows and knees felt the dampness of the ground soak through her clothes.

Listening.

"Christmas, where are—"

"The hills, I said. I'm at Jerusalem Ridge. Drive," she answered Spaceman, who'd joined her new channel. "We need the sheriff out here. Get on it, and get cell reception." She almost added: *shut up and just do it*, didn't want to be distracted with an argument, and didn't want to hear any further chatter. Bad enough that she heard Brick again bellowing for her to keep back.

Focus!

As she cleared the next clump of grasses her stomach rocketed up into her throat. There were Hemi and Renegade, down, more than a dozen yards away. They didn't appear to be moving, and they were not covered in Alpha's blue paint. They were covered in red. Piper stood and then instantly dropped in a crouch as more bullets chewed into the ground. It sounded like the barrage came from above and was aimed behind her—maybe the shooter was midway up on the ridge. He was definitely still in the area, and unfortunately still active. Maybe he was firing warning shots.

"Spaceman," Piper said as she keyed the walkie-talkie. "*Listen to me. Listen.*"

"I'm on my way to you."

"No. *Listen.* Get in your car and drive until you have cell reception.

47

Call for an ambulance, call for the sheriff. The shooter is still out here. We've two down. *Really* down. Injured. Maybe worse. Hemi and Renegade are really down."

She heard the thud of footsteps coming up behind her. Another series of shots. A glance over her shoulder—Brick. He skirted the grasses, hunkering, then standing up, looking, crouching again when more shots rang out.

"Someone's shooting *at* me," Brick said. "What the hell kind of game is this?" He looked around her and saw Hemi and Renegade. "Shit. That's blood. Are they dead?"

"This isn't a game anymore," Piper said, edging forward, leading with her gun. "Where's Hot Sauce?"

"North," Brick answered. "I don't know where Gonzo is. Harold's at the cabin, eating again." He poked his walkie-talkie, and she heard him call Hot Sauce and Gonzo, warning them of live fire.

"I'm going to see if Hemi is still breathing."

"Wait. I got something, Christmas." She overheard Hot Sauce respond and ask if Brick was serious about live fire.

"Serious as a coma. Bullets," Brick answered. "That wasn't paint. Where are you, Hot?"

"I'm not waiting, Brick," Piper said.

"I can't cover you," Brick cut back, keeping his voice low. "I got paint. If the shooter's still out there, we're meat. I only got paint." To Hot Sauce: "Where the hell are you? Did you bring a real gun?" To Piper: "Says he has paint. Says he's heading to the cabin, going for help. Still nothing from Gonzo."

Listening, hearing Brick's heavy breathing and her hammering heart, she glided forward, fast and cautious, gaze darting beyond her fallen friends, looking up at the hills, guessing that the shooter had the high ground, but she couldn't identify his post, couldn't tell how high. The hills were barren in places, but mostly they were grass and moss covered, a few thin trees here and there, and some bushes that would provide good cover. She looked again and still didn't see him. One shooter? Two?

Piper risked it, standing now and running toward Hemi and Renegade, making herself a target, and somehow reaching her friends unscathed, crouching to be small. They had on vests, but ones designed to lessen the impact of paintballs, not to stop actual bullets.

Kill shots, center torso, three in Hemi, two in Renegade. Their paintball guns lay at their sides. The left side of Renegade's face was torn off by a round. The ground near Hemi's right hand was disturbed like he'd been clawing at it; his death had not been instant.

"Spaceman," Piper keyed her walkie-talkie. It had a range of thirty miles, long-range, but not top of the line. Spaceman should still be able to hear her.

"Christmas," he came back.

"How far do you have to drive to find cell reception? Or to borrow someone's landline? How much time are we looking at?"

"I don't know. I sent Harold in my car. I'm on my way out to you. I see Hot Sauce heading my way. Brick—"

"Brick's with me. Hemi and Renegade—"

The gunfire started again, coming fast and from above like maddened bees, and this time aimed at her.

CHAPTER SEVEN

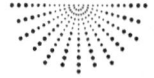

10 A.M. SUNDAY

Piper rolled behind an arrow-wood shrub so dense it gave her good cover. Brick slammed in beside her.

"How did you bring a gun?" Brick was short at five-six, stocky-looking, but all muscle. He'd picked up the name for his cement-block build and being immovable when he wanted to be. His aim was steady, eyesight incredible, perfect for a top-notch, medal-plastered sniper. "Not that I'm complaining, Christmas. Wish I would've brought one. But why did—"

"Sheriff," she stated, parting the leaves and trying to see a glint of metal on the nearest hill—that had to be where the shooter was, based on the latest barrage. "I carry twenty-four-seven. Handcuffs too, and my badge. What do you think we have up there?"

"A hunter maybe," Brick speculated. "Maybe Renegade or Hemi shot at him by mistake. Maybe that scared him, and he started shooting back. Maybe it's just an ugly accident or misunderstanding that got out of hand. Hemi can be jumpy. Hemi—"

"—is dead. Renegade, too."

"Dead." The word was spat out like a piece of rancid meat. "I saw. I don't want to think about it, and—"

"And that many shots? Not an accident. Besides, Hemi and Rene-

50

gade would've only shot paint at him. No reason to kill someone over paint." Her gut roiled over the loss of her friends. She had to concentrate to stay focused.

"No way to call out from here, Christmas. No cell signal."

"Harold's driving for help."

"Harold's fast," Brick returned. "Collects speeding tickets. He'll raise someone. Hot Sauce said he's going for help, too. Hell, dead. A fun weekend off. Dead."

"Spaceman," Piper said, adjusting the volume on the walkie-talkie. The bush they crouched behind had a sour smell and it nested on her tongue, the air feeling uncomfortably heavy. Head pounding. Stomach flipping. "Spaceman—"

"Coming," Spaceman said. "Fifteen minutes out. Maybe twenty. You're on the far side of my land, right up against county property. Not easy to get there."

That's what he'd told her he liked about his grandfather's property —overgrown, choked vegetation, perfect for paintball games, private and peaceful. Except it wasn't peaceful now.

"We've definitely got an active shooter," Brick said at Piper's shoulder. "Still targeting us. Spaceman, can't tell if there are one or two. I'm guessing one with a semi-automatic. What the hell is a shooter doing on—"

"County land?" Spaceman finished. "If he's on the ridge it's not my property."

"Maybe the shooter's not on your land, but Hemi and Renegade were killed on *your* land. So what's a—"

"No idea. Christmas, do you have eyes on him? What's he look like? Tall, thin? Hair—"

"No eyes yet." Piper couldn't see movement on the slope, no glint from a gun, but she felt certain he was there. Gonzo was thin and tallish. Was Spaceman thinking Gonzo was responsible? "Spaceman, Gonzo isn't responding on either channel. Could he be the shooter? Do you know if he's got some issue going on that—"

Brick poked her shoulder and peered through the gap in the bush. "Ain't Gonzo. He's whacked sometimes. Takes depression meds some-

51

times. Prozac. Ain't no way he'd shoot at us. Especially not at Renegade. He's in love with her."

"Then why can't you raise him?"

"Maybe Gonzo's been shot, too," Brick said.

Piper frowned, realizing that could be a possibility. Hemi dead ... not from a skirmish in the Middle East, but to some crazed stranger in the Kentucky woods. Renegade, too. Gonzo maybe.

Gunfire started again, clumps of dirt spitting up where bullets struck the damp ground.

"That was close," Piper said. "But I don't think the shooter can actually see us here unless he changes position. I can go up the hill over there." She pointed in the direction of a scrubby section. I've got an idea where he is."

"Yeah, I've got a pretty good idea, too. His cover is better than ours. Not a good risk, Christmas. And you know it." Brick nudged her again and pointed east. She followed his finger and saw a deep shadow away from the base of the ridge. "Cave," he said.

Keen eyesight. Piper hadn't noticed that it was more than a shadow.

"Let's head for it, see if the shooter comes down."

"Yeah, moving might draw him in if he wants to kill us that damn bad," Piper said.

"That cave would give us an advantage we need. Or it could be our saving-grace hidey-hole until Harold and Hot Sauce bring some cops."

Piper drew her lower lip into her mouth and peered through the branches, again considering a path up the hill.

Brick seemed to sense her waffling. "You go up, and you'll be an easier target. You might get lucky and nail his ass. But he drops you, and I'm left alone. I got paint, Christmas. Paint ain't gonna take him down."

"Listen, Brick—"

"*You* listen. He drops you, I'm next. And you ought to give me your gun. I'm a better shot."

"With a sniper rifle, you are." She would not surrender her pistol.

"Don't try to be a hero, Christmas."

Piper really wanted to go up and find the shooter—or shooters—but Brick made sense. She wasn't thinking wholly straight; she was thinking about Hemi. This wasn't a good time for a knee-jerk reaction, but she really wanted to get the guy. Hemi should not be dead. But she shouldn't do something stupid and join him in the hereafter.

She nodded toward the cave. "Okay. Go."

Brick fast crawled toward the shadow, staying below the sawgrass and sweet spire. Piper was behind him, elbows propelling her, pistol still gripped in her right hand. More gunfire came as they cleared one clump of grass and disappeared behind another. The shooter was visually tracking them. She prayed it wasn't Gonzo.

"Rifle, Spaceman. Good range to it," Brick said. "Probably got a scope." Piper saw he'd keyed his walkie-talkie as he crawled. "Semi-for sure, but maybe a bump-stock to make it full auto. Lot of mud spitting up, big rounds. Hunting gun maybe. You armed?"

"Yeah," Spaceman cut back. "I've got an old Glock."

The shooter definitely had an automatic or semi- from the rate of fire, Piper agreed. Another two dozen yards and they'd reach the cave. Didn't seem far, but it might as well be a gauntlet.

"Move," she told Brick. "Now."

A glance up as she reached the next clump, and she finally saw a glint of metal from a gun barrel. She estimated the shooter was about three hundred and fifty yards away. Brick had been right, while Piper could find some cover low on the hill, to get close enough for a good shot on him—to *really* see him, she'd have to cut through open terrain and give him too much of an advantage.

"Move, Brick," she urged him. "Almost there." She crawled through blood, a streak of it. "You're hit?"

"Yeah. Not bad," Brick said. "I don't think it's bad." He crawled faster as if to prove the point, reached the shadows, and disappeared.

Piper stayed out a moment, covering him, hoping Harold had made it to a spot with reception and had called for an ambulance. Though Hemi and Renegade were beyond needing it, Brick was not. She didn't know the emergency capabilities of the nearest towns, and couldn't guess how long it would take to get medics and sheriff's deputies out here.

She watched the hill, aimed for where she'd seen the glint. Nothing there now. Perhaps he'd moved or had ducked down and was reloading. Taking advantage of the cessation, she raced into the cave after Brick, stooping inside the entrance, looking out, and discovering by rotted timbers just beyond the entrance that it was a mine. The air had a damp funk to it that was filled with the decay of wood and other discarded things. It overpowered the smell of her sweat.

The gunfire started again, aimed at their previous position. The shooter must have taken his eyes off them for a moment and hadn't seen them cut into the shadows. Piper's view of his position was restricted now, and that vexed her.

She took a deep breath of the unpleasant air and looked over her shoulder at Brick, sitting propped up against a wall, holding his leg. The diffuse light reached in just enough that she could see his khakis dark with blood.

"Really not bad," he said to her. "I've had worse."

She set her pistol down and shrugged out of her pack. Inside was a pocketknife, and she crawled to him and used it to cut his trousers.

"Honest, I'm fine. I got it, Christmas."

"Let me—"

"I can take care of it myself. Just watch out for our shooter. He might come in pursuit."

"I don't think he saw us move. He's still shooting at the grass." But she needed to keep her attention on the hill. She'd learned in the military to eliminate the threat before helping your downed comrades. "You good?"

Brick pulled his own backpack loose and took her pocketknife. "I said I got it."

Piper scooped up her gun and turned back to stare out the mouth. The mine ceiling seemed lowest at the entrance; farther in it rose, maybe a natural feature of the earth and rock. This part of Kentucky was riddled with abandoned mines. She wondered if this was marked on Spaceman's old map and she'd just not noticed it amid the faint small print.

"Spaceman. Spaceman," Piper coaxed on her walkie-talkie.

"Fast as I can." She heard his reply through the earbud. "Harold has to have contacted someone by now, the way he drives." Spaceman sounded like he was huffing, running. It wasn't that the distance between here and the cabin was all that far, it was that the route was choked with trees, bushes, ruts, and a myriad of tangled grasses. It didn't allow for all-out speed.

"Brick's hit, not sure how bad," she reported. "We found a mine and—"

"Great! The mine. I know exactly where you are. I've got an old fluorite mine on the property. I'm hurrying. Stay put."

Piper kept her post and waited, listening for movement outside, listening to Brick making a soft growling sound. Time crept by, filled with nothing happening that she could see. Was the shooter moving?

"Come on, come on," she whispered. "Where are you?" She meant both the shooter and Spaceman. "Where? Where?"

She knew there had been many fluorite, lead, and zinc mines in Kentucky right across from Spencer County. From WWI until the 1970s more than half of the fluorite mined came from Kentucky, much of it culled from shallow deposits. Mining trickled to nothing when it became cheaper to buy the mineral from other countries. It basically stopped altogether by the mid-eighties, when the sites were abandoned.

Fortunately, Piper thought, no one had boarded up this forgotten mine.

"Why is it called Jerusalem Ridge?" she whispered.

Brick softly chuckled. "I asked Spaceman that the first time I was out here. It's Biblical. Man who lived around here in the eighteen hundreds—Buck Monroe—climbed to the top and said the view was good, like the new Jerusalem that John the Baptist saw. So he called it Jerusalem Ridge. 'And I saw the holy city, new Jerusalem, coming down out of heaven from God,' some verse in Revelation. Something like that. Jerusalem Ridge."

"It's quiet out there," Piper said. Too quiet. Too—

Another burst of gunfire changed that. She couldn't tell where it was aimed, her sightline too limited, but it sounded close. Maybe the shooter had caught sight of Spaceman.

"Christmas," Brick whispered. "Can you see anything?"

She shook her head. "Sawgrass."

One more burst, and the firing stopped again. She listened. It was eerily silent outside for several minutes. Time crawled.

Was the shooter coming, or leaving?

Piper keyed the walkie-talkie and kept her voice a whisper: "Spaceman, are you out there?"

Nothing.

"Spaceman, I want this guy. I don't want him getting away." Spaceman had said he was fifteen to twenty minutes out, but that was at least fifteen to twenty minutes ago. "Where are you?"

Nothing.

Shit and two is four.

Then a whisper: "Christmas, wait for me."

Piper was relieved Spaceman was still among the living. But she wasn't sure she would wait for him. The shooter had killed two of her friends, maybe three if Gonzo was down, too. He'd wounded Brick, tried to kill her. And the firing had stopped.

Too quiet.

Too unnerving.

If the son of a bitch was leaving the ridge, she needed to go after him. Any sheriff or police on the way might not get here in time to catch the killer. She pictured how she could slip out and go the long way around to come at this from the other side of the ridge. Up and over county property, surprise him. She had to be fast. Not reckless, something strategic.

A deep breath and she edged out into the shadows.

Nothing.

Quiet.

Another step and the gunfire started again.

"Shit." Piper slipped farther back into the mine. Where was Spaceman?

"Spaceman. Spaceman."

No answer.

Had the shooter got him, too? How long until deputies and medics could get out here?

"Shit and two is four and four is—"

"Christmas?" It was Spaceman.

"He's still out there, Space. He's still active. We're still in here. Where *are* you? Did you get lost?"

"Did you see him? Eyes on him, Christmas? Does he look tall and—"

"Nope. No eyes. He's got cover."

"Wait for me. Seriously. Wait. I got turned around out here."

Piper peered out again and still couldn't spot the shooter. About three hundred and fifty to four hundred yards away, she was certain. A semi-automatic rifle with a good range to it. Maybe fitted with a bump-stock like Brick suggested ... which was illegal. But killing people was even more illegal.

She wanted to take the shooter alive to discover why he'd killed her friends and what he was doing out here. Why he was still shooting. He couldn't explain the crime if he was dead. She worried that if Spaceman went after him that might happen. Tall, thin, Spaceman had asked ... what if it really was Gonzo?

She crept out once more. The ground in front of the mine took the bullets. She stepped back in, plotting to move faster next time, dart to her right for cover so she could climb, heave a rock first to distract him. From the trajectory, it appeared he'd moved lower but was still at a range of about three-fifty yards. Not a misunderstanding or an accident—the shooter was bent on killing them. Why? She could call out to him, beg him to stop. But that would only highlight her position and make her an easier target.

"Christmas!" Brick called to her.

A glance behind at Brick. He was holding a bullet between his bloody fingers.

"Look what I dug out," he said, as if he'd found some prize. "Thirty round mag. Left a hole." He dropped the bullet next to him. He'd wrapped his leg with strips from his shredded t-shirt and was standing against the wall, his head less than an inch from the ceiling. "Told you it wasn't that bad, feels better with it out. A little better anyway." A pause: "Very little better."

Piper wondered if he'd bothered to disinfect the blade from her pocketknife. She returned her focus to the ridge. "Brick, did you—"

"Fireball Whisky. Got a couple of airplane bottles in my bag. Stung like a mother. Got one left to drink when we get out of this."

She supposed that sterilization would have to suffice until he got to a hospital where they could clean the wound and repair the damage. How long until medics arrived?

"I'm almost there," Spaceman reported over the walkie-talkie. "Five minutes, ten. I got hung up in some thistles, got a little off course. Found my path. I think I'll come up from the far side of the ridge, county's land, get the high ground on your shooter. Eyes on him yet?"

"No, I say again," she returned. "High ground is a good idea. I'll—"

"Back here, Christmas. I found an answer." Brick had his cell phone out to use the flashlight function, shining the beam along the ceiling deeper in. The mine roof appeared higher, but Piper realized that was because the ground sloped down and the rock above remained constant. "Mines have ventilation shafts. I think I see one back there. It's some sort of hole anyway, light coming down. I can boost you up and—"

"Perfect," Piper quickly agreed. She'd come out at a higher elevation and not where the shooter would expect. It might be her best opportunity to take him alive. She didn't want to put it all on Spaceman.

"I'm almost there," Spaceman said again. "Damn these bushes."

"C'mon, Christmas," Brick encouraged. "Ain't waiting for Space. Let's try this."

Piper didn't want to wait either. On his own land, Spaceman might be lost. She holstered her gun so she'd have her hands free, followed

Brick, who heavily favored his leg. The air was even fustier farther in and thickly scented with rotting vegetation, roots that had traveled down from bushes and trees overhead that had died, green and brown moss. There were discarded, rusted tools along the left-hand wall, as if the workers walked out some decades past and never came back for their equipment.

She spotted the ventilation shaft at the edge of Brick's beam.

"Sunlight's coming down. See? Narrow, some old roots in there, but you're little. I'll give you a boost. Think you can climb it and—"

"Yes," Piper cut back. She'd manage to climb out because she had to. Because Spaceman wasn't here yet. Maybe Spaceman could take the shooter down. Or maybe the shooter would add Spaceman to his tally. It was time to leave this hidey-hole and go on the offensive.

She liked that idea.

Brick laced his fingers like a stirrup, and she put her right foot up, hands on his shoulders. He started to lift her, and then her plans were dashed as the ground opened under them and they plunged into blackness.

CHAPTER EIGHT

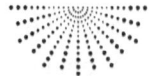

10 A.M. SUNDAY

Oren was back in Fulda, parked near the end of a long blacktop driveway, even with the white wooden sign that read: BUDDHIST CULTURAL CENTER. A red line of paint had been drawn through the "Cultural." Above it someone replaced it with the crudely lettered: *TERRORIST*.

The front of the white saltbox had been defaced with more spray painted words. In red: *Go Home; Anti-Christ; Scum; Poison;* and *Evil.* In green: *Gay; HOMO; Sickos; Death;* and *Athist,* which Oren figured was atheist misspelled. There was black spray paint, too, symbols like Xs and squiggles, swastikas, and something that looked like a crude skull. The graffiti extended only up the first floor, the second level unmarred, no doubt because the perpetrator hadn't brought a ladder. It was one of the worst cases of vandalism he'd seen in the small county.

Chris Hagee's house stood directly across the street. Oren wondered if Chris was watching from one of his windows. More, he wondered if Chris was responsible for this. How could the retired farmer not be?

"Thank you for coming, Chief Deputy Rosenberg," Anthony Delaney said. Tall, willowy, with intense brown eyes, the bald monk

60

had donned his orange robes and sandals. Anthony didn't always wear traditional monk garb; Oren had seen him in jeans and sport shirts. Maybe he was trying to look formal since he'd summoned the sheriff's department.

Oren took out his cell phone. "I want to get some pictures, talk to you and the people staying here. But I'd like to wait until Detective Meredith arrives so we only have to go through all of this once."

"Of course," Anthony said. "Again, thank you for coming. There's more."

Oren raised an eyebrow.

"Our vegetable garden has been ruined. The car's tires slashed. The birdbath is missing. The mailbox ripped off the post."

Anthony's father had lived in this saltbox for decades and was found dead amid his outdoor Christmas decorations on New Year's Day. The elder Delaney had two sons—Anthony and Zachary, the latter being found guilty of murder ... several murders ... and was sitting in prison waiting for trial. Anthony had inherited the house.

Anthony had been living at a temple in Thailand, where he'd gained the title Bhikkhu, which Oren learned meant a fully-ordained monk. Anthony had come back for his father's funeral and soon after decided to stay and open the Cultural Center in the saltbox.

Oren wondered what the local Buddhists did for operating money. Anthony didn't have a job, outside of maintaining the Cultural Center, but maybe the money he inherited along with the house was enough —at least at the moment. Conrad Delaney wasn't poor and had been a bit of a miser, but he didn't leave a veritable fortune, so it wouldn't last indefinitely. Maybe some overall Buddhist organization funneled money here. Maybe he got donations. Small Spencer County wouldn't likely fork out enough funds ... especially if people listened to Hagee and his camp. Curious, maybe he'd come right out and ask Anthony. But not today.

Oren noticed Anthony peering across the road at Chris' house.

"Did you see him do it?" Oren asked. He'd meant to wait for Basil, but he couldn't stop that question.

Anthony shook his head. "I used to wonder if I should have sold this place, donated the money to my father's church or something he loved, moved back home to Thailand. I was happy there. I just thought I'd try this. I thought I'd be honoring my faith and principles while also honoring my father if I stayed here in this house."

"I'm sorry this happened," Oren said. He meant it, and thought he should say more, but left it at that. It was a large, fine house on what he guessed was a little less than an acre. Lots of room for gardens, but too much grass to mow in his opinion. And the biggest downside was the narrow-minded neighbor directly across the street.

"It might have been him." The young monk continued to stare at Chris Hagee's house. "But, no, I didn't see him do it. We didn't see anyone do it. So very quiet, the vandal. It might have been Mr. Hagee. He doesn't care for us. Maybe he just walked across the street and did it out of anger. Mr. Hagee doesn't want me—us—here. I used to get along with him. Before. When I was a kid. I'd mow his grass sometimes. My brother and I—" He let the thought drift.

Basil Meredith's midnight blue Nissan Rogue pulled in behind Oren's Explorer. Esme Meredith was driving and their kids were in the back seat. Basil got out of the passenger side and walked around to the driver's side, leaned in the open window and kissed his wife. He was wearing a pale green long-sleeved shirt, black tie, black pants, and a madras plaid sport coat. He'd been at church when he returned Oren's call, saying the service was just ending and he would be over immediately. Oren and Basil lived only a few blocks apart in Santa Claus, and Oren said he'd give him a ride home.

The detective waved as his wife pulled away, then gaped at the house, shook his head, and approached. Oren met him halfway, putting some distance between them and Anthony.

"Hagee, right?" Basil asked, his voice low. "He did this."

Oren shrugged and talked softly. "Chris would be the natural first guess."

"But—" Basil prompted. "You're thinking no." Basil had been hired by the sheriff in May. He'd been a decorated detective covering gangs, drugs, and high-profile crimes in Chicago and had answered the detective job ad because he wanted to move his young family away from the big city's gun violence. He was nearly as tall as Oren, built like a weightlifter, and black, which marked him as a noticeable minority in basically white Spencer County.

Oren scratched his head, looked across again to Chris Hagee's house. "The more I think about it … it's likely Chris instigated it, got one or more of his buddies to paint the place up. Hell, I got to believe he was involved somehow. But this—" He gestured to the garishly vandalized saltbox. "All of this took a lot of effort, stealth, and time. Chris is lazy. He's a talker, a complainer, a rabble-rouser. But he's not much of a doer. He might have orchestrated it, but he didn't physically do it himself."

They walked toward the monk.

"There is more on the side by the garden," Anthony told Basil. "The profanity worse. And on the side of the garage. A little on the back of the house. It looks like the paint ran out there."

"Any broken windows?" Oren asked. "Any damage inside?"

"Nothing inside," Anthony answered. "I think we would have heard someone inside the house."

"When did you notice this damage? How early?" Basil had his phone out, recording the conversation and taking video of the vandalized sign and the front of the house.

"Early. Before six. I came outside for a walk before breakfast, which I begin preparing at six. And I was outside last night around nine, went to sleep a little after ten. So this happened after ten last night."

"And certainly before six this morning. And you waited nearly four hours to call us. Why the wait?" Basil strolled up the driveway, taking more video. Oren and Anthony followed. "Why didn't you call us right away?"

"I meditated first," Anthony said. "For quite a while. I needed to think about this house, my life. I needed to think about a lot of things. There are three guests staying here, and I meditated with them, too. We all looked for answers. When we were finished, I called Oren."

"Did you find any? Answers?" Oren asked, the thought just coming out. He scowled, hadn't really meant to ask it aloud.

63

Anthony stared at his toes a moment. "Yes, important ones. I decided not to let this vandalism stop me or chase me away. I decided not to let hate and lack of understanding win. I decided to end my second-guessing of staying here and to continue my commitment. And I found peace before I called you."

"Peace? *Gornisht helfn.* I would have found a big helping of angry," Oren mused.

"If I allowed myself to be angry at this, it would be as if I held a hot coal in my hand, ready to throw at the one who wronged me. I would be the one getting burned."

Basil whistled low. "Hate was definitely involved with this, Mr. Delaney."

"Anthony, please," the monk said. "Yes, I understand there was hate."

Basil continued to film the house. "Something like this happens again, Anthony, you call us right away. Before you meditate on it. Understand? Doesn't matter that you're able to accept this, not get angry over it. This sort of stuff can escalate."

"It has escalated. This is worse than the times before," Anthony admitted. "This time I called you because my insurance requires a police report."

Oren and Basil swung to sandwich him.

"This wasn't the first time?" Oren asked.

"No," Anthony replied. "But the three times before were minor compared to this."

Oren frowned. "This is the fourth."

"Yes. Once just the sign, which we repainted. Once just the tires, which we were able to have repaired. Once it was eggs ... a lot of eggs, which we washed off. But this." He paused and studied his toes again. "This time, I need our insurance company to help. I'm not sure how I'm going to clean the siding, get rid of the foul graffiti. I think it might have to be painted over, and that will not be cheap. And the tires will have to be replaced this time. The birdbath ... that was valuable to me because my father had made it. Insurance would cover most of this. But I need the police report to file." He sighed and stared at Hagee's house. "Buddha said: 'Silence the angry man with love. Silence the ill-natured man with kindness.' I have tried these things, Detective, Oren. I must try again and with greater effort."

"Do you have video surveillance?" Basil asked.

Anthony shook his head. "Of course not."

"A home security system? Motion sensor lights?"

"No."

"You should think about all of those things," Basil said. "Especially after this."

Anthony gave him an almost wistful smile. Oren translated that to: "no."

Basil took a deep breath and continued. "You said you have three guests staying here."

Anthony nodded.

"I'd like to talk to them. Inside, out here, doesn't matter."

"I will get them."

"I'll also need the names and contact information of anyone who stayed here in the past few weeks, particularly when your other incidents occurred."

"I will consider that."

"And the dates of the previous incidents," Basil said.

"Mind if we walk around?" Oren gazed at the spot on the front lawn where Anthony's father had been found New Year's Day. "Take some more pictures, note the rest of the damage."

"Please," Anthony said.

"Malicious mischief," Oren said after Anthony retreated inside. "As rotten as this is, the best we can charge is malicious mischief."

"There are degrees of mischief." Basil took more video of the front of the house and then started toward the side where the damaged garden stretched. The detective scowled. "This is a shame."

Plants had been ripped out of the ground. This early in September the tomato vines had been heavy with ripe fruit, most of it smashed. Flowers had been trampled in the beds behind the house, and Oren pointed out where the birdbath had been.

"I see where they ran out of paint," Basil observed. "We're going to find out who did this."

They spent nearly an hour talking to Anthony and his houseguests, the latter no more helpful than the monk had been. Basil repeated all his questions: what goes on at this center; who comes and goes; anyone not happy with their reception here; anyone watching the house; any complaints from neighbors; any threats?

"Just Mr. Hagee," was the consensus on the last three.

"And those threats?" Basil prompted.

"Just words," Anthony said. "Mr. Hagee said if I didn't go back to Thailand, I would be sorry."

Oren and Basil took a few more pictures and notes, then drove across the road to Chris Hagee's.

"He's home," Oren said, after he knocked on the door and rang the bell for the sixth time.

"Saw the curtain move," Basil said. "I'll work on a warrant, but no judge is going to bother with this on a Sunday. Not for vandalism."

"And the courthouse is closed tomorrow for the holiday." Oren knocked again, a little louder. Called out: "Chris, we need to talk to you." To Basil: "But I bet Judge Vaughn wouldn't object to chatting with us tomorrow after breakfast. He never misses the Monday buffet, holiday or no. Snag him there. Wouldn't have to wait for things to open back up Tuesday."

Basil stepped off the front stoop and looked up at the second-floor windows. Oren knocked again. "Search warrant for the house and the garage, looking for spray paint cans, a birdbath. And a warrant for his phone records and computer, see who he's talking to, see if he sent any emails about decorating the Cultural Center across the road." Basil turned and looked at the front yard. "Neglected."

Oren had noticed that on his previous stop. The grass was long, and the weeds along the front flowerbed and at the edge of the driveway were high. "Chris' wife is staying in Owensboro. Maybe she did the yard work."

"Or was the reason he did the outside work," Basil said. "It's nice to do, yard work, relaxing. I didn't have a yard in Chicago. Don't mind the mowing."

Oren knocked again, rang the doorbell. "Chris!"

Finally, the door opened, but only wide enough for Chris to stick his face out.

"I heard you the first dozen times," Chris said. "Can't you let someone sleep late on Sunday?"

Oren doubted Chris had been sleeping, but he looked tired, the collar of his sport shirt rumpled, a shadow of whiskers on his face.

"Need to ask you some questions, Chris," Oren began. Basil stepped up behind him.

"I ain't answering your questions, Chief Deputy Rosenberg," Chris snapped. "Sheriff'll be back Tuesday, you told me. I'll have words with her then about—"

"Need to ask you about what happened across the street, Chris," Oren interrupted. He figured he'd get Chris talking, then turn the conversation over to Basil, stand back and listen.

"You mean all that paint? It's an improvement, don't you think? Added some color." Chris grinned, then his face took on an angry cast. "I didn't do it. I don't know nothing about it." A pause: "I ain't upset about it, either. Like I said, an improvement. If them Buddhas don't like it, they ought to move."

"Do you know who might have—"

"Done it?" Chris glared. "A hero. A God-fearing soul, Chief Deputy Rosenberg. Someone who doesn't want Buddhas operating on this little road in little Fulda. But it wasn't me. No way in hell I'd set foot on that property."

"You want them to leave," Oren said flatly.

"Hell, yes. Everybody in town knows I want them to leave. But I'll get my *neighbors* to leave by legal means. I don't need graffiti to get my message out. When Sheriff Blackwell gets back Tuesday, she and me will talk. She'll get 'em to shut down and go back to Thailand. I've got notes about what goes on over there."

"Mr. Hagee—" Basil started.

Chris' eyes narrowed. "I didn't do it. And that's all I'm saying, and

67

all you need to know. I didn't do it. Y'all have a good Sunday." Chris slammed the door.

"That was unfriendly," Basil said. "We can't force our way in, make him talk to us, we don't have a warrant."

"We'll get a search warrant tomorrow," Oren said. "We got enough to show cause. Let's stop at the some of the neighbors and chat, and then go to Nang's for lunch. My treat."

Basil stepped back and looked up at the second floor again.

Oren joined him and saw Chris pull back the curtain on a corner window and shake his fist, which seemed like a comical, theatrical gesture. Then Chris opened the window and leaned out.

"Met your granddaughter, Chief Deputy Rosenberg. She and me had a nice discussion the other night at the bar. She promised to do something for me when the courthouse opens Tuesday. You better remind her about that promise. I'll check up on her, I will. I know the law."

Oren stopped himself from asking about it.

"Now, like I said, y'all have a good Sunday and be getting your asses off my property!" Chris slammed the window and disappeared from sight.

"We're getting our asses moving," Oren said. Then much softer: "But we'll be back."

CHAPTER NINE

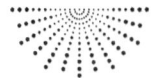

10:30 A.M. SUNDAY

Piper heard more gunfire, but it sounded like it came from a long distance away. She also thought she heard a train chugging past, and then beer glasses clinking, but some part of her knew that neither of those last two was possible. Unfortunately, the gunfire was likely real.

She couldn't see anything.

There was only black.

Was she blind?

Finding it difficult to breathe, she registered that her face was against something hard and damp. She tasted dirt and smelled something fetid, realized that small rocks poked against her cheeks, but they didn't hurt.

Piper didn't hurt anywhere.

She remembered falling. Brick was boosting her up, and then the ground collapsed under his feet. He must have fallen too. She didn't remember landing.

"Brick?" She spat the dirt out of her mouth. "Brick!"

No answer.

She rolled onto her back, breathing easier now. How far had she fallen? Flailing around with her right arm, she tried to find her walkie-talkie but only connected with little bits of rock and clumps of dirt that crumbled in her fingers. She went to reach with her left arm, felt her fingers move, but her arm wouldn't cooperate, wouldn't budge. Was it trapped under something?

Shit and two is four.

"Brick?"

Piper reached with her right arm across her body, rolled a little, and touched her left arm. It wasn't caught under anything. It was wet. Her left arm was wet and sticky and when she wrapped the fingers of her right hand around her left wrist, she discovered that she could pick up her arm, and then could let it flop back down. She couldn't move the arm on its own. A little more prodding revealed that her left arm was broken above the elbow, badly, bleeding, and a bone poked through her t-shirt sleeve. It felt jagged. Her shoulder was oddly forward, and she felt another break right below it.

And four is eight.

"Brick!"

It *should* hurt, her arm. She should be in agony, but she wasn't. Why the hell wasn't she feeling pain?

Too much blood around her. Piper had to stop her arm from bleeding, but the task seemed impossible, not being able to see anything but black. Black and now a hazy circle of gray above, maybe where the light filtered down through the air hole Brick had discovered and that she'd planned to crawl up through.

So, she wasn't blind, but she was in a hole. How deep? How far had they fallen? Why didn't it hurt?

"Brick!"

Still nothing.

Lightheaded and dizzy.

She pressed on the wound, trying to get the blood to stop. Pressure was the key. Pressure and patience, and neither worked.

Panicking, she fumbled with her right hand, undid her buckle, and awkwardly tugged her belt off and sat up. Piper had thorough first responder training years ago at Fort Campbell, repeated it when she was stationed overseas, and took it a third time through the Indiana

Department of Law Enforcement Academy last spring as part of her sheriff certification. She was pretty good at first aid.

Why the hell wasn't she hurting?

A fall with a hard landing, a broken arm, she should hurt.

Might be on an adrenalin high, she thought, which would supersede pain receptors and could explain why she wasn't aching. It would probably hurt like hell when the adrenalin rush wore off. She should take advantage of the high.

All the blood loss? She was feeling lightheaded. If she didn't get her arm to stop gushing, she'd bleed out and die in this hole, her body likely never found. Again, prodding her left arm with her right hand, she determined where the blood was coming from and wrapped the belt above that spot, which was a little below her mangled shoulder. She tightened it, and tightened it again, feeling with her right fingers, which were slippery with blood, feeling, until finally it seemed like the flow had stopped.

I am so screwed.

Her left arm just dangled there. She pictured it looking like a coiled ribbon hanging over the edge of a birthday present.

"Brick?"

He had to be near, right? She tentatively felt around with her right hand, brushing against the canvas of her backpack. It must have come off during her fall. Next to it, something plastic. Ah, her broken Splatterking. She kept exploring with her fingers in the darkness, finding her walkie-talkie—broken and useless, tugging her pack closer and fumbling to open the flap, then dumping the contents out and feeling over them. Water bottle, useful; plastic covered map, useless; package of Goldfish crackers; box of raisins; handcuffs; sheriff's badge; bag of paintballs with some of them broken open; cell phone. She knew there was no cell reception, but it had a flashlight function. Where was her gun? Where was Brick?

"Brick?" she tried again.

Her paint and blood-covered fingers trembled as she played over the phone's keys, everything slick, found the light and pressed the button. Holding her breath, she shined the beam around, playing it across the stuff the backpack had disgorged, across the stone floor and its dusting of dirt and rocks, then the blood—lots of blood. She really didn't want to see her arm, but she angled the light and looked anyway.

Dear, God, that's awful. I am so absolutely screwed.

She turned the beam and it settled on Brick. He was only about five feet away, laying on his stomach, head twisted to the side, eyes closed. Breathing. Piper gulped in the fetid air with relief. He was definitely unconscious, his back was at an odd angle, his right leg twisted and the knee bent in a direction it shouldn't go.

Breathing. But for how long? It looked like his back was broken, his leg too.

She swept the beam around the chamber—small, everything rocky, no passages leading away that she could see, but there was the section in the ceiling they'd fallen through. It was twenty-five or thirty feet overhead, and no way to climb up to it unless you were a spider that could manage the horizontal stretch. She'd not brought a rope or anything that would mimic climbing gear. Why would she have thought to pack a rope for a weekend of paintballing in the woods? And even attempting to scale a wall with only one functioning arm wouldn't happen.

Absolutely screwed.

Someone had to be looking for them, right? Spaceman if he hadn't been shot. And whoever Harold had managed to summon.

Focus on something she *could* do.

Piper wanted to help Brick somehow. He was still breathing. Moving him might cause more harm than good. She also had to help herself. She'd lose her arm if she kept the tourniquet on longer than a few hours. Her cells dying would release toxins—she knew that from her first responder training. The toxins would ruin the arm. And if she loosened the tourniquet, she'd bleed to death. Her thoughts fragmented.

What's one arm? Better to give that up than die.

So screwed.

Brick was still alive.

She breathed evenly, deeply, felt a twinge of pain. Had she cracked a rib or two or three?

Her arm was of more concern.

Cauterize it; she'd have to do that if she couldn't find a fast way out of here. Cauterize it and she could ditch the tourniquet, save the arm. But how? She had nothing to light a fire. Maybe Brick did. Piper was having trouble concentrating and didn't know whether that was from blood loss or terror.

Piper had always considered herself a bit of a bad ass, downrange assignments in the Middle East, racing into danger when others were running from it, chasing murder suspects in Spencer County, getting shot at. But now? Right now, she was terrified.

In a hole in the ground in the middle of the woods, no cell reception, no one knew Brick and she were here, bleed to death or lose her arm. Lose her life maybe anyway ... that was a real possibility. Brick could lose his, too. The hole in the ground might as well be a grave.

Shit and two is four.

Get it together.

Get it together.

GET IT TOGETHER!

Piper thought about Nang and what he'd be cooking at his Quick Stop; about her aging dog and cat at her house—she needed to make it back for them; about her father, the police chief of Santa Claus; about Oren who would have to fill out her term. She pictured Teegan and cursed herself. It had been the dispatcher's birthday yesterday and she'd forgotten, should have thrown her a little party in the break room, should have done something, but she was so excited about this weekend away.

This weekend from hell.

And four is eight.

Move!

She crawled to Brick, her left arm dangling uselessly, though she felt the bones moving around inside it, an unsettling sensation. Another twinge of pain, this time in her legs. Brick's backpack hung on one shoulder. She looked again to make sure he was still breathing.

He was, but his breath hitched now and again, like he was struggling. Didn't know if she should wake him up, or try to anyway. Better not, she decided, better just try to summon help.

"Stay asleep," she whispered.

His walkie-talkie was halfway under him, tucked into his paintball vest. It would be broken, too. But she'd check, just in case. Piper laid the cell phone down, the beam shining away from Brick, but giving her enough diffused light to work with. She oh-so-carefully tugged the walkie-talkie free. It was damaged, but miraculously still in one piece.

Work. Please please please work.

Thirty-mile range. Spaceman would be in range and could hear her ... if he hadn't been shot. It made a squelching sound, working.

"Spaceman," she said. "Spaceman."

Static.

"Spaceman!"

She sat the walkie-talkie down and one-handed opened Brick's backpack, careful like it was the casing to a bomb and she didn't want to disturb the wires inside. Actually, she didn't want to do anything that would jostle Brick. Piper reached her right hand inside, fingers contacting the plastic-coated map, a small bottle which she figured was a Fireball Whisky, a water bottle, a box which she pulled out to discover was Cracker Jack, and a pack of cigarettes, which excited her. She'd forgotten Brick was a smoker, and if he had cigarettes, he had something to light them with. She found two more cigarette packs before she came to the lighter, sat back, and contemplated what to do next.

She reached for the walkie-talkie and felt the bones move again inside her arm. There was a slight throb, dull, the hint of pain trickling down from her shoulder. Maybe she could cauterize her arm. But she still had time to worry over that.

"Spaceman, are you—"

Static.

Shit.

"Christmas! Where the hell are you?" His voice through the walkie-talkie sounded like heaven.

"In the mine. Brick and me, we fell through the floor. The shooter—"

"Down. He's down. Help is coming, Christmas."

She kept the conversation short as she felt a numbness in the fingers of her left hand, and an ache traveling up and down her arm from her shoulder to her wrist, and then a lance of pain settling in deep and threatening to take her breath.

The adrenalin rush fading and reality crashing over her.

Piper gasped at the piercing pain that raced through her limbs and nested in her chest.

Everything hurt.

Absolutely everything.

She couldn't think.

And then the world was black again.

CHAPTER TEN

NOON SUNDAY

"I'm probably not pronouncing it right, but I'll have the *cải xào nấm*. And this looks new, the *rau muống xào tỏi*," Basil said, glancing up at the menu above the counter in Phan's Quick Stop.

"What is it?" Oren wondered. "That new one?"

"First time on the menu." Nang grinned. "*Rau muống xào tỏi*, which Detective Meredith pronounced fine, is a special water spinach. I just discovered a market in Owensboro that carries it. I fry it with garlic. It is an excellent side dish. The *cải xào nấm* is bok choy served warm with shitake mushrooms over rice and with soy sauce." He looked at Oren. "I recommend both."

Oren liked Nang's food, but he was iffy on ordering something that might have too many mushrooms. He didn't care for them on pizza either. "It's good, right?" He looked down at his cell phone and sent a text. "The spinach?"

"Very," Nang said.

"Okay. I'll try that water spinach then, but I'll pass on the *nấm*. And give me three spring rolls." Oren looked at the menu again. "And a bowl of beef pho soup. I'm hungry, skipped breakfast. And a big mug

76

of coffee. Black, one sugar. No, two sugars. Maybe something for dessert. We'll see."

"Do you have green tea?" Basil looked out the window when he saw a red Mustang convertible pull up to the pump. The driver was an elderly woman under five feet, wearing a bright paisley headscarf. She got out, put on a white glove, and punched the Premium button as she grabbed the nozzle.

"The only brand I carry is Tan Cuong Green. Fragrant, and it has a sweet aftertaste. Most people want a jolt of caffeine."

"He's paying today." Basil pointed at Oren. "And I don't do much caffeine."

"Sit. I'll bring it over when it's ready."

The woman in the scarf came in to pay for her gas. She took off the glove and put it in her pocket.

"I see you got those pay at the pump things," she said. "I won't use them. I don't trust them. I like cash." She passed over a fifty and Nang gave her change. She pushed four dollars back. "And I want two scratch-off lottery tickets, the ones with flags on them."

Oren—and most everyone else in Spencer County—knew that Nang was passing through Fulda a few years ago when he stopped at this station for gas and a lottery ticket. The Quick Stop was for sale at the time. Nang had won enough on the lottery ticket to buy the store, and did just that because he took it as an omen. The place previously had offered hotdogs, soft pretzels, and soda, and he was quick to take them off the menu.

Nang grew his three-table Vietnamese restaurant into a business that also catered reunions, weddings, and the like; installed two more pumps outside; recently added the pay-at-the-pump option with video surveillance; and opened a full-service garage on the property. Nang had a two-year automotive degree from across the river, but his passion was Vietnamese cooking: the Quick Stop let him use both professions.

"No, make it three lottery tickets," she said, adding two more dollars. "You have a good week, Nang."

"You, too, Margaret. Tell Ian hello."

77

Oren knew that Nang sold a lot of lottery tickets to people hoping to catch the same lightning. He'd probably buy a couple on his way out. The ones with the flags on them.

They picked the closest table, and Oren sat so he could watch the front door ... force of habit. Nang brought the tea and coffee.

"It will be a few minutes for the rest."

"No hurry," Oren told him. "We've got time today." He wanted to talk to Basil about the graffiti and Chris Hagee. It wasn't a staggering amount of damage moneywise to the saltbox, he suspected, but the thought of it burned in his chest. So Bhikkhu Anthony Delaney was not angry. Oren harbored enough anger for both of them. His phone beeped with a return message.

"I sent a note to Millie," Oren told Basil. "I'm curious what favor she's doing for Chris Hagee. She's going to join us. Said she didn't want to talk about it over text."

The bell jangled and a twentyish couple holding hands came in, both in jean shorts and t-shirts, skin tanned, hair streaked by the sun. They ordered at the counter and picked the table closest to the restrooms. Then they pulled out their cell phones and started to surf. Oren wanted to tell them to talk to each other. Didn't young people do that anymore?

He saw Basil looking at them, scowling, maybe likewise disapproving of the couple's detachment. Then the detective stared at the space in front of him. The placemats had photos of Vietnamese temples on them. Basil's displayed the Tran Quoc Pagoda in Hanoi. He sipped some tea, took out a pen, and made random-looking doodles on the pagoda. Then he drew a swastika like had been painted on Anthony's house.

"Right before I left Chicago the aldermen were breathing down the department's neck to be more aggressive about graffiti. They were mostly concerned about the Ryan, Eisenhower, and Kennedy expressways. You drive those routes into the city and see graffiti. It's ugly. The taggers have to scale walls and dodge cars to put it up. We didn't make many arrests along the expressways because the taggers were so hard to catch. But the arrests we made stuck. The Illinois Department of Transportation cleans it all up, but it isn't as big a priority as filling potholes and picking up trash. Sometimes the graffiti stays up for days."

"But the aldermen kept pushing?"

"Oh, yeah. The aldermen, they were hot about it because they didn't like the notion of people driving into the city seeing all the concrete defaced. Thought it was a bad 'welcome to the Windy City' vibe."

"We've always had some graffiti here," Oren admitted. "But not a lot, all things considered." He took a long drink of the coffee and made a contented sighing sound. "And we've caught people at it from time to time. It's vandalism, not serious really, but it can wreck property value, hurt feelings, and can be a bear to clean. What was done to Anthony Delaney's house was outright awful, and probably the worst I've seen here."

Basil drew "V" birds in the sky above the temple. "In Chicago there's a Graffiti Removal Program, and private property owners can call it, no charge for the work. A blast truck comes in with baking soda under high water pressure, gets the paint off brick and stone. They have a paint truck that takes care of covering up the graffiti on vinyl and wood. No one should have to put up with their property being tagged."

"Nice," Oren admitted. "No such thing here. Not enough of a problem, and not enough of a budget."

"Obviously. At least Mr. Delaney has insurance." Basil sipped more tea.

"That's something, I suppose."

"Streets and Sanitation worked with us, and we adopted a graffiti-busting grid system. Crews would patrol the five wards. There were almost two dozen units in the graffiti-fighting fleet, and a couple of trucks were set up with chemical tanks to help strip off the paint. The department always took it seriously, despite what some of the aldermen thought. Murder, theft, kidnapping, those are always the biggies. Vandalism doesn't seem like such a serious crime in comparison, but it is a crime, and the doers need to answer for it."

79

"So how long did it take?" Oren nodded to Nang as he approached with a tray, steam curling up from the dishes.

"Take?"

"For someone to get their place cleaned up?"

"Ah, I get you. Well, despite having a dedicated task force, because of the sheer number of graffiti calls it took about four days to respond to any one complaint. But, like I said, folks got their places cleaned up free of charge."

Nang served the young cell phone couple who hadn't said a word to each other. Then he tended to Oren and Basil, arranging the plates on the table and bringing more tea and coffee.

"Thanks, Nang," Oren said. "This looks great." He went after the soup first, then stopped halfway through and tried the water spinach. He was surprised at how tasty it was and made a mental note to order it again. He watched Basil eat. The detective was fast, but Oren wasn't about to match the pace. He wasn't in a hurry.

Basil pulled out his phone and searched for something. "I've been reading a lot about Indiana's various laws, seeing what compares and what contradicts with Illinois. Yes, whoever vandalized Anthony Delaney's house can be charged with malicious mischief. But we can do better than that." He nudged his empty plates aside, picked up his pen, and circled the swastika he'd drawn on the pagoda.

"Hate crime," Oren said.

"Damn right," Basil replied. "It definitely fits the classification of a hate crime." He looked at the screen on his phone and read: "The definition includes: 'an offense in which the person knowingly or intentionally damages property because of the color, creed, disability, national origin, race, religion, or sexual orientation of the owner or occupant of the affected property.' The FBI has a similar definition." He put the phone down. "Definitely a hate crime. Worse, Anthony Delaney's house could be considered a place used for religious worship, and that ups the mischief charge even more."

Oren whistled.

"So," Basil continued, "while a regular malicious mischief charge in Indiana could net the doer a fine of several hundred dollars and few days in jail, our Delaney tagger could be looking at up to six years in prison and a ten thousand dollar fine."

"I want the guy," Oren said. "The guy who put up the paint, and Chris if he instigated it. I bet we could get District Attorney Scales to push for the maximum. He'd probably be happy to get a case like this. Something different to work with."

Basil made a few more doodles on the placemat. "Despite all the ugliness of it, the disrespect for property, I saw some graffiti in the neighborhoods that was art. Incredible what some of the taggers could do, the colors, blending, pictures. The murals especially. Honestly, I saw places where the graffiti improved the look of a building, made something drab and dirty into something beautiful. Essentially improved the block."

Oren nodded. "I see some good stuff painted on trains. The Hoosier Southern Railroad is a twenty-two mile length of track that runs from Cannelton over in Perry to Lincoln City and Santa Claus. When I'm stuck at the crossing, I count the freight cars going by. Habit. Lots of them have names spray painted on them, love notes, slogans, some cartoons. Saw a really nice-looking Snoopy on his dog house once. Lots of blues and white. A little black, sometimes yellow. But mostly blues and white. Once in a while you see the outline of words or of initials, and a half-finished illo, like the train moved on while the artist was still working. Always wondered if someone else in another city would finish the design."

The bell above the door jangled and Millie came in, waved to Oren, headed straight to the counter, and ordered.

"Try the water spinach," Oren called.

"My daughter says she wants to be a cop when she grows up." Basil shook his head.

"Runs in some families," Oren replied. "My father, now my granddaughter."

"So, it skipped a generation."

Oren nodded. He didn't want to discuss his daughter.

"I was just getting in the car when you messaged me, Pops, was going to go grocery shopping." Millie smiled broadly as she sat. "I'll go shopping after this. Couldn't turn down lunch at Nang's and a chance to gossip about Mr. Hagee."

"So gossip," Oren encouraged.

"The short version is a guy named Henry Tucker got a few free drinks at G's Bar, and Chris Hagee got so hot about it he called the department. And, lucky me, I caught it."

"It's not about the free drinks. It's about Anthony Delaney." Oren shifted in his seat. "We talked to Henry Tucker a little while ago, and he didn't mention the G's Bar incident. Henry lives a few doors down from Anthony Delaney's, which was vandalized this morning. Henry said he didn't see or hear anything regarding the vandalism, but mentioned how nice Anthony and his houseguests have been to him. Said he'd like to know who spray-painted the house, is worried it'll spread down the road. He's definitely friendly with Anthony. His son and Anthony used to go to high school together. He asked if we thought Chris Hagee did it."

Basil leaned back and waved at Nang for another tea refill. "I hope you didn't try to arrest Henry for drinking on the house, Millie. That's not illegal."

"I know it's not. Chris Hagee wants the *bartender* locked up, not Henry Tucker." Millie shook her head. "Did you know that in Indiana it is illegal to serve someone a free drink and not give the same deal to everyone else? Not kidding. It's a real law. Don't expect it gets enforced much, if at all. Chris Hagee really pressed me on this. In fact, he showed me the law. I'd never heard of it. I had to file a report, take a bunch of statements. Going to the DA's Tuesday with it. Great, eh? How'd he even know about the weird law—"

"I know how," Basil cut in. "You know that MSN page that pops up when you go online? If it's your homepage? They had an article a few days ago about antiquated laws on the books in each state. That was the one listed for Indiana. I read it because I skim stuff like that. I bet he read it, stuck it in his brain, and called it up when he was at the bar last night."

"I'm obligated to put this on DA Scales' plate," Millie huffed. "I can't just ignore it."

Oren crossed his arms and scowled. "Like I said, Henry didn't mention the bar incident when we talked to him earlier. But we didn't know about it to ask him. He was worried about the vandalism at Delaney's though. Really thinking he might get spray-painted next."

"Because Henry Tucker likes his Buddhist neighbors? Sheriff Blackwell isn't due back until Tuesday morning," Millie said. She smiled her thanks as Nang set her lunch down. "Should we call her? Let her know what's brewing?"

"Can't," Basil said. "She's in the middle of the woods, Kentucky, playing Army. There are no cell towers, no reception. Primitive. Relaxing."

"Paintball," Oren supplied. Softer: "So young she's still playing with toys." He noted Millie glower. "Besides, Chris Hagee isn't earth-shaking enough to bother her over."

Millie dug into the water spinach. "Oh, this is so good."

"When she comes back, she won't shut the Buddhists down," Oren continued. "They haven't caused any problems, and the only thing wrong with their Cultural Center is that it's right across the road from a blustering bigot."

Basil looked up from his placemat. "I want the search warrant, see if Hagee's got spray paint, see what he's been emailing and to who. See if you're right, that he didn't do it, but incited it. See just who he might have talked into vandalizing the Delaney house." He met Oren's gaze. "I haven't been to G's Bar before."

"Me neither. We should go."

"I've nothing planned the rest of the day except mowing my yard," Basil replied. "And that can wait anyway. It's going to rain again."

"At least the sheriff's got three days away from all this crap," Millie said. "She's getting to have a little fun with her Army friends."

"Yeah," Oren said. "At least someone in the department's having fun."

CHAPTER ELEVEN

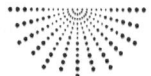

2 P.M. SUNDAY

Gunther pulled a face when Basil and Oren walked into G's Bar. He was wiping off a table near the front window and thrust the towel into the band of his apron, spun on the ball of his foot like a drill team marcher, and retreated toward the back.

"Gretta," he hollered. "The sheriff's here." A pause: "Gretta! They're gonna haul you away in handcuffs! The squad car's out front."

Oren was surprised the place was so busy, being the middle of a Sunday afternoon in a town so tiny it wasn't counted in the past census. A man and a woman who looked to be in their thirties were playing pool, and another dozen patrons—two seated at the bar, and ten paired off at five small tables—stared at him. He took off his hat.

He thought the place smelled good, of polished wood, fried onions, and hamburgers. Maybe he should have suggested having lunch here instead of Nang's. Though he was on an eternal diet, he had a fondness for grease and carbs.

"Spent some money on the inside," Basil noted.

Oren had thought the outside was rundown and in need of some new paint and a whole lot of nails to shore it up. But the inside looked like a team of remodelers from one of those TV reality shows had swept in and made everything shine.

"Looks pretty nice," Oren admitted. "Probably why they're doing a good business."

Basil lowered his voice: "Only in a county like this would a dozen customers be considered a good business."

Just as the patrons lost curiosity in watching Basil and Oren, Gretta Mueller came through a door in the back and renewed everyone's interest. The customers again looked on intently, and Oren heard a man at the bar say: "Twenty bucks they arrest her." "And Gunther, too," another put in.

"Not here to arrest anyone," Basil said. He nodded politely to Gretta. "Miss Mueller."

Gretta's hair was more white than gray, long and pulled back in a banana curl ponytail that hung down to below her shoulder blades, pretty, like it had been styled. She wore makeup, tasteful—a little mascara, a coppery brown eyeshadow that had a faint glimmer to it, some rose color to her cheeks, dark pink lipstick. A gold necklace had a heart charm dangling from it that matched her earrings. A second, longer gold necklace featured a cross. She had on an expensive-looking dark blue pantsuit; an apron with damp spots covered most of it. Maybe she'd come here after church and had been doing dishes in the kitchen.

"Good afternoon, Oren," she said in a chilly voice, then turned. "And you are—"

"Basil Meredith," Basil supplied.

"*Detective* Meredith," Oren added. He had gone to high school with Gretta, though they'd traveled in different small circles. She'd hung out with the smart girls, the ones not so pretty or thin or athletic. High school seemed to divide itself along pigeon-hole lines. He knew she'd gotten a full-ride scholarship to Purdue—it had made the local news—and came back to the county when she was done with her master's, started teaching. He also knew she lived in Fulda, in a farmhouse she'd inherited from her parents who died about twenty years ago. Her brother Gunther lived with his wife in Rockport, in a small

85

brick house a few blocks from the Sheriff's Department and right across the street from an insurance office where Oren had his policies. Gunther owned that office, but this summer had passed the management of it along to his son, probably about the same time Gretta opened the bar.

"You're the big-city hire I read about in the newspaper this summer, right? Your wife writes romance novels? I think I've read one or more of them."

Basil nodded. "I used to work for the Chicago Police Department."

Gretta snorted, a half-laugh. "Bet you never had to arrest a bar owner in Chicago because she gave out a few free drinks."

"We're not here to arrest anyone," Basil repeated.

Oren pointed to the empty table Gunther had cleaned. "Do you have a few minutes to sit and talk to us?" He saw that Gunther had drifted close and was listening, and he also noticed that the brother and sister looked quite a bit alike, much more than they had when he went to high school with them.

"Sure." She reached behind her back and undid her apron, took it off, and handed it to Gunther. The outfit was actually a linen blazer over pants a few shades lighter and complimented by a cream-colored blouse with black pearly buttons. Oren figured she'd definitely worn it to church this morning, as it was definitely not bar attire. "What would you like to drink, Detective? Oren?"

"Diet soda," Oren answered. "Don't care what kind."

"Ginger ale," Basil said, as he walked to the table and selected the chair that would give him the best view of the bar.

Oren took the one where he could keep an eye on the front door, force of habit.

"Gunther—" Gretta gestured with her head.

"I'll get them." Curtly, to Oren: "That'll be five dollars for both, pay up front, no freebies, no discounts. Freebies and discounts are illegal." Then he was gone to get the drinks and make a phone call.

Basil put a five on the table.

"It shouldn't be a crime to give out a few drinks," Gretta said, as she settled into a chair and started tracing a whorl in the tabletop. "I own the place, I set the prices. And if I want to—"

"No, it shouldn't be against the law," Oren said. "But it is against the law in Indiana."

"Some obscure damn thing that I looked up on the internet after Chris Hagee complained," Gretta huffed. "I shouldn't be arrested for—"

"We really don't want to talk about that this afternoon," Basil said. "That's all a matter for the DA, and it is up to him."

"Then why are you here?"

Gunther brought the drinks and took the five.

"Would you get me a glass of water?" Gretta asked him.

"I think they should arrest that jerk Hagee," Gunther said, as he retreated behind the bar.

"That's what you came out here for?" she pressed. "To talk about Chris Hagee?"

"Yes," Basil admitted.

She crossed her arms and let out a breath. "That stupid son of a bitch," she pronounced. "He's always been a little bit of a pain in the ass, but he was tolerable before. Close to cordial sometimes."

"Before Anthony Delaney opened the Buddhist Cultural Center?" Oren asked.

"Yeah. Chris was tolerable—mostly—and had a little gaggle of friends. Before the Buddhists."

"Redneck friends is what he had." Gunther brought Gretta a tall glass of water with ice, beads of moisture glistening on the outside. He placed a round leather coaster down that said "G's" on it, then handed her the glass.

"Chris and Joan started coming here about a week after I opened, usually around four in the afternoon for an early dinner," Gretta said.

"Usually twice a week," Gunther supplied. "Mondays and Wednesdays. Every once in a while on Saturday night if we were running a sandwich special. Past several times he's only been here by himself." He spun and went to another table, where a man had raised an empty mug.

87

"What did he talk about," Basil prompted, "when he came in?"

"Lately, the Buddhists," Gretta was quick to answer. "The damn scammy credit card refinancers from India that seem to call everyone, and the Buddhists. Listen, I'm Catholic. Gunther's wife is Presbyterian, and my nephew claims to be a pagan and has an altar to Thor in his apartment. I don't care that there are a bunch of Buddhists living in Fulda. I taught Anthony Delaney in high school. Good kid, smart, a little distant, needed focus. If he found that focus in Thailand, that's okay. Luke said: 'Do not judge, and you will not be judged. Do not condemn, and you will not be condemned. Pardon, and you will be pardoned.' Chris used to go to my church. But that was some years ago. I think he forgot all the scripture."

The couple started another game of pool. Someone fed a dollar into the jukebox. George Strait began singing *Amarillo by Morning*.

"Did you know he has a petition going around?" Gunther was back, hovering. "He had a bunch of names on it that I saw when he waved it at me. I almost signed it to get him to shut up, but I figured that would encourage him. We told him not to pass his petition around here."

"A petition regarding the Buddhists?" Basil pulled out a notebook and wrote in it.

"Yeah," Gunther returned. "And they never did anything to him as far as I know. They've not bothered anyone in town."

"Anthony Delaney has always been friendly," Gretta said. She smiled softly, and Oren thought she might be remembering days from school. "But his brother, Zachary—" She let that thought hang.

Gunther paced behind Gretta. "I feel sorry for him, you know, Hagee. The man's got to be damn unhappy to stir up things like he's doing." Another customer raised a hand, and Gunther hurried away.

"Did you ever hear Chris threaten anyone?" Oren recalled Chris' comment that the monk might end up dead like his father. While it hadn't come across quite as a threat, it nevertheless bothered him. The worst thing that Chris had done—that Oren was aware of—was steal sleigh bells. Conrad Delaney had been found dead in the big sleigh in his front yard on New Year's Eve. Chris had discovered the body and called the sheriff's department ... but not before he'd taken the antique bells that had hung on the sleigh. He returned them upon threat of arrest when the theft was noticed. Maybe Chris had done other things, but nothing that had crossed Oren's desk besides a few drunk and disorderly complaints.

"Do you know much about his family, Oren?" Willie Nelson started singing *Pancho and Lefty*, and Gretta tapped her thumb in time with the mournful beat. "The apple and the tree, you know."

"I know his father and uncle owned a farm over by Pedigo. The uncle's still alive, and the farm's still going, but I'm not sure who's running it. I know Chris bought his own farm shortly after high school, his dad giving him some money and co-signing a loan. He leases his land now, has someone else work it. Considers himself retired."

"Chris' grandfather and great-grandfather were members of the KKK. I don't know about Chris' dad. Maybe he was, too," Gretta said flatly. "My mom told me that, about the KKK. She was friends with Chris' mom. Ida, I think her name was. She said Ida found robes up in the attic when she was cleaning after some funeral. The Klan gatherings had gone out of fashion some decades before, and they'd tucked that unfortunate bit of family history away in an old chest. Ida took the robes out and burned them. It's the apple, you know, not like Chris had a choice, being born into a family full of prejudice."

Chris' prejudice had always been visible to Oren, but he hadn't known the roots of it. He listened and watched Basil make more notes.

Gretta went on. "I just believe that some of that hate and prejudice trickled down to Chris, that he didn't have much of a chance to duck it, you know. It's in his blood. How thick? I don't know. There's degrees to prejudice, Oren, Detective. He probably doesn't like either of you much because you're Jewish, and you're black. But he doesn't have a petition circulating about you. The Buddhists? I don't know why they tripped his trigger. Maybe they were just convenient. Maybe Chris needs to be upset about someone who doesn't fit into the mold of what he considers American. Maybe Chris just wants to be both-

89

ered about something and they're an easy target because they're right across the street. One of those souls who isn't happy unless he's unhappy. But, honestly, why the hell did he come in here last night and cause trouble for me? I would've given him all the free drinks he wanted if it would've kept him in check."

Oren thought it looked like Gretta was about to cry. She pulled her lips into a straight line and closed her eyes. When she opened them, it seemed like she was looking at something far beyond the interior of her bar.

"Henry Tucker," she started. "I'm seeing him, you know. Henry goes over to Anthony Delaney's once in a while. Henry's youngest son is around Anthony's age, and they went to school together. Henry goes over there with his son, and they've had Anthony over to their house for dinner a few times. I was there once. Henry's boy still lives at home. Dale should be out on his own—he's almost thirty. But Henry doesn't push him, and doesn't mind that he's thinking about being a Buddhist. So what if I give Henry a few free drinks? What the hell is wrong with that? It's my bar. And what the hell is wrong about Henry being friendly with Anthony Delaney? What the hell is wrong with Chris?" She started crying then and got up from the table, stood behind her chair. "Do you two need anything else?"

"No," Basil said. "Thanks for taking the time."

"So, I'm not going to be charged with anything, right?" Gretta asked.

"Not our call," Oren said.

"It'll be up to the district attorney, and I can't guess what he'll do," Basil said.

"Well, not that Hagee'll ever show his face in here again, but if he comes back, I'm not going to serve him," she said. "I can refuse to serve him, right? Or can I get charged for that, too?"

Basil grimaced. "You can't refuse service based on race, color, religion, or national origin."

"What about because he's an asshole?"

"No court is going to uphold a right to refuse service for any discriminatory reason," Basil answered.

"Piss." Gretta headed to the back of the bar.

Oren and Basil left and stood by the Explorer as they watched Henry Tucker edge his Sonata into the dirt parking lot across the blacktop road. Rain softly pattered the asphalt.

"See, I couldn't have mowed this afternoon," Basil said.

Lightning flickered overhead and thundered answered.

"Looks like we're really going to get dumped on," Oren replied.

Henry locked his car and started across the road.

"This is convenient," Basil said, nodding toward Henry.

"Nice that something is." Oren raised a hand. "But I'll bet that Gunther called him, asked him to come by."

Henry waved and headed toward them. Oren knew Henry was one of the managers at the power plant, was probably in his mid to late fifties, as much as a decade younger than Gretta Mueller. He didn't have a lot of hair, nothing on top, just a ring of brown streaked with gray that ran around his head like the tonsure of Robin Hood's merry man, Friar Tuck. He'd been married for nearly thirty-four years, his wife dying eighteen months ago from leukemia. Oren thought it fine that Henry'd found someone else in Gretta, even if she was older. Shouldn't be illegal for Gretta to give Henry drinks either, he figured. That law needed to change.

"Hey, Oren." Henry stopped a few feet away. His blue jeans looked new. He had on a pressed long-sleeved shirt, mustard yellow with faint red lines running through it, a bolo tie. In Oren's mind, the man's polished Chelsea boots, more a throwback to the Beatles and the Sixties, contrasted with the rest of his Western-flavored attire. Church attire? More likely he wanted to impress Gretta. "Is Hagee causing trouble here again?"

Oren shook his head. "We're just out here—"

"Not to arrest Gretta, I hope. I think Hagee has his head up his—"

"Just out asking some questions," Oren interrupted.

"And getting wet," Henry observed.

"Speaking of questions …. When we talked to you earlier today, you didn't mention Chris Hagee being at G's Bar, stirring up trouble over a few free drinks," Basil put in.

"Well, you didn't ask me about it. And, quite frankly, I didn't want to talk about that. Leaves an awful taste, you understand, what he did, calling the sheriff because Gretta gave me free beer. Awful. You only asked about all the paint at Anthony's house."

"True," Oren said.

"Do you think it's related? Do you think Hagee is going to paint up G's next? Put swastikas and stuff all over it?" Henry stabbed the ball of his foot against the lot and spit. "He wants her arrested, all because she gave me a few beers. Three glasses of beer. But you can't arrest her if you arrest him first, right? If you get him first—"

"That's not how it works," Basil said.

"Hagee should be in jail. You know he put all that paint on Anthony's house. I should've told you I saw him do it."

"But you didn't see him, did you?" Basil asked.

"No, I didn't. Anthony told me he didn't see anyone do it either. Sneaky S.O.B. who did it. I told Anthony he better put a camera up by his front door. I ordered one off Amazon a couple of hours ago. I'm one of their Prime members, so I should get it delivered tomorrow. I'll put it up right away. If Hagee throws swastikas up on my house, I'll have video to catch him. You can arrest him then, right?"

Basil didn't reply, but Oren nodded.

"You have a good afternoon, Henry," Oren said as he opened the driver's side door.

"One without free beer," Henry returned. "One out of the rain."

Basil settled into Oren's Explorer and whistled low. "Beats covering gun violence downtown, drugs, gangs. But it's still ugly."

Oren turned on the windshield wipers and pulled out of the parking lot. "I know Piper sent Diego out to answer some of Chris' complaints this summer. Just to frost his muffins, because Diego's—"

"Not white," Basil said.

"She was poking the bear," Oren said. "Chris and I go back. Hell, I go back with a lot of people in this county. Like I said, prejudice in degrees … or maybe its selective prejudice. Yeah, I'll go with selective prejudice. I'm Jewish, Chris doesn't mind me so much. But, then, I don't live across the road from him. He might not get along with me if I did. In fact—"

The dispatcher called, interrupting.

"Sheriff Blackwell is in surgery in Hartford, Kentucky," Zeke reported. "I don't have all the details yet, but it's something about a cave-in and multiple fatalities. Sounds pretty serious."

"*Gornisht helfn,*" Oren spat.

CHAPTER TWELVE

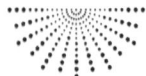

8 A.M. MONDAY, SEPTEMBER 7TH

The eggs tasted awful. Piper took another bite and revised her opinion. They didn't taste like anything, no flavor, felt funky on her tongue, and maybe weren't even real eggs. But she was so hungry she ate them anyway. The cup of oatmeal was worse. Ugh. She nudged it away. Piper reached for the coffee and held her nose over it before taking a sip. It was passable, but not as warm or strong as she liked.

"You didn't have to stay here all night," she told Nang, setting down the cup. He'd just returned from the cafeteria, carrying a plastic spoon and a container of black cherry yogurt that looked more promising.

"Yes, I did." He pulled back the top and gave it to her.

It tasted decent, so she practically inhaled it.

He'd slept in the chair in her room. Her father, the chief of police of Santa Claus, had volunteered to also stay, but Piper managed to talk him into going home. She wasn't hurt *that* bad, she'd convinced him. And Santa Claus and Wrinkles needed him.

But she was indeed hurt that bad. She was just good at putting up a hale front.

She'd lost a lot of blood and had needed a transfusion when she

94

was brought in yesterday afternoon. The hospital happened to have an orthopedic surgeon on staff for the holiday weekend, so she was taken into surgery almost immediately. Her shoulder had been dislocated, her arm broken in three places—one a nasty compound fracture. She had four cracked ribs, suffered a concussion, and was in shock. Piper had overheard one of the nurses say she was surprised it wasn't worse.

Now she had a titanium rod in her arm and plenty of screws to keep it there. They'd stapled the skin when they were done with the rod, from her shoulder to her elbow, wrapped it, put her in a splint contraption, and gave her a lot of antibiotics and pain meds.

If everything went well, she'd get the staples removed in three weeks, and x-rays sometime after that to make sure the bone was starting to heal. More x-rays a few months later, then some physical therapy sessions.

Restricted duty for up to six months, the surgeon had told her. No driving until given the okay. While she could manage an Explorer one-handed, the surgeon had explained if there was an accident and the airbag in the steering column went off, the force would further injure her broken ribs and arm. Besides, the prescribed pills would make driving unsafe.

She closed her eyes in frustration and settled her head into the pillow.

The bed should be uncomfortable, she knew. Hospital beds always were. But it felt like she was floating in pudding, a not unpleasant sensation; the pain meds were that strong.

Nang hovered, while she concentrated on not crying. It wasn't that she didn't want to appear weak in front of him. If she cried, he'd press her. She just didn't want to talk about what was crushing her heart.

Hemi.

Dead.

She moaned inside.

Her brother from another mother, she used to call him. She cursed herself for losing touch with him when she'd left the Army. He was young, she was young, and she figured they had plenty of time to

95

reconnect later and catch up on each other's lives. Years. But all those years were gone now. Too many missed opportunities.

Renegade was dead.

Brick probably wished he was dead. He'd been brought in after her, as it took a while to stabilize and retrieve him. This morning they shipped him off to a special trauma center in Louisville. "No way he'll ever walk again," she heard someone at the nurse's station say. "He's probably going to be a quad." Piper translated that to quadriplegic.

All because they'd gone to play paintball over the Labor Day weekend in Spaceman's woods.

If their objective hadn't been the ridge, they might not have run afoul of the shooter. If they'd slept in and went out later, maybe the shooter would've been long gone. If they'd picked another weekend—

And who the hell was he? Charles Robert Weger?

Sheriff's deputies at the scene said the shooter—Weger, thirty-one, of Hartford, Kentucky—was dead. Two deputies who interviewed Piper last night asked if she knew Weger, showed her a picture, asked if she'd seen him before. No to both. The deputies, thorough but appropriately sympathetic over the deaths of her friends, rattled off plenty of questions.

They admitted they'd found no motive yet. Weger'd had an expired hunting license in the pocket of his camouflage pants. Beer bottles littered the ground near his perch. It all might have started as an alcohol-fueled out-of-season hunting weekend that for whatever reason turned south, like a scene in an episode of *Criminal Minds*.

Piper would follow the case, stay in touch with the Ohio County Sheriff's Department. She had to know why her brother from another mother was dead, Renegade too, and why she and Brick had almost joined them. She had to know why a fun weekend shooting blobs of paint at each other turned into a tragic nightmare.

She stared at a big, clear plastic bag on the floor against the wall. It contained her broken cell phone, ruined Splatterking, badge, and backpack. Her gun was in secure storage somewhere in the hospital. She'd get that back when she left.

An overnight bag sat next to it. Nang had packed a change of clothes for her. What she'd worn yesterday had been cut off. Four bouquets of flowers and Mylar balloons covered the windowsill—from Nang, her father, the department, and the Rockford police chief. They muted the scent of hospital antiseptic. The largest, shiniest, and ugliest balloon, a honeybee wearing glasses and sporting Band-Aids, read: Bee Well Fast! She thought she'd leave that one behind for housekeeping.

Hemi would get flowers, Renegade, too … but not any they could enjoy. Piper allowed herself to spiral into melancholy.

"You look nice in pink," Nang said. Piper knew he was trying to get her to smile, a futile endeavor. "You should wear more pink."

Her hospital gown was a faded magenta, one too many trips through the laundry with a gallon of bleach. The footies were pink, too.

"I don't think I own anything pink." She used her right hand to key the bed so she sat up straighter. "Thank you for staying."

"Thank you for not dying." Nang's voice was soft, his expression serious. "Spencer County needs its sheriff." He leaned over the bed and kissed her. "I need its sheriff."

Piper thought his touch felt like pudding; the pain meds had deadened everything. Her hand grasped his and squeezed.

"I need to get out of here," Piper said. "I need good coffee, some *hu tieu* and *bánh xèo*. I want to see Camaro and Marmalade and sit in my backyard with you. I should figure out where I want to put a goldfish pond. And I want to know why this happened."

She also wanted to attend Hemi's funeral, but that wasn't practical. As he was originally from Anaheim, California, she knew his body would be flown back for a service and burial there in a few days. Flying was on her "you shouldn't do this for a while" list. *Probably for the best*, she thought. She didn't know anyone in his family. Maybe there would be a memorial at Fort Campbell later.

"I need to get out of here," Piper repeated.

Nang stood there with no reply.

Spaceman and Gonzo arrived shortly before noon. Gonzo handed her a large stuffed chartreuse sloth with dangly legs. He wore an oversized San Francisco 49ers t-shirt and baggy cargo shorts that quit at his knees. The outfit made him look almost skeletal. He had a scraggly shadow on his face, like he hadn't shaved for a few days. A Cowboys ball cap sat backwards over his unruly hair.

"You get better soon, Christmas." Then Gonzo waggled his fingers and disappeared.

"I was worried he'd been shot," Piper said, since they hadn't been able to contact him by walkie-talkie yesterday. More, she'd been worried that he had been the shooter: Gonzo always seemed a little off to her.

"Yeah, well, we found him after the cavalry arrived," Spaceman said. "He'd turned off his walkie-talkie and was wading in the creek, drinking pineapple rum. Admitted he went off his meds for the weekend. Admitted he'd been going off his meds for a while. Not inviting him to paintball again, Christmas. Gonna get him some help at the base, maybe get him to consider leaving the Army, find a different path. Hell, maybe the Army'll force a discharge on him. I think he's really gonna be screwed in the head when it finally sinks in about Renegade." He held out a big garbage bag. "We're going back to the base tonight. Harold's gonna drive Gonzo and Hot Sauce, I'm going solo, gonna visit my grandfather first for a few hours. Thought I should stop by and see you, too. Christmas, you look awful. Really awful. This whole weekend was awful."

He slumped in a chair, holding the garbage bag between his knees. "I'd never killed a civilian before, Christmas. Never shot at anyone other than insurgents. Sheriff told me it was a good shoot, justified. Local paper wants to do a story on me, like I'm some kind of hero. But I ain't talking to them. That's why I'm going back to Campbell tonight. Screw the piddly rest of my leave, you know. 'Sides, it was Hemi that wanted to go to that old tavern. That was on his bucket list, not mine. Shit."

Nang backed quietly out of the room.

"It was all supposed to be fun, before Hemi had another six-month tour, Renegade and Gonzo were going to get twelve-month assignments, probably Afghanistan, Bagram, you know. I was getting ready to leave the service at the end of December, take a three-month assignment first. Hot Sauce was to go to Grafenwoehr next month. Shit."

Piper and Spaceman didn't say anything for several minutes. A medicine cart clattered by out in the hall. Someone laughed. Machines beeped.

"Did you know Renegade has—*had*—five sisters?"

Piper shook her head. "Rene and I never talked much about family."

"Five sisters, and she was the—" He counted on his fingers. "The third kid. Her youngest sister, Mindy, just turned eighteen and joined. Renegade was hoping she'd get assigned basic at Campbell. But Mindy drew Fort Jackson in South Carolina. Family's from Madison, Wisconsin. Renegade will probably be buried up there. I really could have seen her as a general down the road. Barking orders and making all the big decisions." He stared at the floor. "Glad I'm getting out, Christmas. Selling cars, new and used, I can do that. Hell, I might like it. I killed a civilian. Shit."

And two is four. Piper wanted to ask him about the shooter and how it had gone down, but figured that could wait for a Facetime chat, put some days between all of this. "What's in the garbage bag?"

He stood and opened it, reached in and pulled out Hemi's fancy paintball rifle. "Rescued this for you. Harold and me ... we got enough paint gear, and we're not inviting Gonzo again. Hot Sauce doesn't need it either. We all figured Hemi would want you to have this. When we get together again, you'll have something fine to play with. Might be a while, though, because of their tours. Or maybe just me and you can go out and shoot when you're all healed." He put the rifle back in the bag, then stood and propped it up against the wall next to the door. "Got a half dozen or so paint grenades in the bottom. We should've mentioned the grenades, said something about you getting a vest, too." A pause. "Shit, Christmas, you look awful. Hey, I better get going. You take care of yourself. And you and me, we can catch up when I'm out after the first of the year, when you're all fixed up.

Maybe I can get you a deal on a car, that little thing you drove out to the cabin, that's a—"

"A suggestion of a car," Piper finished. It's what her dad called her Smart Fortwo. "I've got other cars. I'll tell you about them sometime." She had a big garage filled with collector cars and motorcycles that a Navy veteran known as Mark the Shark had willed her, along with her house and her pets.

"After I get out," he said. "We'll have some coffee and talk, and maybe I'll have that cabin all gussied up. I have a lot of plans for improvements, if I don't decide to rip it down and build over from scratch." Spaceman saluted her and stopped just outside the door. She heard him talking to Nang, but didn't catch what they said.

She closed her eyes and imagined she was low-crawling with Sybil Ludington through pudding. In her dream the landscape changed to hardscrabble ground, and she was crawling on a downrange assignment a world away from here, then across scrubby land outside of Henderson, Kentucky, in pursuit of serial killer Zachary Delaney. The landscape changed again, to a muddy swath on Spaceman's property, blue and yellow balls filled with paint exploding all around her.

CHAPTER THIRTEEN

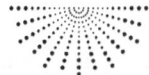

9 A.M. MONDAY

Oren had a mound of scrambled eggs on his plate, along with orange slices and blueberries in a bowl next to it. He sipped his second cup of coffee.

Basil likewise had eggs, though not as many, sprinkled with cheese and mushrooms. His fruit plate was larger.

"That was easier than I thought it would be," Oren said. He took a big forkful of eggs and savored the taste. They weren't *plain* eggs, though they looked it. The cook must have done something special to them. Maybe used cream instead of milk or put in some subtle spices. "Judge Vaughn didn't take much convincing, but I wager that's because of the way you worded all the paperwork." He grinned. "And maybe because he doesn't care for Chris Hagee."

Judge Vaughn was eating breakfast five tables away with his teenage daughter, and had only skimmed the warrant before signing it.

"I told you I was good with search warrants," Basil replied. He reached for the carafe and poured them each a glass of orange juice. "I'm going to bring Esme here some morning. Surprised Rockport has such a nice buffet. I've been stopping at St. Nick's Diner in Santa Claus. But I'll come back here. Much better."

"Only two places for breakfast in town," Oren said as he shoveled more eggs. "Here at the country club, where there are actual tablecloths, and that little greasy spoon near the office. Don't have to be a member to eat here. If you did, I might just have to join for the privilege. I come out here for breakfast once a week and on special occasions, like when they have prime rib. It is a tad pricey."

Basil smiled. "Pricey? Never been to Chicago, have you?" A pause: "Did you hear when Sheriff Blackwell is coming back? I should've asked you right away."

Oren shrugged and dove his fork in for more eggs. "I talked to Paul when he got home last night. He said they were keeping her today, probably tomorrow, and that she can't come back fully to work for a while. Zeke and one of his friends are going down tonight, getting her car back up here. Apparently she's worried about it sitting in the woods, and she's not going to be able to drive for a while. Zeke said she's asking about what's happening in the county. He told her about the vandalism. She wants me to call her."

"And?"

"Yeah, I'll call her, but after the warrant is served, this afternoon maybe." A pause: "Zeke ordered some flowers and balloons from the hospital gift shop yesterday. We'll need to chip in."

"Sure. Damn shame her weekend with friends turned out so badly. Shootings and a mine accident, a lousy vacation." Basil downed the orange juice in one pull and cleaned his plate. "I shouldn't," he said, "but I'm going back for a little more."

"I shouldn't either," Oren said. "But I probably will, too, when I'm done with this." Oren wouldn't match Basil's speed at eating. He definitely wasn't in a hurry this morning, and wanted to relish the food and the fresh orange juice. The rest of his day was going to stink, no reason to get to the awful stuff earlier than he absolutely had to. "And I think I'll have one of those cinnamon rolls with the icing. I shouldn't do that either."

He had the search warrant details to the left of his plate, and scanned them while Basil was getting seconds. Oren admired Basil's work on the warrant paperwork; it had been thorough.

It included looking for the stolen birdbath and the missing mailbox, spray paint cans, plus any sort of paint cans and paraphernalia that might've been used in the vandalism. It covered receipts for the purchase of spray paint and paint-related supplies, which could be key in tying Chris Hagee to the graffiti even if they couldn't find the actual paint cans. It also detailed "electronic devices" capable of holding communications between individuals who could be involved —cell phones, tablets, computers.

Finally, it specified the petition he'd been circulating and the spiral notebook with his observations about the Cultural Center. Oren wanted to see the names in both of those as they might lead to people who disliked the Buddhists enough to vandalize the saltbox at Chris' behest. It was a "no knock" warrant, which meant they could enter the house if Chris refused to cooperate … which Oren thought could be a possibility. But he hoped it wouldn't come to breaking down the door. They'd also gotten a separate warrant-subpoena for cell phone records, which might carry call logs, text messages, and geographical locations that could be incriminating or exculpatory. Chris didn't have a Facebook account, so they couldn't find his sympathizers that way.

It equaled a lot of work in response to one spray-painted house. *A lot of time and effort for a relatively minor crime in the overall scheme of things*, he thought. But it was necessary. Too bad Piper had taken the long weekend off to play paintball with her Army buddies. If she'd stayed in the county, she'd be dealing with this kind of paint instead of paintballs—and she wouldn't have needed emergency surgery.

Basil came back with more eggs, fruit, and a second plate with a monster-sized cinnamon roll that he set in front of Oren. "I picked out the best-looking one," he said.

Oren raised an eyebrow.

"Because something's up with you," Basil went on. "Beyond Chris Hagee, the Buddhists, and the search warrant. You are not in a happy place."

"You're a good detective," Oren said.

"It's in your eyes."

Oren reached for the roll, pulled off a piece, and stuck it in his mouth. "That search warrant, you'll need to execute it at the Hagee place without me. Solo, or take whoever you want with you. Your choice. Body cam footage in case Chris raises a ruckus, and we'd want visual evidence of that."

"Because you are—"

"Going to Owensboro when I finish breakfast. I got a call last night from my father's memory care center. They want me to sign some forms. They're putting him in their hospice program today."

Basil lowered his gaze. "I am so sorry, Oren."

Oren frowned. "I knew it was coming. Just didn't think it'd be this quick. Maybe they'll give me an idea of how long he has left." He washed the bite of roll down with coffee, which suddenly tasted bitter. "While I'm over there, I'm going to look up Joan Hagee, Chris' wife. She's staying with a sister in Owensboro. I figure if someone did the spray paint job for Chris, Joan might know who that could be. Maybe her names will match with ones on Chris' petition. Worth asking her, you know. I'm going to be in town anyway."

"Sorry about your father," Basil said again.

"Yeah, thanks. Life sucks sometimes."

CHAPTER FOURTEEN

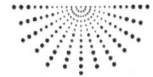

10 A.M. MONDAY

Basil turned on his body cam when he got out of the Explorer. He'd opted to come out alone. Rocco had been available, but Basil wasn't terribly fond of him. Rocco had been with the department a lot of years and had a good set of skills, but he talked incessantly and often insipidly, and Basil wasn't in the mood for that this morning. He'd get enough vexing chatter from Chris Hagee.

Chris' pickup was in the driveway, parked right against a garage set back from the house. The search warrant also covered the pickup and a Chevrolet Equinox, both registered to Chris, according to the DMV.

Basil pushed the doorbell button and waited, looked out over the lawn that still needed mowing. Maybe Chris' mower didn't work. Maybe the doorbell didn't work either. He knocked.

He could just go in; Basil had the tools to open the door without damaging it. The no-knock warrant meant he didn't need Chris' permission. It was expected, however, that the property owner be given a reasonable time to answer. And he preferred things this way.

Basil waited, knocked again, and tried to look in the front window, but the shades were drawn. What was a reasonable time in Chris' case?

This was a nice piece of property, big house, two car extra-deep garage, a shed that looked in good shape, a barn farther back that even from this distance he could tell needed a new coat of paint and some shingles replaced. Probably worth a fair amount of money, all of it, especially since there was acreage attached that was being leased to a farmer who grew soybeans. If he owned something like this, he'd keep his job with the sheriff's department and farm it himself on weekends as a hobby, hire someone to help part-time. Basil was going to put in a nice-sized vegetable garden across the back of his yard in Santa Claus come next spring, and his wife wanted to plant a few cherry trees. They were thinking about a small fish pond, too, going all-in on the rural life. He grinned when he thought about his friends in the Chicago Police Department—they'd have a good laugh over his *Green Acres* lifestyle.

He knocked one more time. Nothing. Well, he'd let Chris sit inside and stew for a while, come back and give the man one more chance.

Basil decided to start with the truck, garage, and the shed, likely places to find paint. If Chris saw him looking around, he might come out. Basil preferred to talk to the man before just going in and digging through everything.

He stopped at the pickup. It was an orange Chevy Colorado, a mid-sized extended cab, probably a recent model from the apparent lack of wear. A glance in the bed showed an off-white tarp with green spatters on it covering something. He reached over the side and lifted the tarp, stared at a dozen cans of spray paint, all missing the lids, black, red, and green. Those were the colors sprayed on the house across the road. He pulled the tarp back farther and saw the mailbox that had been broken off the post, Delaney stenciled on the side.

"Bingo." Basil made sure the cam was angled so it would pick up everything. He'd thought all along that Oren was wrong about Chris being too lazy to vandalize the place himself, but he hadn't argued the point then. Hate was a powerful encourager, and Chris certainly hated the Buddhists enough to have a burst of energy.

"I didn't do it. And that's all I'm saying, and all you need to know. I didn't do it." Basil recalled exactly what Chris had said when Oren and he were out here yesterday. The detective had learned early on that people lied all the time. Evidence, however, spoke the truth.

Like hell you didn't do it.

He spun and returned to the front stoop. Maybe Chris would be more amenable to answering the door now. Basil knocked, waited, knocked, and then reached in his pocket for a tool to open the door.

"Sheriff's department!" he announced loudly as he stepped inside. The small foyer opened to a living room that smelled like a frat house after a party. The couch had a rumpled throw on it, and the coffee table in front of it was covered solid with beer cans and bottles— cheap brands. An ashtray overflowed with cigarettes. Pizza boxes were stacked under the table. Pages from the little county newspaper were scattered on the floor. Nearly-dead houseplants sat on a shelf that extended across the front picture window, the dirt inside caked and cracked; they hadn't been watered for quite a while. Basil left all of these things alone as they weren't really covered by the warrant.

A padded straight-backed chair stood near the front window; a side table next to it held a spiral notebook and binoculars. *Probably the notebook Oren talked about*, he thought. Basil did a slow circuit of the room so the cam could pick up everything, then he opened the note-book. Yeah, that was on his list. He carried it into the kitchen.

"Sheriff's department!" he announced again. "Chris Hagee!"

The large, modern kitchen held newer stainless steel appliances. It, too, looked like a leftover party with dirty dishes piled in and on the filthy sink, more beer cans and bottles, same frat house stench. Basil reached across the sink and opened a window; the slight breeze didn't help much.

"Sheriff's department! Chris!"

Maybe he was out in the barn or had driven somewhere in his Equinox. That both of Chris' vehicles were American-made called up the old jingle: "Baseball, hotdogs, apple pie, and Chevrolet." Chris probably wouldn't drive a foreign-made vehicle.

The kitchen table was small, seating for two, the island bigger and with padded bar-style stools. A laptop had been left in front of one. Basil placed the spiral notebook on top of it; he'd take both with him.

In his experience, people who committed hateful crimes often communicated with others via email, bragging or looking for encouragement. There might be useful evidence on the laptop.

A lot of work for a malicious mischief charge, but Basil was amped up about this. It was the most interesting thing he'd worked on the past few weeks, and the hate angle festered. Basil was limited to looking in places where items on his list might be located. He couldn't open drawers in search of the missing birdbath, but he could in trying to find the receipts for the paint. The inclusion of receipts basically gave him *carte blanche*, as people could, and did, stash receipts everywhere. Given that broad leeway, he opened cabinets, looked under the sink, and when he'd made a casual pass through everything in this room, he moved to the dining room.

"Sheriff's department!" he periodically called. "Mr. Hagee!"

In Chicago he'd found evidence of multiple crimes while conducting searches. Once while looking for a particular gun used in a gang-related shooting, he opened a silverware drawer and found drugs and drug paraphernalia. He'd been operating within the scope of the warrant, as the gun most certainly could have fit in that drawer. Contraband, he was allowed to seize it even though it was not specifically listed, and in that case it led to requiring a second search warrant to hunt for more drug-related materials. He doubted Chris was into drugs. The man sure liked cheap beer though.

"Chris Hagee!"

If Basil managed to find all the items on the list, he'd be required to stop searching, the hunt considered complete. A warrant was not a license to keep poking into every crevice of the man's life.

Drawers, closets, bins, boxes, Basil found only a few receipts, but nothing for spray paint or paint-related items. They were all for big things—the microwave, refrigerator, and stove, all of which apparently had been purchased less than a year ago. The man probably threw all the lesser receipts away. Basil spent close to two hours searching, as the house was large, had a basement and beer-and-wine cellar, and he had nothing else on his work schedule today. Too, he hoped by taking his sweet time Chris Hagee would come in so they could talk. Maybe he was out walking his property.

He found a cell phone in the downstairs bathroom; an iPad on the dresser in the bedroom—which was the tidiest room in the house and contained only men's clothes; and the petition to "Relocate the Fulda Buddahs" in a desk drawer in the study. He took all of these and added them to the spiral notebook and laptop. He found no other computers in the house.

Basil intended to go through the items when he got back to the department, no reason to do it here. He'd really hoped to talk to Chris, but he could do that another time. The paint cans presented enough evidence for an arrest warrant.

Maybe he'd find the paint receipts in the pickup's glovebox to put the icing on everything.

He carried the items out to his Explorer, returned to the house and locked it, then paused on his way back to the truck to complete his search when he saw a young man at the end of the driveway.

The man was barefoot, dressed in blue jeans and a plain white sport shirt unbuttoned at the collar, and his head was shaved. He carried a bowl of tomatoes and held them out toward Basil like an offering.

Covering crimes in Spencer County, Indiana, was an entirely different animal than working in downtown Chicago, Basil thought.

The bald man bowed deeply.

CHAPTER FIFTEEN

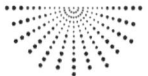

11 A.M. MONDAY

Oren tipped his hat when Joan Hagee stepped out on the front porch. Her sister's house was a gable-fronted cottage on the west side of Owensboro, covered with baby-blue vinyl siding and ornamented with black shutters and bright white window boxes. He thought the place looked like something out of a children's book. The whole place was neat, the lawn trimmed close, the flowerbeds numerous and weeded—a contrast to the Hagee place in Fulda.

"What brings you to town, Oren?" Joan gave him a suspicious, narrow-eyed stare. Her clothes had that new look to them: beige high-waisted culottes with pressed creases in the front, a pale green short-sleeved blouse, and shiny leather loafers with not a hint of scuff. She wore a dainty silver chain that ended in a clover charm. Small pearl earrings peeked out from a layered pixie cut, a new hairstyle and honey-blonde color since he'd last seen her.

"I want to talk about Chris," Oren said, watching her bristle and take a step back toward the door.

"What's he done now?"

"We're investigating a vandalism incident," he began. "Just gathering some—"

"Let me guess, he did something to Anthony's house. Right? Anthony Delaney?"

Oren offered her a slight smile. "Joan, we don't know if he did anything. We're just investigating right now. But there was some damage to the house, and I know Chris took exception to—"

"—Anthony," she finished. "He took exception to Anthony because the boy went away to Thailand and came back as a Buddhist monk. He doesn't fit Chris' image of what a neighbor should be. He's been hot about it ever since Anthony returned for his dad's funeral and told us he was going to stay, do something with that big saltbox." She crossed her arms and glowered, but Oren knew she wasn't mad at him. Joan's ire was focused on her husband. "He had problems with Anthony's father before that, but usually only around Christmastime. Didn't like the decorations in the front yard. I'll admit the spotlight hit our bedroom window. But he didn't have it on every night."

She shifted her weight from one foot to the other and made a tsking sound. "So, what did Chris do? What kind of damage?"

"Spray paint, a few other things. But, like I said, we don't know that Chris did it. We're investigating."

"Anyone get hurt?"

Oren shook his head. "Just property."

"So why come all the way over here? What do you need from me? I sure as hell didn't paint anything. I haven't set foot in Fulda for almost two months."

Oren studied her a moment. She was plain-looking, almost pretty, but her stern expression marred her overall appearance. Chris told him Joan had been gone two weeks. Oren instead believed Joan, two months. "It's possible that Chris only encouraged someone to vandalize Anthony's house, that he didn't actually do it himself. I'm hoping you know some people who Chris might've been talking to about the Buddhist Cultural Center. He'd started a petition, and—"

"Oren, I'd love to help you, but …. Oh, I'll give you some names and numbers of the people we used to invite over for New Year's Eve and such. How would that be? Or you could just stop at some of his neighbors and ask them. Stop at his brother's too. Chris was trying to

111

rile up everyone on the road, swing them to his side against the Buddhists."

"I'd appreciate that list," Oren said.

"Chris always had some kind of issue with anyone who wasn't white, Christian, and who didn't vote Republican. Just the way he was made. And it just took me too damn long to get tired of it. Wait here and I'll get something to write on."

She went back in the house, and Oren turned and looked out onto the street. It was a nice neighborhood, seemed like everyone in eyesight kept their yards in *Better Homes & Gardens* shape. It smelled good, too, of cut grass and flowers. Yesterday's deluge had been kind to the greenery.

Shouldn't have come here first, he thought. He should have gone to see his dad right away, signed the damn paperwork, visited. He'd just wanted to put it off, as if by postponing the act his dad could avoid hospice and live longer.

Joan came back with a small pad of paper and a black marker. She jotted down names and put question marks where she couldn't recall an address or phone number. Oren recognized most of the names. It wasn't a terribly long list. They would be easy to look up in the county directory.

"Anthony was a great kid growing up," she said. "And he's turned into a nice man. I've no problem with him. In fact, I'm sorry he has to deal with Chris. Did you know that Chris takes issue with your sheriff's department, too? It's mostly because you haven't made him happy and kicked Anthony back to Thailand, but also because you're—"

"Jewish."

"Yes. And because your granddaughter is Jewish. And because your new detective is black. And because a Hispanic deputy—"

"Diego."

"Came out to the house a few times to answer Chris' complaints. He was nice about it, patient with my husband. Look, Chris is narrow-minded, and I used to be able to ignore it, especially because he was working in the fields, out of the house for so many hours a day. But since he retired, retired too early, was around all the time—"

She shuddered. "I just got tired of all of it, you know. And he's gotten worse about it through the years. Like his hate just builds up and it spews out of his mouth in cruel words. I'm done with it. I have a lawyer, and I'm filing for divorce. Chris knows. I called him last week. He doesn't believe I'm really doing it, but he will when the papers get served in a few days. He can have the house for all I care, won't have to sell it. We'll split up our savings and investments, and I'm going to take my share and move to Mississippi."

"Mississippi? You have family there?"

She shook her head. "Don't know a soul there. Laurel, Mississippi. Town looks friendly. I watch this home-remodelers show on television, and there's a couple in Laurel that takes rundown little houses and turns them into something amazing. I think I'd like something amazing in my life."

Her face softened, and Oren thought she looked much closer to pretty now.

"Honestly, I hope Anthony Delaney sells his dad's house and moves out of Fulda, maybe back to Thailand if that would make him happy. Chris would stop stirring up trouble, won't have a heart attack over it, will quit nagging people to sign his silly petition." She lowered her gaze to the wood slats in the porch. "Chris isn't all bad, you know. Never was, though he's gotten more intense about things. I still love him in a way. I'm just not going to live with him anymore. Laurel, Mississippi. I hope he didn't vandalize Anthony's house. I really hope he didn't. Now, you have a good day, Oren."

"You too, Joan. And thanks."

The list she'd provided might be helpful, especially if there were names on it that matched ones on Chris' petition, which he was certain Basil would find. Oren was still confident Chris hadn't spray painted Anthony's house. But he was equally confident that Chris had a role in it.

On the way to the nursing home, Oren stopped at a convenience store and bought two cans of Coke, his dad's favorite soda, and a small bag of Cheetos popcorn.

He signed the paperwork that had been set aside at the nurses' station, went to his dad's room, popped the top on one of the cans, and placed it and the popcorn on the bed tray. Condensation on the red aluminum sparkled in the sun coming through the window.

"My birthday's Thursday," Oren started as he settled into the chair. "She'll probably bake me a cake, have some friends over, tell me after they leave that I should retire. Push me. I'm going to be sixty-six. She doesn't understand I need to work." He popped the top on the other can and took a sip. He liked the feel of the chill against his fingers and held the can to his cheek for a moment. "I don't want to retire, Dad. I don't like working for a twenty-three-year-old, but I like what I do. She's not awful, Piper Blackwell, really tries, and I'd genuinely like her if the roles were reversed." He leaned back in the chair, took another sip. "She's twenty-three."

Oren glanced out the window, then returned his attention to his father. "Thursday, I'm going to be forty-three years older than my boss." He laughed, an odd sound. "But she's got a birthday coming up, too, and so I'll go back to being forty-two years older than my boss. Never thought I'd work for someone younger than my granddaughter."

He told his dad what he knew about Piper getting hurt in an abandoned mine, some broken bones, surgery, two people getting shot and dying.

"It'll probably be a while before she can come back to the office. So, I'll go back to being in charge temporarily." Oren had been the acting sheriff when Paul Blackwell stepped down for his cancer treatments. Oren had run for the office the following election, but Piper beat him. He still swore people saw the Blackwell name and thought they'd been voting for Paul. "Biggest thing on my plate is a house spray-painted in Fulda. Paint, a mailbox broken, and a birdbath gone. A hate crime, of all things."

Oren drank the rest of his soda, stood, and looked down on his father in the hospital-style bed. The old man hadn't awakened through the entire one-sided conversation. The nurse downstairs had said the elder Rosenberg was sleeping most of the time now, barely eating, that he'd gone downhill fast in the four days since Oren had last stopped in. He would be moved to a different wing now that Oren had signed the hospice paperwork, which included a DNR order.

He wondered why his dad just couldn't stay here, in a familiar room. Insurance coverage maybe. Hospice meant they were cutting out all but one or two of his prescriptions, wouldn't resuscitate him if his heart stopped.

When it stopped.

The nurse gave Oren a guess of several days to two weeks.

"I'll be back tonight after I get off work." He leaned down and kissed his father's forehead. The elder Rosenberg still didn't stir. "Maybe I'll take a long lunch break tomorrow and come over then, too."

Oren stared at the old man's heavily-lined face, willing the eyes to open, the mouth to speak.

"I'll bring you a grilled cheese tomorrow," Oren said, knowing his dad probably wouldn't wake up to eat it. "And another can of Coke. We'll sit and talk for a while."

CHAPTER SIXTEEN

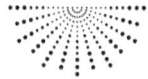

NOON MONDAY

These tomatoes are for Mr. Hagee. Is he home?" The young man held a small bowl with a few Heirloom, beefsteak, and cherry varieties.

Basil recalled walking through the Cultural Center's garden and seeing the ruined plants, the smashed fruit. They must have been able to salvage something, and had opted to share. He turned off his body cam.

"No, he's not home. And, honestly, I'm not sure giving him anything is a good idea."

"Buddha said, 'With gentleness overcome anger. With generosity overcome meanness. With truth overcome deceit.' Reaching out to Mr. Hagee *is* a good idea," the man insisted. "I will also offer to cut his grass."

"Okay, I get that you want to be neighborly," Basil returned. "It' a nice gesture, but Mr. Hagee isn't home. Come back when he is."

"But you were in the house. I saw that you—"

Basil sighed. Truth overcomes deceit. "Exercising a search warrant. That's why I'm here. Mr. Hagee doesn't have to be home for me to do that. Sheriff's business."

"Because you think he put graffiti on the house." It wasn't a question. "He doesn't like us. We would like that to change."

"I don't think Mr. Hagee likes a lot of people."

The young man nodded and looked both ways before crossing the road to return to the Cultural Center. Basil noticed the vandalized sign had been taken down and was certain it would be put back up when it was repainted. He watched until the tomato-bearer disappeared into the house.

Basil radioed Zeke, who was on his dispatch shift. "I got some stuff from Hagee's, and I'll be on my way to the office soon. Any other calls I need to answer while I'm out?" He saw the same baldheaded young man exit the Cultural Center's side door and go to the garage. He had on tennis shoes now. Curious, Basil watched him while Zeke ran through a list of call outs that Rocco was handling. A few moments later the man eased out of the garage on a riding lawnmower and started cutting the side yard.

"Hey, Zeke, has Oren come back yet?" Basil didn't want to call Oren and maybe interrupt his time with his father. "No? Okay. See you in a little while."

Maybe Chris Hagee would soften to the Buddhists if they really did come over and cut the grass. Basil clicked on his body cam again, turned, and went to the pickup, discovered the doors were unlocked, opened one and looked inside. The truck had a funky musty smell, likely coming from the crumbled food wrappers and crushed beer cans. So, Chris drank while he drove; he just hadn't been caught at it. Cigarettes filled the little ashtray. A glance in the glove box revealed the usual—sunglasses, packages of gum, tire gauge, a couple of maps, registration. No receipts. He searched under the seats and in the extended cab—more trash.

Basil would bag up the spray paint cans and take them with him. He didn't want Chris coming back and possibly tossing them out. A lot of work for a vandalism case. Pity that someone could be so angry he'd spray paint graffiti on a house, damage property. The Buddhists had done nothing to Chris that he could tell ... other than just being across the road. And practicing a philosophy to which he objected.

117

He went to the garage, tried to raise the door, but it wouldn't give. Basil returned to the truck and pushed the button on the garage door opener attached to the visor. The door rhythmically clicked as it rolled up, revealing a cavernous bay that held a riding lawnmower, assorted tools, a snow-blower, hand-tiller, objects covered by tarps, and a man hanging by his neck from a rope tied to the rafters, a stepladder tipped over beneath him.

Basil stared and tugged in a breath.

"Zeke," Basil radioed. "Call Dr. Neufeld. See if she can come out to the Hagee house. Tell her to make it as soon as possible."

"Somebody dead?"

"Yeah," Basil answered. "Chris Hagee. Better let Oren know, too." If Oren was still with Joan Hagee, he could deliver the news in person if he wanted. She didn't need all the specifics right now.

Basil didn't have all the specifics yet.

He returned to his Explorer and got out an evidence kit, gloves, and booties, which he put on as he stepped inside the garage. *Dead less than twenty-four hours*, he thought. Not dead so long that he could taste it. He'd been around enough bodies to learn that if someone has been dead a while the smell is so strong it lodged in your mouth and you tasted it. Chris' body didn't have an atrocious pong yet; mostly what Basil smelled was gasoline from the lawnmower, tiller, and nearby gas cans. It was warm today, and the garage had been sealed, so that might make it a little harder for Dr. Neufeld, the county coroner, to determine a close time of death. But she was good; Basil had been impressed after working with her regarding the August murder of a comic shop owner. He figured she could get a pretty close TOD estimate.

Even though Basil had his body cam on, he took additional pictures with his phone. The body from every angle, the tipped-over stepladder that suggested Chris set up the noose, stood on a rung, and jumped.

Can't be charged with malicious mischief if you're dead, Basil thought. Can't be upset with your Buddhist neighbors, either. He spotted three over-sized beer cans crushed nearby. Tall-boys, they were called. Had Chris imbibed until he had the courage?

Basil walked slowly through the garage, recording everything on his body cam, at the same time continuing to take pictures. More empty beer cans in the back. More cigarettes in an ashtray. A toilet that wasn't attached to anything sat in the open, the tank lid coated with dust … maybe it was supposed to be installed somewhere in the house and Chris just hadn't gotten around to it. There were a couple of fishing tackle boxes and a case for a manual typewriter. A shoebox held packets of flower seeds. It was an interesting assortment of things.

The tarps covered various objects—a stumpy outdoor grill with an exaggerated Indiana Colts helmet as a cover; a snowmobile so rusted in places it likely hadn't been taken out in a decade; an impressive red tool shelf that was empty and so pristine it probably had never been used; and an antique manual push mower likely worth something to a collector.

Basil didn't find a suicide note in the garage. There'd been nothing that would pass for one in the house—he would have noticed. Maybe Chris hadn't planned it out enough to write something. Maybe he'd been drinking and thinking. He shivered. Basil had seen a lot of bodies, in the military and in Chicago, even some in sleepy Spencer County. But in all of that, he'd never covered a suicide.

His radio crackled. Zeke said the coroner was on her way and Oren was stopping back to see Joan Hagee and would come by as soon as he was done there. Did he want Rocco dispatched, too?

"No. I'm good here," Basil replied. He took another pass through the garage to confirm there was no note. He found two more stepladders at the back. Selecting one, he carried it next to where Chris hung, set it up, and climbed. Basil wanted a closer look at the corpse before it was taken down.

Chris had been wearing blue jeans ripped on the right knee, and black high-topped tennis shoes, the toe tops scuffed. His brown tie-dye t-shirt had a printed image on the front of a retro diner flying an oversized

119

American flag on a tall pole, motorcycles out front, and a big Route 66 shield sign semi-transparent like a cloud that hovered behind everything, some spots of dried blood on the cloud. Maybe the shirt was something Chris had picked up on a cross-country vacation. Basil took a few pictures. There was a tattoo on Chris' right forearm of an eagle profile against a field of red, white, and blue, a wedding ring on his left hand that looked imbedded because the fingers of that hand were swollen. Looked like he'd broken his nose, too, dried blood in the nostrils. Had he picked a fight with someone before he decided to end it all?

Basil was careful not to touch Chris or anything on him. Chris belonged to the county coroner now. Basil didn't want to contaminate anything with his own DNA; he'd already contaminated the ladder by using it. He wondered how soon Dr. Neufeld would schedule the autopsy. Even an obvious death—old age, suicide, house fires— required one in Indiana, unless it occurred in a hospital, nursing home, or other care center under expected circumstances. This would be classified as an unattended death. He was thankful Oren had gone to notify the wife; Basil had always disliked doing death visits.

One more look at the body. Take in all the details before it really started to stink.

Finished, he turned off the body cam, climbed down, carefully replaced the stepladder, and returned to his Explorer. He didn't keep the cam on constantly, as he was well aware of the expense. The cams had been paid for through a bequest, but the real cost was in storing and managing the footage. He'd read where the cams cost the Baltimore Police Department more than $2.5 million one year. Piper had demanded that every deputy be judicious in the cams' use. He wouldn't have used it during his search of Chris' place—not for a vandalism incident—if the home's owner was not such a volatile and perhaps litigious soul. Good thing Basil had used it, especially in light of Chris' death.

Basil intended to sit in the car and wait for the coroner, but he saw four men, all baldheaded and casually dressed, cross the road and stand at the end of the driveway. Anthony Delaney was among them.

It was a straight shot down the driveway to see Chris hanging. Basil's Explorer and Chris' pickup didn't block the entire garage opening.

"Okay," Basil said. "I'll have a chat."

Anthony held up a hand in greeting as Basil approached. Basil pulled out his notebook; he might as well ask them questions until Dr. Neufeld arrived. Keep everyone occupied, and maybe he'd learn something interesting, like who might have killed Chris Hagee.

It certainly wasn't a suicide.

CHAPTER SEVENTEEN

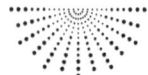

9 A.M. TUESDAY, SEPTEMBER 8TH

Dark Italian Roast tempered with a hint of cream filled an oversized mug displaying a black and white image of an antique steam engine. The blend came from Nang's store, and it was her favorite coffee, rich-tasting and full of caffeine. She held her nose over it and inhaled, likening herself to an addict getting an overdue fix. The mug had been a Christmas present from her father. Zeke poked his head in the doorway and interrupted her moment of bliss.

"Need anything else, Sheriff?" His face showed a mix of emotions: eagerness, trepidation, concern. He'd brought her the coffee moments ago, even though she made it clear she was perfectly able to go to the break room and pour it herself.

"No, I'm good. Thanks."

"You let me know if you need to go home, okay? I can get a deputy to—"

"I'm good," Piper repeated. "But I'll catch a ride with you when your shift's done, if you don't mind." She would follow the doctor's orders about not driving.

Zeke smiled. "Sure." He edged in and leaned against the doorframe.

122

"But if you get to hurting too bad, need to leave earlier, you let me know and I'll—"

"I'll let you know." She hadn't meant the words to sound brittle. "Thanks, Zeke," she added in a softer tone. "I appreciate your help."

The phone rang and Zeke disappeared to answer it.

Piper had been released from the hospital yesterday right after the lousy evening meal. They'd suggested she stay another night, but weren't demanding about it. She needed to get out of there. Sitting in that hospital bed, all she was doing was thinking about Hemi, Renegade, and Brick.

Nang drove her home to discover her Smart Fortwo already in the garage. Zeke had retrieved it right after his shift ended, in addition to house- and pet-sitting for her while she was away for her terrible and short vacation. They'd agreed on a price for the service, but she'd up that amount. Zeke had passed the above and beyond mark.

Nang had spent the night and argued strongly this morning about her not going to work. Piper would've let him win if Chris Hagee hadn't been found hanging and Basil hadn't insisted it was murder.

Too much to do, too interesting to stay home. Besides, at the department there would be plenty of people available if she needed help. Nang drove her to the office, continuing on to his Quick Stop, vowing to come back to her house tonight bearing a gourmet Vietnamese dinner. Piper looked forward to that.

She took a sip of the coffee and wrapped her right hand around the mug to absorb the warmth. Her left hand was useless because of the sling contraption, and the fingers were swollen. Another sip. Another.

"Heaven," she whispered. Just the right temperature. She took a big gulp and held it, then let it slide down, paused, and drank more until she finished it. Good coffee mollified some spot in her soul. She'd never touched coffee until joining the Army, where it became a ritual every morning. Piper recalled liking Army coffee, but that was before she frequented Starbucks and later discovered the superb varieties Nang carried.

Piper listened to Zeke talk to a caller complaining about dogs fighting on the road near the Saint Meinrad Archabbey and monastery. She heard him dispatch a deputy. He answered another call and Piper let the conversation drift away.

Her arm hurt. A lot, from the shoulder to her elbow, an annoying, pulsing ache. Her ribs hurt too, and there was a dull throbbing behind her eyes. But all of it was manageable without taking more pain pills. They made her a little muzzy and a lot sleepy. She wanted to accomplish something useful today and at the same time keep her mind off things. That was probably the real reason she didn't want to stay home. While total rest would likely do her good, it would also give her too much time to think about Hemi, Renegade, and ponder Brick's dreadful fate. She'd called the hospital in Louisville last night to check on Brick, but couldn't find anyone who would give her a report— other than to say he was alive. Maybe Spaceman could find something out. She'd call him tonight.

Too, she wanted to find out more about the gunman, Weger. Why he was on the ridge, why he'd opened up on them. Dead, he couldn't just come out and explain his actions.

I need more coffee.

Piper had sent Basil and Oren to Evansville, where Dr. Neufeld was performing an autopsy on Chris Hagee. The coroner had been able to get it scheduled right away. Piper wanted someone in attendance to get the results as fast as possible, though she knew full lab work could take a couple of weeks, especially a toxicology screen. Oren usually liked to take the autopsies, as he and the coroner had been good friends since grade school. She'd been told it gave the two an opportunity to gossip about her. But Basil had discovered the body and wanted to follow through, so she sent them both.

With all the pictures and body cam footage, it sure screamed suicide. But she'd only looked through the video once. She was going to view it again, slower, as soon as she started on her second cup. Piper eased away from the chair and steadied herself. Her trussed arm set her a little off balance, or perhaps that was due to residual pain medication. She grabbed the mug and went to the break room for more coffee. Two bins on the table held items from the crime scene.

The small one held Chris' laptop, cell phone, iPad, petition, and a spiral notebook. The other contained the assortment of empty spray paint cans. Two tubs for two separate crimes. A whiteboard set behind a table awaited notes and photos from the case. The board had been the first acquisition Piper had made for the department.

Were they two separate crimes? The vandalism? The death of Chris Hagee?

Why had Weger killed her friends?

Think about Chris Hagee. Just Chris. Don't think about Hemi. Renegade. Brick. Shit, the image of Hemi and Renegade shot dead blossomed. *Think about Chris.*

She could well imagine Chris being depressed enough to do himself in. Piper had skimmed Oren's report, saw that Joan Hagee was filing for divorce. Chris was an unhappy, unsettled man, and the divorce news could have pushed him over that edge and into oblivion. If she hadn't taken the three-day weekend-to-disaster in Kentucky, she might have responded to Chris' complaint about the Cultural Center herself. While she wouldn't have removed his Buddhist neighbors, maybe she could've mollified Chris enough so he wouldn't have hung himself.

But Basil said Chris *didn't* hang himself, that it only looked that way. She believed in her big city detective. Therefore, Chris Hagee was murdered. A murder investigation could keep her mind off Hemi and Jerusalem Ridge, at least for a while.

Chris likely had plenty of people who didn't like him. They might have a big suspect pool.

She returned to her office, intending to watch Basil's video again, but paused to take care of something important, though not quite as pressing. She logged onto Amazon, bought a Prime membership, and then quickly hunted for gifts for Oren and Teegan. Her father had always gifted the deputies in the department with a little something on their birthdays, and he reminded her when he visited in the hospital yesterday that Oren's was coming up. Thursday. And she'd missed Teegan's, not even sent the goth dispatcher dyed-black carnations. Buy two gifts today, get them delivered tomorrow, try to wrap one-handed in the evening, and bring them in Thursday. She didn't shop long, spent more than she'd wanted to, hoped her selections were appropriate, and then cued up Basil's video.

She studied every frame, from finding empty spray paint cans in the pickup bed to his entering the living room that looked like a party had taken place, to the dirty kitchen, to every room, to the garage where Chris dangled. There was a shot of four baldheaded men at the driveway before Basil had paused the footage, no doubt they'd come across from the Cultural Center. Buddhists were known for being peaceful, but Piper had learned about just how bad the graffiti was. Could one of those men have been angry enough to hang Chris from the garage rafters?

Piper shook her head. Not likely. A soldier in her unit had been fond of quoting Buddha, and he'd repeated a few of the sayings so often they were still stuck in her brain. One she remembered in particular was "Hatred does not cease through hatred. Hatred ceases through love." The people across the street from Chris Hagee would not have hated him enough to kill him.

She replayed the video where Basil had climbed the ladder for a closer look. Piper wanted to figure out what her detective had spotted. What had Basil found that made him think Chris did not commit suicide, but was murdered?

"What and what and what and—"

"Sheriff Blackwell?" Zeke stuck his head in the doorway. "Can I get you another coffee?"

"I'm good."

"Do you need—"

"I'll holler."

The phone rang and he disappeared.

Piper watched the video again. The image wobbled as Basil set up the stepladder and climbed it, and then looked up into Chris' fixed gaze. She zoomed in on that. She'd learned all about petechial hemorrhage, little red spots that appear in the eyes. All sorts of things can cause the condition: leukemia, straining, asphyxiation, strangulation.

Hanging counted. The first murder she'd covered—Anthony's father —had been strangulation complete with petechial hemorrhage.

Chris' eyes definitely showed petechial hemorrhage. P-e-t-e-c-h-i-a-l, Oren was fond of spelling for her. But petechial spots didn't necessarily mean murder.

Was it his clothes? The rip in the blue jeans? The t-shirt looked clean other than a few spots that might be blood. What spoke murder to Basil Meredith? What had he seen that she didn't?

One more time.

And then she watched it again after that.

Chris' arm looked a little odd, the right one.

She rubbed her eyes, finished the second cup of coffee, stopped in the restroom, went for a third cup, and told an inquisitive Zeke that she was still doing all right. She watched him take a 9-1-1 call.

"What is your emergency?" Zeke used his professional-sounding voice. It was on speaker, so Piper could hear the woman on the other end, saw the caller ID: Jennifer Morris. "How can I help you, Jennifer?" Zeke's fingers keyed the software to pinpoint her location. Another keystroke would dispatch a sheriff's deputy or an officer from the Santa Claus or Rockport police departments if it was within one of those towns. His finger hovered over that key.

"I'm not Jeni. My parents took away my cell phone. I'm here at school and I had to call you using Jeni's. I need my cell phone back. That's the emergency. That's why I called."

The point of origin of the call was the high school. Zeke did not send a car.

"Who am I talking to?" Zeke continued.

Piper was pleased with her dispatcher, a good hire. He was eighteen and had wanted to be a deputy, but he was a few years short of the required age. Instead, she had given him the dispatcher job. He was also a tech guru, and therefore a *truly* good hire.

"Crystal. My name's Crystal."

"Crystal—"

"Just Crystal. I go by Crystal."

"I need your last name, Crystal."

She made a huffing sound.

"Crystal Ann Bardimosi. B-A-R-D-I-M-O-S-I."

Piper smiled. An uncommon last name, they should be able to track down the home address rather easily.

"Crystal, I see that you called 9-1-1 Thursday with the same complaint. And the Tuesday before that." Piper watched him scroll up a screen. Those calls had come in after three, and Teegan had fielded them. "And Friday, too, pretty late in the evening."

"Yeah, I did, and the b— lady who answered my call wouldn't send anybody. But I can't go any longer without my cell phone. I'll just die if I don't get my cell phone. I'll just die, you understand? I need you to make my parents give it back. Arrest them if they won't cough it up. It is theft, you know. A crime."

"Crystal, this line is for emergencies," Zeke returned. "And your cell phone—"

"—is most certainly an emergency!" Crystal's voice rose in obvious irritation. "And I'll call you again and again and again until you do something about it. And again and again and again. I'm not kidding."

"Tell her we'll send someone out right away," Piper said softly.

"Hang on, Crystal. Can you tell me what class you're in? The room number? We'll get someone over there immediately."

"Old man Denby's history class. But the phone is at my house, not here at school. Gotta go. Old man Denby's coming back from the john." Crystal disconnected.

"We'll take it," Piper told him. "Don't ping Rockport. It's their jurisdiction, but they'll ignore it."

Zeke dispatched a deputy. "Stop at the principal's office for an escort to Mr. Denby's history class," he radioed. "Pick up a Crystal Bardimosi. B-A-R-D-I-M-O-S-I. On a charge of—" He looked at Piper.

"Disrupting Public Services."

"Disrupting Public Services," Zeke radioed. "She's a habitual 9-1-1 caller for frivolous complaints." He smiled at Piper. "Hope that'll teach her. Can't use 9-1-1 for stuff like that, could interrupt a real emergency."

"After she's brought in, I'll call the parents," Piper said.

"You really going to charge her? Lock her up?"

"Probably not, but I'll scare her." Piper shrugged. "We'll see if Crystal's attitude changes when we get her in here, and see if her parents can calm her down. I'm going to send some kind of message to the girl regarding the use of 9-1-1. Now, I gotta get back to the video."

"If you need any—"

"I'll holler."

Piper had MP training from Fort Campbell, had been sheriff of Spencer County for a handful of days beyond eight months, and she'd read a lot of police-related manuals ... was always reading them, it seemed. But her detective had years more experience, commendations, and decorations; and she'd hired him for all those reasons. He'd seen something in Chris' garage.

What had she missed from the video?

She went to key the cam footage up again just as Zeke put a call through to her office. She grabbed it, thinking it might be Oren with autopsy results. Too soon for the results, she realized as she said: "Spencer County Sheriff."

"You shine," Nang said. "How are you—"

"I'm not fine," she returned. "I'd be lying if I said I'm fine. But I'm doing okay. I'm drinking coffee and working ... at my desk, just reviewing things, not moving around much. Moving around a lot seems to be a bad idea. But I'm okay. I'll be better tonight if you make something with chicken and bring some flavor of ice cream. Chocolate. A chocolate flavor. And if you help me take a shower because I'm not supposed to get this damn thing wet and I'd really enjoy hot water pounding my back. And if you'd stay the night and—" *And I hope Zeke isn't listening to this conversation.* Her door was open and she was just around the corner from his desk; he could hear if he wanted to. She took a swallow of coffee. "And you'll be pleased to know the Vanderburgh County Sheriff caught your drive-off from the other night. Apparently the guy drives-off from more than a few stations, including one yesterday in Evansville."

Piper let Nang get a few words in and watched the video as he talked. Maybe it wasn't any *one* thing Basil had noticed, but a few things. Maybe it was the blood on Chris' knee where his jeans were torn, and maybe it was the swollen fingers of one hand but not the other. Maybe it was the way his right arm hung and the bruise on his face. Piper had myriad bruises from her fall in the abandoned mine. One on her face looked like she'd been punched. She knew she looked awful, hadn't bothered with any makeup. She only saw the one bruise on Chris.

What had Basil—

And then she spotted it, or was pretty sure that's what it was— something about the ladder Basil had stood on to get a closer look at Chris. Not the ladder that was on the ground near the body. Something about the ladder Basil had set up.

"And two is four," Piper said softly.

CHAPTER EIGHTEEN

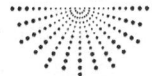

11 A.M. TUESDAY

Dr. Annie Neufeld started the autopsy nearly two hours late, a first for her. Basil had been told that she usually liked to start as early as possible, often before the scheduled time, and was sometimes finished before a sheriff's deputy arrived to watch.

"Car trouble, sorry. I finally gave up on the thing. Ford ... Fix Or Repair Daily. Or is that Found On the Road Dead? Gave up on it and had to take Bebe's Toyota, after I drove her to work. She had a court case today she couldn't miss, and then I had to stop and get gas, put air in the back tires. Called and got them to hold this room for me." Annie put on her mask and began, her voice now muffled. "I'm going to have to get a new car. Or maybe a little SUV. I'll start shopping after I'm done with Mr. Hagee. Not a Ford this time. Anything but a Ford. I think I'll get something red."

"I thought she'd retired, your wife," Oren said.

"She had," Annie returned. "But Bebe got bored and unretired. She closed her practice half a dozen months ago, but then she ran out of hobbies. Instead of reopening her office, she's gone into partnership with Harlan Cook."

Basil saw Oren cringe. Basil had never spoken with Cook, but he'd heard around the office that the man had a reputation for being an

131

ambulance chaser and for getting drunk drivers off. Harlan *Crook* was the department's nickname for that lawyer.

"Harlan. Really?" Oren scratched his forehead and walked to the counter, stuck his fingers in the Vicks VapoRub jar and smeared some under his nose. Basil had been around a lot of dead bodies. Chris' wasn't horrible yet; he'd forego the Vicks. There were enough antiseptic odors in the room to mask it.

Annie made a clucking sound, muted by her mask. "Harlan's not that bad, Oren, and he's great at finding snags in arrest reports for drunks. It's his specialty. My Bebe will help him stay on the right path. Besides, I suspect the partnership won't last all that long. Bebe'll figure out something else to do. Retirement? Not her thing though, probably never."

"Not mine either," Oren said softly.

Annie laughed. "Your birthday's Thursday, right? Sixty-six?"

Oren nodded.

Basil made a mental note of that. He'd have to come up something appropriate, maybe a gift certificate to that place with the excellent breakfast buffet.

"Well, your wife's going to hit you up with the retirement card again."

"I know."

"And she'll—"

"Don't want to talk about it, Annie."

The coroner fell silent and went to work.

Basil noticed Chris' clothes on the counter, bagged and ready to be sent to the state lab for testing. He'd requested the testing because he knew this was a murder investigation. He padded over and picked up the bag with the Route 66 t-shirt. He saw the blood spots.

"You say murder." Oren had come up behind him, so quiet Basil started.

"Yeah. Hell, yeah, it's murder. Dr. Neufeld will confirm that in a little while. Look." He pointed to the blood spots on the t-shirt.

"And—" Oren prompted.

"Blood's from his nose, I bet. Broken nose. Bled onto his shirt. It could have been from an accident, falling. But from what I've heard of Chris Hagee, I'd guess he got in a fight with someone. Blood on his knee. Pants ripped at the knee. He didn't get those injuries from hanging himself."

"Okay, I'll maybe give you that. What else?"

"A couple of things, actually. All sorts of things." Basil picked up the bag with the jeans and looked over his shoulder. Annie was scraping under Chris' nails and taking a sample of skin cells from his face. She hadn't pulled back the sheet yet, but he'd asked her to take samples from his skinned knee, too. Shouldn't have asked, he realized after she gave him a dirty look. Annie was clearly a professional and didn't like being told what to do—didn't need to be.

"Tennis shoes." He picked up that bag and pointed to the tops of the shoes that were scraped and dirty. Turned the bag over to show the dried mud in the grooves in the soles. "And the ladder, which I took pictures of, the one I used to get a closer look at the body. There were shoe prints on that ladder, dried mud. Muddy shoe prints on the ladder that had been under Chris, too."

"Because it rained the day before Chris was hung. Muddy shoes from all the water."

Basil nodded. "And the shoe prints, I have a picture in my phone. Just the balls of the feet from the ladder. Those muddy prints don't match the tread on Hagee's tennis shoes in this bag."

Oren made a humming sound. "So you think someone else with muddy feet hoisted Chris up and hung him."

"Yeah. That's exactly what I'm thinking."

"But Chris could have climbed the ladder another time, with different muddy shoes."

Basil shook his head. "Nah. Murder. If the murderer was smart, he would've wiped down the ladder. And, yeah, you're right. Chris could've used the ladders at an earlier date and left the mud from different shoes. Except these tracks are for a considerably wider foot than Chris has."

Oren whistled. "Sherlock. Anybody ever call you Sherlock?"

"A few people in Chicago," Basil returned. "I fingerprinted both the

ladders, quite a few things in the garage. Chris' truck inside and out …
though the rain complicates it a little. There are some elements of
latent prints that aren't water soluble. I used some ORO—Oil Red O—
and got some partials. I'll run it all through the database this afternoon, compare it to Chris Hagee's fingerprints. And I want to go back
out and check for more prints."

"Did you get anything from the spray paint cans?"

"They were wiped clean, which I thought odd, even the plunger
caps and nozzles. Assuming the person who used them wore gloves,
there would be prints from whoever stocked them on a store shelf. So,
they were truly wiped clean. The tarp? I couldn't get anything off that.
Too wet. The graffiti incident, that's somehow related to Chris
Hagee's murder, I think. For some reason if Hagee had spray-painted
his neighbor's house, I don't think he would've bothered to wipe off
the cans. He might have bothered to dump the spray cans, though, not
leave them as evidence." He paused: "And there were a lot of beer cans
inside his house that he hadn't wiped clean. I've had those fingerprinted, too. I'm curious if he had company over, and who that
company was."

Oren whistled again. "And you didn't find any receipts for the
paint. That's okay. I know where he likely bought them. He wouldn't
have gone to Owensboro, would've stayed in the county. I'll go to the
hardware store and check."

Oren smiled and Basil figured that was a good indication the chief
deputy was enjoying the challenge of the investigation.

"So Chris Hagee was murdered. I'll wager we've a long suspect list.
A lot of folks didn't like the man. Hell, I didn't like him either," Oren
said.

"But a lot of people did, or at least agreed with him. He had almost
three hundred unique signatures on his petition to remove the
Buddhists."

Oren crossed his arms, let out a deep sigh. "That's more people
than live in Fulda."

"Hate," Basil said. "That's a lot of hate. Or people just not knowing
any better."

"I've got something," Annie announced. "You should take a look before I get into him."

Basil and Oren returned to the table.

"Bruising." Annie had drawn back the sheet all the way. "I'm taking pictures before I cut him open. Here and here and here." She made a face. "When we took him down yesterday, he was red in some places, early bruising, some blue. Now it's blue-black. It can take hours before the deep colors come into a bruise, even if the fellow is dead. And it's swollen, a lot of blood involved. That helps me pinpoint the time of death, which by the way, I'm estimating at between midnight and four yesterday morning, not dead all that long before you found him, Basil. Maybe I can be even more precise once I'm inside. But I'll never give you better than a two-hour window."

Two hours would be good, Basil knew, and the only time in Chicago he got a better TOD was when the death had been witnessed. Spencer County was fortunate it had a coroner who was competent to conduct an autopsy, he mused. It was an elected position, and so even a grocery clerk could run for the office. Most small communities had to contract with an outside medical examiner to handle autopsies.

There were bruises on Chris' chest and stomach, on his upper right arm, on the right side of his face, and on the front of his thighs. Dr. Neufeld gave a detailed description of them so her recorder could pick everything up.

"A fight," Oren said. "Someone really beat him up."

"No," Basil said. "That was my first guess, seeing the broken nose. This was worse than a fight."

"A fight wouldn't have hurt as much," Dr. Neufeld said. "I'd say he was struck by a car, or maybe a tractor or other piece of farm equipment. I'll know more when I get in there, see what kind of organ damage there is. But it looks like he was run over, a lot of broken ribs. You found him hanging, but he couldn't have put himself up there. His right arm is cracked near the shoulder, right here where this discoloration is, and the collarbone is cracked. I don't think he could have tied the noose and lopped it up over the rafters with that arm, let alone moved a big ladder. Someone ran over him."

"And then hung him," Basil added.

"To make it look like Chris killed himself. So it would look like a suicide instead of murder," Oren finished. "Pretty amateur job of covering a murder. Maybe the killer didn't think we'd figure it out. Maybe they were panicked, in a hurry."

Basil saw the chief deputy smile again.

"Interesting, Annie," Oren added.

"And it's up to you to solve," she cut back.

Basil saw her look directly at Oren.

"I heard Sheriff Blackwell is pretty much out of commission, is lucky she's alive."

"Up to us to solve," Oren said. "Yeah, this is our case."

"If you two have enough to go on, get out of here and let me finish. I'll get plenty of pictures, and call you with the results when I'm done. Tox screens will take a while, but you know that." She used a spray attachment to clean off the body, and then she pulled over a tray with tools laid out. "You going to see your dad today, Oren?"

"After we go back to the department, and I drop Basil off. Late lunch with Dad. I'm going to get us grilled cheese and Cokes."

"His favorite," she said. "He'll like that."

"I don't drink Coke," Basil said. "But I like grilled cheese. We can go back via Owensboro, and you can introduce me to your dad. It's not far out of the way. You drive. I want to sit and think about who ran over Chris Hagee."

"And then hung him because they didn't want to take the credit," Oren said softly.

CHAPTER NINETEEN

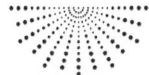

2 P.M. TUESDAY

"Oren's tracking the spray paint," Basil said, as he sat across from Piper in the break room. He had Chris' laptop open; Zeke had finessed his way past the passwords.

Piper looked down at the spiral notebook and opened it. "Because the graffiti is connected," she said. It made sense to her, everything involving Chris Hagee was connected—his dislike of the Buddhists, anger over free beer, being distraught about his wife leaving him, and no doubt myriad other things in his unhappy, unsettled life.

"Yeah, everything connects somehow. Oren thinks he knows where the paint was bought," Basil said. "He's at the hardware store."

"He could've done that with a few phone calls."

"Yeah, but he needs to be moving, busy, and he needs to be alone. He's running down some other things, too."

Piper crooked her head in question.

"That's right, you haven't heard. His dad's dying. Fast. I doubt he makes it past the weekend. Oren's broken up about it. Don't blame him, I saw it. I went with him for lunch, tough to see an old man all faded and shrunken and not recognizing his son. Nurse told me Oren went over there last night, brought his uniform in a hanging bag, slept in a chair, and then left from there to come to work this morning. I

137

wager he does it again tonight, too. I got the idea Oren and his dad were real close."

Piper felt like crying. She was the sheriff of Spencer County because she'd thought her dad was dying, didn't re-up at Campbell like she'd planned so she could take care of him and be with him at the end. She let her dad talk her into running for his vacated office to give her something to do while he was going through chemo. Then he beat cancer the second time, and after that survived a heart attack. Despite how healthy he seemed now, and his working as the police chief of Santa Claus, she still thought of him as fragile with a tentative hold on life. Piper knew Oren's father had been career law enforcement, and no doubt inspired Oren into the field. The two were indeed close. Oren hadn't mentioned to her just how bad his dad was faring.

"Oren needs to take a few days off, spend them with his dad. He doesn't need to be coming in here."

Basil shook his head. "Yeah, he does need to come in."

"We can cover this ourselves. We don't need—"

"But *he* needs," Basil countered. "I saw him. He needs to be occupied and keep his mind off stuff. At least keep family stuff at bay for a little while."

The image of Hemi dead on the ground beside Renegade hovered in her head. Death was a soul-shaker.

"I get it. I really do. Okay." Piper needed to stay occupied herself so she'd not dwell on Hemi, Renegade, and Brick.

She started scanning the notebook, Chris Hagee's "Buddah Journal" as he'd labeled it on the first page, dated back to April fourth. Basil turned his attention to the laptop. In the background, Piper heard Zeke field a 9-1-1 call about an accident in Santa Claus; he deftly dispatched a car from that police department.

Anthony Delaney had returned to Spencer County in January, for his father's funeral and to handle the estate. It was around the end of the month that he'd decided to stay and do something different with the house. But the journal didn't start until months later. Maybe April was when Anthony had hung out the sign and named the place the Buddhist Cultural Center. She remembered he'd checked with the county zoning laws to make sure it was legal—which it was, but there'd been no item in the news about it springing up, only a few photocopied flyers put out at the grocery store in Rockport.

Probably hung out the sign right around the first of April, and Chris started his journal a few days after that, she thought. Chris seemed to be a busybody and noticed everything going on along his little country road.

The first entry was lengthy.

Ap 4, 3:30: Saw Billy and his wife Lola stop by. Likely on their way to somewhere else, looked like they were driving in from the east back where their house is. She was carrying some big casserole dish covered in aluminum foil. They go to the Catholic church, ain't a reason in the world for them to go see the Buddahs. Anthony opened the door and talked to them. There he was, bald and wearing orange. Orange like a prison jumpsuit except it was a robe like a Gaysha girl would wear. It's his Buddah priest outfit. He let them inside.

Almost an hour Billy and Lola was inside. Maybe Anthony was trying to convert them, teaching them a chant or something. Anthony was always friendly when he was a kid. He was not a Buddah worshipper then. He mowed my grass in the summer and I gave him $10 a whack. Wish I hadn't paid him so much. Wonder what they all talked about for an hour. Too bad I wasn't a fly on the wall watching.

"This is sad stuff," Piper said. "Maybe Chris shouldn't have retired. Maybe if he'd done something with his time other than spy on his neighbors, things would have turned out differently for him."

"Most of his recent emails make mention of the Buddhists, but he spells it B-U-D-D-A-H-S. It might be because he didn't know how to spell it, or it might be intentionally wrong to degrade them some more. And most of the emails are to his wife, Joan." Basil kept reading. "It seems he thought if he could get the Buddhists to go away, she'd come back. I count one hundred emails since the first of August to her, average of three a day. Each one basically says the same thing, that he's working on cleaning them out of Fulda, that's he's working on the sheriff to do it for him, and that he has more names on his petition."

"And what does she email back?"

"Only one email in return from her, August twenty-fifth. Maybe there are more and he deleted them, I've not gone through his trash yet," Basil said. "She wrote: 'Chris, leave me alone. I'm filing for divorce. Leave Anthony Delaney alone, too'. Of course, there might've been phone calls exchanged between them, maybe messages left. I haven't dug into his cell phone yet or phone records. Going to take a good chunk of time." He tapped his thumb against the table. "There are some other emails farther back, to different people. We'll compare those names to the petition and that journal. He didn't have a Facebook page, but he may have posted to other sites, comment sections and things like that. I'll work on a browsing history after I'm done with the emails."

"Zeke can help."

"He's pretty amazing," Basil admitted. "Where'd you find him?"

Piper thought back to her first meeting with Zeke the Geek. "He was president of the high school computer club and was helping some senior citizens with genealogy research. A couple of those seniors ended up dead. Zeke was helpful when we were investigating their murders."

Basil nodded. "I read about that case. Mark Thresher, right? He's the one who willed the department money for the body cams and the police dog."

And gifted me with a beautiful house and old cars and motorcycles. "Mark the Shark," Piper fondly corrected. "Zeke is awesome."

She continued to read the journal entries, finding one of the later ones especially sad.

Aug 22, 2:30: Joan pulled into that Buddahs driveway. That driveway, not ours. Thought she made a mistake. She pulled right up to the walk, went to THEIR door. Ain't right. She looking pretty. Gray pantsuit she sometimes wears going out—when WE went out. Don't see anything sticking out of that tote bag she has. Purse in her other hand. She sets it down, knocks, oh look who's there, Anthony, right away, like he was WAITNG For Her. MY wife! Damn Buddah wearing his orange prison robes again smiling, had her come in. WTFH WTFH WTFH, my Joan goes to see the damn Buddahs, NOT ME!!! I should go over there and (there was a section where he'd scribbled out a couple of sentences so hard he'd dug a hole in the paper) *Why's she going to see them again??? Holy Hell and All. Maybe she'll get them to move. Maybe. Yeah, that's it. Maybe. Talking to them about moving so she can come home.*

The entry didn't say how long Joan was at the center. Her first visit there, June 12th, well before she'd left Chris, lasted thirty-two minutes according to the journal.

Piper wondered if Chris did go out and talk to Joan after her August 22nd stop at Anthony's. Maybe he had, and he just didn't write anything about it. She also wondered why Joan had lied to Oren, telling him she hadn't been back to Fulda in more than a month. People lie, she knew. Maybe Joan had come back even more recently, like the weekend Chris died.

Zeke came into the room at three when his shift ended. "Crystal's mother called, thanked us again for not arresting her daughter. Said Crystal's grounded until Thanksgiving. And no cell phone."

"Bet that'll hold," Piper said sarcastically.

"Take you home, Sheriff? Ready to go?"

"Not yet." Piper was tired, aching, really could do with a pain pill and an easy chair, but didn't want to leave the case just yet, it was that interesting. "I think I'm going to stick with this another hour or so, get through this notebook and some other things."

"I'll wait," Zeke said. "I'll be in—"

"Go home Zeke," Basil interrupted. "I'll take Sheriff Blackwell home in *one* hour." Piper caught the emphasis on the one hour. She appreciated her detective looking out for her, but it was her decision, not his, when she would leave. She was in charge. Maybe she'd stay here a long while today just to prove that.

"Okay," Zeke said. "You call me at home, Sheriff, if you need—"

"I'll be fine. Thanks."

Piper eased away from the table and went to the whiteboard, lightning fingers of pain flickering through her arm and making her think maybe she should've left with Zeke. Her chest was throbbing, too. She pulled a chair next to the board, set the journal down, then the petition, and started jotting down names from Chris' written entries.

Suck it up, Christmas. Get through it. She flexed the fingers of her good arm.

"I don't see a single name on the petition that matches the center's visitors Chris recorded in his book," she said.

"No. But he might not have caught all the visitors," Basil said. "Chris wasn't at his house twenty-four-seven. Sometimes he went to the bar, sometimes he went shopping. All that beer in his house ... that didn't magically appear. I figure he went shopping quite often. And he had to go other places to collect signatures for his petition."

"Granted," Piper said. "But from these two sources there are no overlapping names." She drew a line down the center of the whiteboard, and on the right-hand side jotted:

- Jeffrey Morse
- Gregg Hammer
- Bebe and Annie Neufeld

There'd been a nasty notation next to those names, but Piper passed it by. Chris apparently hadn't liked gay people either.

- Henry and son Tucker *****

Five stars because there were recordings of five visits.

- Billy and Lola Krupp ***

Three visits all in June.

- Son Tucker ********

142

Eight recordings of separate visits. Oren had mentioned that the son—Dale—had been a schoolmate of Anthony's. She wrote Dale in parenthesis.

- Joan **
- Gretta Mueller
- Gunther Mueller **
- Missy Pearson
- Young man in a red t-shirt
- Young man in a Coors Beer t-shirt **
- Young man wearing an Indianapolis Colts jersey
- Sort of young man wearing brown shorts and one of them muscle shirts
- Meter reader **
- UPS delivery ********************
- Two women Jehovah's Witnesses

Chris had made a note that the pair of Witnesses first visited him, and he encouraged them to go across the street to see Anthony, said the monk needed a new perspective.

- Gunther Mueller's boy
- That funny-looking woman from the Sheriff's Department ******

Piper wrote *Teegan* next to that; she knew her dispatcher had been over there several times, and was searching to see if Buddhism was right for her.

- Michael or Mike Grisham or Grishward or Grisword ******

Chris had written that he couldn't quite recall the last name of the man who usually brought Culligan water bottles around because the well water along the road didn't taste good.

Oriental gas station guy.

Piper suspected that was Nang.

- Lance Larkspur **
- Danny Olson
- Young black man in a blue t-shirt
- Young black man in a green t-shirt
- Woman in a hippie skirt
- Young black man in a red and white striped muscle shirt, might have been the guy in the green t-shirt earlier

There were more unnamed people, but Piper left it at that and returned to the table. "No way to identify the nameless people Chris wrote about without getting Anthony in here. He can provide names for at least some of them." She closed the notebook. "This lists when each person visited, how long they stayed, except for Joan's last visit, and if they brought anything with them—backpack, suitcase, grocery bag, and on and on."

"I'm interested in two days for starters," Basil said. "September fifth, the day before the graffiti, and the sixth, the day before I found Chris hanging from the rafters."

Piper underlined: Meter reader, UPS delivery, Dale Tucker, and Coors Beer t-shirt for the fifth, and Lance Larkspur for the sixth. She decided to go through the notebook one more time, carried it over to the table, and sat. More stabs of pain shot through her arm.

Basil got up and started writing on the left-hand side of the whiteboard.

"So far, we know Hagee comes from a racist roots, believed he was all-American," he said, writing on the board. "He retired from farming nearly two years ago. He drank a lot of beer, liked pizza. A lot of beer and pizza." He stopped and grinned at Piper before continuing his list-making.

Christopher Paul Hagee

- Born into a racist family

144

- Believed he was patriotic
- Retired from farming 23 months ago
- American-made vehicles
- American-made appliances
- Heavy beer drinker
- Soon-to-be divorced
- Started petition against the Buddhist Cultural Center
- Frequently called Sheriff
- DUI in March 2018, successfully fought in court
  —Harlan Cook
- Disturbing the peace in August 2018 at Rudy's Tap, dismissed
- Disorderly conduct in May 2019 at Phan's Quick Stop, no charges
- DUI in February 2020, successfully fought in court
  —Harlan Cook
- No children
- Rents his farmland in Fulda
- Formerly attended Catholic church
- Registered Republican
- No guns registered
- No pets
- Two joint bank accounts with wife
- One joint checking account with wife
- Individual IRA
- $1,400 in a shoebox in the closet
- $56 in wallet found on body
- Murdered/staged as suicide

"Those are the things we know about Chris Hagee," Basil said. "On the surface, he was a husband, farmer, redneck, bigot, unhappy and unsatisfied man, and that he sprang from prejudiced roots, his grandfather a member of the KKK."

He paused. "Like him or not, all of this just scratches the surface. Over the next few days I'm going to dig a lot deeper. The victim was more than those things, and the more I discover about him, the closer I'll get to his killer. I've not interviewed his neighbors yet, not specifi-cally *about* him. When we were out there before, it was only to ask about the graffiti and damage to the Delaney house. I'll start on the neighbors in the morning, right after I see Judge Vaughn about another search warrant, this one for Hagee's safe deposit box. I'm hoping there's a will inside and names his beneficiaries."

"Because they could be suspects," Piper said. The initial search warrant had been signed before Chris' death and targeted information relating to the vandalism at the Delaney house. "Money a motive?"

Basil shrugged. "I'm taking his laptop home with me tonight, and have Zeke take a look in the morning, see if he comes up with more."

"I'm limited," Piper admitted. "I guess you'd call it restricted duty. I'll do some phone work in the morning, calling the people who were regulars at Chris' New Year's Eve and Fourth of July parties. Some of them are from out of town and a few of them signed his petition. Joan Hagee will be in the county tomorrow or the day after to start funeral arrangements, but Dr. Neufeld hasn't released the body yet."

"Oren said Mrs. Hagee didn't react much when he told her Chris was dead."

"Apparently not." Piper winced at another, stronger jab from her broken arm. She'd been prescribed pain pills for a reason. She really needed to take one. "Maybe Chris was dead to her when she left him."

Oren came into the break room several minutes later, and Piper thought he looked disappointed to see her still here.

"Thought you were leaving with Zeke," he said.

"I'm doing okay," she said. "Thanks for—"

"I'm taking her home now." Basil stood.

Piper decided not to protest; she really needed to take something so her arm quit throbbing, even though that would send her into la-la land. She felt so uncomfortable she was nauseous.

"I'll ride with you," Oren said. "Then we can turn around and go to Fulda, see if Henry Tucker is home."

"Because—" Piper prompted.

"Because I found out Henry Tucker bought a dozen cans of spray

146

paint four days ago from the hardware store. Red, black, and green, four cans of each."

"Now that I didn't expect." Basil looked at the whiteboard. "The graffiti happened the day after Henry's son last visited the Delaney house. Interesting. Maybe something happened as a result of that visit. If Henry did the spray painting—maybe spurred on by Chris, or maybe because his son Dale was going there too often—"

Oren waved a hand. "I don't think Chris encouraged Henry to do it. Because why would Chris sic the department on Henry at G's Bar if they were friendly and scheming together against their Buddhist neighbors? Henry would be a kindred soul, right? If Henry was working *with* Chris, why do that? Call the sheriff? But—" Oren rubbed his chin. "You know, Chris didn't want Henry arrested. He was real specific about that when he talked to Millie. He wanted Gretta hauled off."

"So they might have worked together, Henry and Chris," Piper said. If she wasn't hurting so much, she would join them—she was that curious. But they didn't need her, both were a hell of a lot more experienced, and this was their case. "Go. I'll find another way home."

Neither man argued with her.

CHAPTER TWENTY

6 P.M. TUESDAY

I don't deserve this treatment." Piper considered herself spoiled by Nang's cooking. Tonight's dinner was exceptional. It had started with hot and sour soup, and then broken rice with spiced grilled chicken that was called something she couldn't remember or pronounce. Red velvet cupcakes sat on a plate in the center of the dining table for desert, and there was a half-gallon of Ben and Jerry's New York Super Fudge Chunk ice cream in the freezer.

"Yes, you do," Nang returned.

Piper had gone with Nang to Indianapolis a month ago, where he auditioned for a national cooking competition. He was chopped in the second round, and he vowed to try again at the coming spring audition. Piper thought he should have won.

"I had to talk my dad into *not* coming over to join us," she said, as she reached for a glass of milk. Piper had cut off the coffee shortly after lunch, and though she would have liked a glass of oaked chardonnay, which would have paired well with Nang's dish, she couldn't drink alcohol with her medication. "I need to spend more time with him, and I will. But not tonight. Saturday, I think I'll spend Saturday with him. Anyway, he came by my office today, stayed for an hour, brought Wrinkles with him. The old pug's not much of a police dog." She grinned. "I showed him a picture of our Belgian Malinois that's being trained. We get him delivered at the end of next week. Now that's a police dog. We named him Thresher, in honor of Mark the Shark."

"Your father's just worried about you."

Piper drank half the milk, set the glass down, and selected a cupcake. Having only one hand to work with was frustrating. She pulled off the paper with her teeth. "Yeah, I get that."

"I'm worried about you."

"I get that, too. But I'm okay, really. It could have been—"

"Worse. You could have died. In that cave, you could have—"

"Yeah." Piper nibbled on the cupcake. If she ate, she didn't have to talk about what happened in Spaceman's woods, which Nang repeatedly asked her about. But she *did* want to think about it. What had made that man fire on Hemi and Renegade, and then on her and Brick? Alcohol? Was he so drunk he wasn't thinking? Had he mistook Hemi's and Renegade's paintball guns for real weapons and thought he was defending himself? The local sheriff's department didn't have lab work back from the shooter's autopsy, which could be telling. It was supposed to be available in a week. And the preliminary report they released to her as a courtesy hadn't told her anything she didn't already know or answer any of her questions.

Piper was so consumed—with grief, anger, and curiosity—that she wanted to dig into the matter herself. Yet at the same time there was this pressing case swirling around Chris Hagee in Spencer County.

Who killed—ran over—Chris? And tried to cover it up with a mask of suicide? Why do that?

Piper had to walk a line with the Hagee case, be involved but not take over. Be the boss, but not be in charge this time. Basil had caught the case and found the body. A decorated police detective with a world of experience, she was stepping back and watching him, not giving orders. Watching ... and at the same time thinking about what happened in Spaceman's woods. Her mind was a busy blur.

"That's not weakness," her father told her earlier, "letting Basil and

149

Oren handle the Chris Hagee case. That's strength and good judgment, trusting the detective you hired, and your chief deputy. It looks like they're working well together. They'll appreciate you for helping, not interfering. For being the sheriff without being the boss."

Basil and Oren thought the graffiti and the murder were connected. She leaned that way, too. Could someone at the Buddhist Cultural Center have been so angry that they ran over Chris? And to shift blame made it look like he'd hung himself? She'd thought that wasn't possible. But Anthony Delaney was the only Bhikkhu at the center, maybe the only true Buddhist, the others just dabblers or curious, looking for direction.

"Okay, if not a penny, a two-dollar lottery ticket?" Nang topped off her glass of milk.

"What?"

"I said, a penny for your thoughts."

"I was just ... thinking," Piper replied.

"Obviously. About—"

"Dead friends, a hanging man, and how bad it would be if I had a second cupcake before that hot shower. And then ice cream afterwards before I crash because I took a pain pill. I'm making up for the four pounds I lost in the hospital."

He nudged the plate of cupcakes closer.

An hour later she sat with Nang on the couch, wearing a pink terrycloth robe with wide sleeves that accommodated her sling. Nang had bought the robe at Walmart in Owensboro on his way back from an Asian grocer in the city. She didn't like pink, but she loved the man who gave it to her. She leaned against him, opened her laptop, struggled to stay awake, and signed into the department account.

"This is an ongoing investigation," Piper said. "I can't share information about an ongoing investigation."

Nang rested his head against the back of the couch, gingerly put an arm around her shoulders, and closed his eyes. "I'm not listening," he said. "And I'm not looking."

Piper didn't want to take the laptop to another room, and she didn't want to shoo Nang away; she was too comfortable against him. It also was the first time today she could actually say she wasn't hurting. Hydrocodone was amazing; she could see how some people became addicted.

She opened the audio file Basil and Oren had recently uploaded from their visit with Henry Tucker. Her finger hovered over the play button. Marmalade, her inherited orange tabby, sauntered in from the kitchen, regarded her and Nang, and then found a perch on the windowsill and started grooming her front legs. Camaro, the aging golden retriever, followed a few moments later, having come in from the backyard via the dog door. He padded to Piper, wagged his tail, and curled between her feet.

She hit play, kept the volume low, and listened. The first sounds were scraping and thunking, and she pictured Basil, Oren, and Henry pulling back chairs and sitting at a table, the recorder probably centered between them.

Oren started: "Vince at the hardware store said you bought a dozen cans of spray paint a little over a week back, a tarp and some other things, too. Red, black, and green paint, four cans each. He remembered the sale because you cleaned him out of red and black."

"So what?"

There was silence then, soft tapping, maybe someone drumming his fingers on the table.

Basil took a turn: "Did your son Dale help you deface the Buddhist Cultural Center, Mr. Tucker?"

More silence, the tapping faster.

"I bought paint. I admit I bought spray paint. I admit that. No crime to buy paint. So what if I bought paint? Nothing wrong with buying a few cans of spray paint. I have hobbies. I use spray paint on the birdhouses I make on the weekends."

Oren: "The Delaney house was spray-painted red, black, and green, Henry. Same colors as the paint you bought."

A scraping sound, like someone moving a chair.

"Do I need a lawyer?"

Basil: "Do you?"

"I wasn't going to hurt Anthony's house. I like Anthony. Dale goes over there a lot, and sometimes Anthony comes here for dinner. I don't want Anthony to know that we—"

Oren: "*We.* So Dale helped you deface the house." His voice did not rise in a question.

"Let's leave Dale out of this." More tapping, fabric rustling. Faintly she heard music playing, from somewhere else in the house. It had just come on, so maybe Dale was home and in another room. "I wasn't going to hurt Anthony's house, honest."

Basil: "But you did. You damaged the house and yard. That was the third time the house was vandalized."

"I had nothing to do with those other times, the eggs and the tires. I heard about them, but those times weren't me. Hagee. You damn well know Hagee did those."

Basil: "But not the spray paint. That wasn't Chris Hagee."

Oren: "Why, Henry? Why do that, spray those awful things on that house if you say that you like Anthony?"

Henry's retort came fast: "Because that asshole Hagee pissed me off. That's why. It's because of Hagee I did it. Him and that damn petition to get rid of the Buddhists, always asking me to sign it, calling me about it, waving the petition in my face, griping about them ... and griping about your department for not doing anything about them. I'd bought the paint a while back for *his* house, Hagee's. I'd planned to write bigot over every blank spot, get that damn big garage of his, too. I was just waiting to get up the gumption, find a time when the damn orange pickup wasn't in the damn driveway. But he was home every damn time I went by, looking out that window with binoculars sometimes, spying on Anthony and whoever else went over there. It was for Hagee, not Anthony."

Basil: "So if it was for Mr. Hagee, as you say, and that you'd intended to deface Mr. Hagee's house, why go after the Cultural Center instead?"

"Do I need an attorney? Should I call an attorney?"

Basil: "That's up to you."

Oren cut in quickly: "So why Anthony's place, Henry? If it was Chris Hagee who pissed you off—"

"It was all on Hagee. All on that son of a bitch. It was because he came into G's Bar Friday night and called the sheriff on Gretta for giving me free beer. Wanted her arrested. *Demanded* she be arrested. Sweet Gretta! She gave me three beers that night. Lord, if that asshole had been there the other nights she treated me, he would've seen her give me beer, sandwiches, chips. Hell, me and Gretta are together, you know. And he wanted her locked up, for nothing! After that woman deputy left, the young one that hasn't been here long, Hagee got all high-and-mighty, wagging his finger and strutting around the bar, saying Gretta was going to be tossed in jail come Tuesday morning. I couldn't take it. I had to get out of there. When I left G's, he was still there, Hagee, all puffed up like a damned barnyard rooster. I went home and got the paint, and I was going to go paint his house. Really, I was gonna go after Hagee's."

Oren: "But you didn't paint Chris Hagee's house. Again, Henry, why did you go after Anthony's instead?"

Tapping. Tapping.

"You don't get it. Anthony's house was dark. Looked like he was sleeping. I know they turn in early. It got me thinking about another way to burn Hagee. Me and Dale— Well, just me. It was just me. Leave Dale out of it. I figured if I spray painted the Buddhist center instead of Hagee's, and did a little damage—"

Oren: "The mailbox, the garden."

"Yeah, and the birdbath. I shouldn't have done the birdbath. I think Anthony's dad made that. I figured Hagee would be blamed for all the damage. Stuck the empty cans in the back of his pickup, covered them up. Thought he might get caught with them, arrested. Hell, he'd be the only one who would do something mean like that. I'm damn well sure he egged the place earlier. See? I didn't intend to hurt Anthony. I just wanted to hurt Hagee. Have *him* get arrested for all of that, tossed in jail. If he was in jail, Gretta wouldn't have to worry about that son of a bitch. If he was in jail, he couldn't bother anybody. He'd be doing this county a favor by rotting behind bars."

Basil: "Dale helped you with the project?"

Silence.

Oren: "Just be honest with us, Henry. That was a lot of damage for one man to do."

"It was *my* idea. *I* bought the paint. *I'll* pay for the damages. Leave Dale out of this."

The silence stretched so long Piper thought the recording was over. She went to turn it off, when—

Basil: "Did you kill Mr. Hagee?"

A sputtering sound.

"Hell, no! Scuttle is he hanged himself because his wife wants a divorce."

Basil: "Did you run over Mr. Hagee?"

Oren: "And make it look like a suicide?"

"Run over? Oren, I couldn't kill a fly. No, I didn't kill Hagee. No, I didn't run over him. I did the stuff to Anthony's house, and I am so very sorry for that. But, no, I didn't kill Hagee. I swear to you. Hagee went and killed himself."

Basil: "Is your car in the garage, Mr. Tucker? You have a pickup truck too, right?"

Silence. Maybe he nodded, Piper guessed, because Basil kept going.

Basil: "Then how about you take us out to your garage and we take a look at your car, truck, and your son's car, too."

"No. Nope. I'm not letting you in my garage. Not without a lawyer. I shouldn't have let you in my house. Now you two need to be going. I want you out of here."

Basil: "You have the right to remain silent. You—"

"Whoa! I said I didn't kill Hagee. You got to believe me. I didn't kill him. I wouldn't kill anyone!"

Basil: "We're arresting you for criminal mischief, Mr. Tucker. What you did to the Buddhist Cultural Center is considered a hate crime; that ups the severity."

Oren, a whisper: "Do not pass go. Do not collect two hundred dollars."

Basil continued reading Henry his rights. Piper closed down the laptop and looked at Nang. His mouth was open, and he was sound asleep. She eased herself away and shuffled into the kitchen.

One more red velvet cupcake, one scoop of chocolate ice cream, one more pill, and she crawled into bed.

CHAPTER TWENTY-ONE

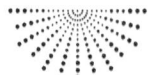

9 A.M. WEDNESDAY, SEPTEMBER 9TH

Piper took the coroner's call in her office. She figured it was autopsy results, since they hadn't come in yesterday. Dr. Neufeld always called about her findings, and then sent both an old-fashioned FAX and an email with the official report. Sometimes she dropped them off in person.

"I'm not finished with Chris Hagee," Dr. Neufeld began.

"Was there a problem?" Piper never knew the coroner to take more than a day for her initial report. Lab results from tox screens were added later.

"No," Dr. Neufeld said. "Well, I suppose. If there's a problem, it's with my lack of specific forensics experience. The bodies that have come my way since you took office have been fairly straightforward—except for that ice pick victim. I've been comfortable with the autopsies and results and signing off on them. I qualify as a medical examiner because I started with a pathology residency and a forensic pathology fellowship. I keep my licensure updated. But at the heart of my training I'm a pediatrician. I need someone with more forensic expertise to look at Chris Hagee. Just to be sure. I mean, Sheriff, I think I have it, but honestly I'm not one hundred percent."

"I don't understand," Piper said. "Hang on a moment." She looked up as Zeke came in with her train engine mug filled with Dark Italian. He placed it on her desk and mouthed: *Need anything else?* And when she shook her head, he retreated to his desk. "Okay, Dr. Neufeld, go on."

"Look, a thorough autopsy determines the cause of death, the manner of death, and the relative time of death. I've got the last of those three locked down to a two-hour window, between two and four Sunday morning. I'd chisel those hours in stone for you, and nobody could give you something more precise—except for your killer. But the cause and manner, I want another set of eyes on. There's a specialist at the Evansville hospital, he's going to take a look later this morning. He's an expert in automotive-related deaths, even wrote a book about vehicular trauma. He's agreed to come in and look. I'll get back to you."

Dr. Neufeld disconnected and Piper stared at the phone. Maybe the coroner was hoping to pinpoint what sort of vehicle had run over Chris Hagee, which might be crucial to find out who was behind the wheel. She wondered how much this expert was going to cost, because the money would be coming out of her department's budget.

She called Nang, figured he'd have made it to the Quick Stop by now. She kept her voice low, not wanting Zeke to hear her frustration.

"I feel worthless," she told him. "I sit at a desk. I'm looking through a dead man's journal, catching up on reports filed from my deputies, staring at my computer screen. I sit at a desk. I sit and sit and sit and sit at a desk. And drink coffee. And you don't need to hear me complain, but I wanted to complain to someone and—"

She listened to him for several minutes and cringed when little pain jolts pulsed down from her shoulder.

"I know, this is temporary, and I know this busywork is stuff that has to get done. But the surgeon said restricted duty for up to six months. Months, Nang. Four at the earliest if I'm lucky. Dear, God, I need to be lucky. I want to be out there, interviewing Chris Hagee's neighbors. That's not practical. So I'm sitting." Piper drank some of the coffee. Could have used a little cream. "Okay, enough complaining. I've an idea for tomorrow. Oren's birthday. I want to do something that'll be good for him, nice for the whole department, actually. Something nice for Teegan, too, since I missed hers. Probably wouldn't have come up with it if I didn't have to sit here at this desk."

She explained. Nang agreed to help.

Piper leaned back and concentrated on the coffee for a few minutes. It was pleasant, waking up next to Nang, having him at the house. Marmalade and Camaro liked him ... though admittedly she'd never seen them dislike anyone.

She'd not envisioned this life in little Spencer County. A year ago, her future was focused on eventually returning to the Army and a posting in Germany, seeing the world, rising higher in the ranks, and putting in her twenty. Maybe more than twenty. Now all she wanted was to sink her roots ever deeper right here, and with a man who was an expert Vietnamese chef and owned a gas station-slash-convenience store in a little town that had a Buddhist Cultural Center across the road from a sad man who'd been hung in his garage.

What would Hemi have said about her embracing rural life?

Piper checked her email, pleased that the Ohio County Sheriff's Department had sent over another report. She pulled up the attachment.

- Charles Robert Weger, thirty-one, of Hartford, Kentucky, graduated at nineteen from Ohio County High School.
- Held back one year in middle school for excessive truancy and failing grades.
- Played on the Eagles football and basketball teams, one year in the band, one year on the cross-country team.
- Attended Jefferson Community College in nearby Shelbyville; received a two-year applied science degree with a focus on automotive technology. Weger worked for various car dealers in and around Rosine; opened his own detailing shop two years ago, specializing in motorcycles and vintage autos.

- Once married after high school to Debbie Henderson, then a senior; didn't graduate. Married one year, with one child in mother's custody Henderson lived in Albuquerque, remarried, kept her maiden name. No child support from Weger. Henderson claimed she that she had not spoken to Weger in seven years.

Piper finished the coffee and continued reading.

Weger had lived alone above a laundromat on Teton in Hartford, was an avid hunter. A collection of guns were found at his apartment: 12-gauge over/under shotgun, Remington Model 700 rifle with a mounted telescopic sight and suppressor, Winchester Model 1912 12-gauge hammerless pump-action shotgun, and a .44 Magnum Colt Anaconda. The gun recovered at the scene was a Bushmaster AR 5.56mm with a bump stock with three boxes of 30-round mags. He had proper paperwork on all the guns, except for the bump stock.

Piper knew bump stocks are now banned, though they used to be legally sold. It could make a gun simulate full-automatic.

No cell phone was located at the apartment or on Weger. There was a landline at his apartment. Laptop was found in his car and is being reviewed. Also in the car was an unopened case of Budweiser; three *Field & Stream* magazines; five remaindered books—*Catcher in the Rye, The Journal of John Swift, Brassey's Dictionary of Battles, In Search of Ray Bradbury,* and *Legend, Memory and the Great War in the Air*; two unopened cartons of Marlboro cigarettes; and a plastic grocery sack containing a package of lemon-flavored Oreos, a half-dozen apples, and three bottles of peppermint-flavored Scope mouthwash.

A well-cared-for German Shorthair Pointer found at Weger's apartment had been turned over to animal control, barring finding a relative or neighbor who wanted to take the dog. Piper assumed it was a hunting dog.

Weger had no outstanding warrants, but had been picked up for various offenses over the past several years: open liquor in his car, overdue parking tickets, excessive speed. There were no records of domestic violence or battery charges, nothing aggressive that would be a tip off that he'd open fire on people.

Weger had a BAC—blood alcohol count—of .06. Anything greater than .08 was legally intoxicated in Kentucky with regards to driving. BAC decreases over time, which meant Weger might have had a higher count when he was shooting. It depended on how quick the sample was taken at the scene. Still, to Piper it didn't seem like the man would have been so drunk that he didn't know what he was doing. The tests showed no other drugs in his system.

Piper closed the file. It appeared that the shooter had at least a relatively clear mind when he killed Hemi and Renegade and shot at her and Brick. Why? Again, the big question. She wondered: had he felt threatened by their paintball guns, thinking them real weapons? Had Hemi or Renegade instigated something? Was there another reason?

Maybe the motive would become clear the more the Ohio County Sheriff's Department looked at the case, checked Weger's phone records, internet presence, and all the things that made up his life. Maybe she'd do a little looking, too; she owed it to Hemi. She started a Google search on Weger, then checked the Ohio County High School online yearbook and looked for news on area hunting clubs.

Zeke was standing in her doorway. Had he been there long?

"Need some more coffee, Sheriff?"

She nodded and held out the mug. *Should go get it myself,* she thought, but Zeke kept offering to help her with every little thing. Take him up on it once in a while. He came back, and she noticed he'd added a little cream this time.

"Hey, Sheriff, Bebe Neufeld's here." He paused. "The coroner's wife, Bebe Neufeld."

"Yes?"

"She's sitting by my desk. Says she's here to see her clients."

Piper had never met Bebe, but she knew the woman was an attorney, and thought she'd retired. Only two people occupied her jail at the moment—Henry Tucker and his son, Dale. With their arraignment scheduled for tomorrow morning, Basil didn't want them released before then.

"Take her back," Piper told him. "If she asks, let her know they're not getting out before court."

Zeke grinned and disappeared.

Piper watched her doorway and saw Zeke lead Bebe down the hall. The woman was thin and stately, in a tweed jacket and matching pencil skirt. Her hair was silvery-white, swept up like a frothy wave caught in mid-break. Large gold hoop earrings, multiple rings on her right hand—the only hand visible from this vantage, the jewelry probably real. A leather briefcase on a strap was over her shoulder. Bebe glanced in the sheriff's office and kept going without changing her stride or her expression.

Piper pulled up the file on Henry Tucker that Basil had put together. It included a note stating it wasn't complete.

Henry Elliott Tucker, 56, Fulda, shift manager at the Rockport Power Plant. Widower, one son—Dale. Graduate of Rockport High School, four years U.S. Marines, member of the Moose Lodge. Spencer County native, lived abroad one year, Italy, after leaving the Marines. No warrants or previous arrests on file.

Dale Jerome Tucker, 29, Fulda, employed at the Rockport Power Plant. Graduate of Rockport High School. Certificate in HVAC—heating, ventilation, and air conditioning technology from Ivy Tech Community College in Indianapolis. Spencer County native. No warrants or previous arrests on file.

Both charged with malicious mischief with a hate crime attachment. The recording she'd listened to last night was included. Basil followed that with a personal note:

I interviewed Henry Tucker on Sunday regarding the spray paint and damage to the Buddhist Cultural Center. He'd said he hadn't heard anything about the vandalism just down the road from his house. He did mention how nice Anthony Delaney had been to him and his son. Further, Tucker said he wanted to know who spray-painted the Delaney house, and that he was worried the vandalism might spread down the road to include his own place.

He noted he'd ordered a surveillance system for his house, and concluded the interview asking if Chris Hagee was suspected of the crime. Henry Tucker lied in that interview. Did he also lie in the second interview when he said he didn't kill Chris Hagee?

People lie and lie and lie, Piper knew. Had Tucker lied twice to her deputies? Basil was at the courthouse right now trying to get a warrant that would allow him to get inside Tucker's garage and check the car and the pickup registered to him, and the car registered to his son. He wanted to see if there was evidence of someone being struck. The warrant would also let him check shoes inside the residence and the garage. Basil wanted to see if he could get a match to the shoe prints on the ladders in Hagee's garage. Getting the warrant signed would be no slam-dunk, since Basil would have to prove probable cause, showing he had a "legitimate and reasonable reason" to search Tucker's property. Gut feelings didn't count.

Her laptop pinged with an incoming email from Basil: warrant secured.

She smiled: her detective was good at his job.

Piper stared into her coffee cup. The Tuckers had been charged with a hate crime, but in her mind their enmity wasn't against the Buddhists who had endured the damage. Their animosity had been directed against Chris Hagee, who was still on the coroner's slab in Evansville. Did Henry hate Chris enough to kill him?

There'd never been a complaint on record for Henry or Dale, not before this. They seemed to be law-abiding rural people who'd just gotten fed up with a bigot neighbor and took the wrong route to deal with it mostly via red, green, and black spray paint. She'd probably go to the arraignment tomorrow, only a block away at the courthouse. She had to post a deputy in the courtroom during any proceeding, a requirement in her county. Maybe tomorrow she'd take the posting herself.

The client meeting hadn't taken long. Bebe stopped in the doorway.

"Do you have a moment, Sheriff?" Her voice was high and musical, birdlike. Piper thought Bebe was birdlike in appearance, too—long neck, beak-like nose, intense dark eyes. Bebe bobbed her head toward the chair in front of Piper's desk, again invoking a bird image.

"Sure, come in. Coffee?"

Bebe shook her head and sat.

"I get it," Bebe started. "I get that my clients made a mistake. Henry Tucker shouldn't have painted his neighbor's house. And he shouldn't have admitted to it. He said he asked about an attorney when your deputies questioned him yesterday."

"But he didn't call one," Piper countered. She remembered the recording. "They gave him the opportunity."

Bebe made a huffing noise. "He's a grown man who did a childish thing, Sheriff. And he's miserable that he pulled his son into it. He's sorry. He's offered to pay for all the damage. And he'll apologize to Anthony Delaney. Henry Tucker was pushed to his limits because of a troublesome neighbor, and he reacted harshly and impetuously."

Piper didn't think it was impetuous; Tucker had admitted to buying the paint a while ago and planning the vandalism, though against a different house. It was pre-meditated spray-painting as far as she was concerned.

She waited, figuring Bebe would eventually go on.

Bebe glanced at the sling and appeared to study Piper's face. The sheriff had made no attempt with makeup to cover the bruises.

"So let's be reasonable about this," Bebe finally said. "My clients made a mistake, they're sorry, and they'll pay for all damages. Let's drop the charges and leave the courts for real criminals. No reason for them to have black marks on their public records. Let them out, and we'll work up some sort of community service agreement."

Maybe someone would consider that reasonable, Piper thought. But Henry Tucker had initially lied to Basil and Oren about the spray paint incident. Basil had written: *Did he also lie in the second interview when he said he didn't kill Chris Hagee?*

"I can't do that," Piper said. "Henry and Dale Tucker are scheduled tomorrow for a 9 a.m. arraignment in front of Judge Vaughn." Basil was no doubt executing his new search warrant at the Tucker house right now. Maybe he'd find a pair of boots that would up the charges against Henry Tucker. Or maybe he'd find a suspicious dent in a car grille.

Bebe stood and stared down at Piper with her dark bird eyes. "I'm sure Judge Vaughn will be reasonable, Sheriff. Age and experience yield wisdom." A pause: "This department could do with a little more of that." She bobbed her head once and left.

CHAPTER TWENTY-TWO

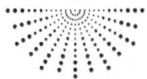

2 P.M. WEDNESDAY

Nothing on the cars," Basil said. "A 2015 Hyundai Sonata and a 2018 Suzuki Equator registered to Henry Tucker, and a 2011 Honda Civic registered to Dale Tucker … all clean. And I mean *really* clean, like they'd recently been through a car wash shiny-clean. Inside and outside spotless. The Civic had dents and dings, which could have been from age, lots of rust along the bottom of the doors, more than a hundred and ten thousand miles on it—just saw that in passing. No damage consistent with hitting either a man or animal. Possible if there was some, it had been repaired already. But they would've had to find a shop that had materials in stock to get it done this fast. Oren's chasing that down, and stopping at likely body shops in Owensboro, too. He's looking for any Spencer County vehicles with front end damage brought in since Sunday."

Unspoken was that Oren would also be stopping in to see his father. Piper had learned her chief deputy had spent last night there, probably would be spending this one, too. She'd tried to reach out to him this morning, but he didn't want to talk about it.

"Found a pair of work boots with dried mud in the grooves that look like a match to prints on one of the ladders," Basil went on. "Dicey, though, because they're partial prints. You only walk on the

165

steps with the balls of your feet. But I'd call it a match. Found another pair that look close to prints on the other ladder, hiking shoes, no trace of mud on them though. Crazy clean and smelling like Lysol, which I found odd. But I'd consider them a match, too … which we can't use as solid evidence because they're only ball of the foot. But it is useful information." He got up and went to the counter, poured hot water into a mug, retrieved a small wooden box, and brought them both back to the break room table where they sat.

Basil pulled a small silver infuser from the box and added khaki green and silver crumbled tea leaves, then let it steep in the mug.

"Smells nice," Piper said.

"Want to try it?"

She shook her head. "I'll stick to my Dark Italian. While that smells nice, this smells better. To me, anyway." She held her nose over her mug as if to verify that. Then she drank some of her favorite coffee and held it in her mouth. This would be her last cup of caffeine for the day.

"This is organic jasmine," he said. "Mellow. Has some pineapple in it to add sweetness. I like it better than the dragon pearl jasmine I usually buy. Found it on Amazon."

"Everything can be found on Amazon."

Basil grinned. "Except enough evidence to charge Dale Tucker with murder."

She stuck out her chin. "Dale?"

"The work boots that I'm calling a match are a size ten, the hiking shoes, a likely match, but mudless, are a size nine. They were both found at the Tucker kitchen back door. When I looked at the shoes in Dale's closet—the young man loves shoes, apparently, there were lots of them—they were *all* size ten. Henry doesn't have as many shoes, and they're size nine, except for two pair. There was a pair of size ten Nike Tanjuns and a pair of size ten penny loafers in Henry's closet. Both those size tens were the same overall footprint as the other size nines; I figure they ran small so he bought the tens."

"The size ten work boots, you think they belong to Dale. Based on the shoes in his closet."

"I do. And when I bagged and brought them here, showed them to our two guests, Henry puffed himself up and said 'lawyer.' Dale opened his mouth to say something, but Henry gave him a look, and repeated 'lawyer.' Yeah, I'm pretty sure the muddy work boots belong to Dale. Got a match on Dale's fingerprints on the work boots and on one of the ladders in Mr. Hagee's garage. I asked him about the ladder, too."

"And Dale didn't answer," Piper said.

"No. Henry said 'lawyer' again. I let Henry place a call to Bebe Neufeld before I came in here to talk to you. Don't want to press them on the Hagee murder until there is more evidence." Basil grinned wider. "Now if Oren can discover if the Tuckers had some quick body work done on one of their cars, we'll be good."

"Might be good anyway," Piper said. "Might be enough, what you have."

Piper heard Zeke field a 9-1-1 call, an overturned truck with injuries near the monastery. He dispatched Diego, the volunteer fire department, and an ambulance.

Basil listened to Zeke too before answering. "Might be enough to charge and hold him a while, but only if the DA is smiling on us. It isn't enough *real* evidence for a murder case. The boot print on the ladder, like I said, is a partial. No way to prove it matches a size ten like the one I got from the Tucker's. A lawyer can argue it could be one of several different sizes—eight, nine, ten, eleven, and that someone else might have a work boot just like that. There were boot prints on the garage floor, but nothing useful. That had so much dirt and sawdust over oil, all the prints were smudged. Only managed some partials on the floor, too. Nothing from the driveway because of the rain. No full prints for a direct comparison. The partial print by itself isn't enough, but it's something. The fingerprints on the ladder are another something. A lawyer can argue that Dale might've helped Chris Hagee with a project in the garage, and that's how the fingerprints got there. But when you put the two somethings together—"

"It becomes significant."

"Yeah, it does. We got a lot of fingerprints in and around the garage and the house. We're still processing all of that. Hopefully we come up with some more matches with Dale Tucker. I'll go back and look some more."

Basil paused and glanced around Piper, and she turned.

"Maybe it's enough, what we have right now. But I don't think so," he finished. "I want more. Maybe Dr. Neufeld can provide that for us."

"I hope so. I aim to be helpful." Dr. Neufeld stood framed in the doorway. She had on blue jeans, white high-top sneakers, and an ash gray t-shirt that had black octopus tentacles descending from her shoulders. Her purse was a denim fanny pack, and she had a manila file folder in her right hand. The clothing told Piper the coroner was done with work for the day, had gone home to change, and then came here.

"Mind if I join you?" Dr. Neufeld didn't wait for a yes. She strode in, sat at the end of the table, placed the folder in front of her, and waggled fingers at Basil. "That tea smells amazing. Are you sharing?"

He got up to get her a cup.

"And where's Oren? He should be here, too, when I go over this."

"Following some leads," Piper said. "He won't be back for a while."

"Any word on his dad?"

"No good word," Basil answered. He fixed an infuser for Dr. Neufeld and put it in the cup. "You'll like this. Organic jasmine."

"I usually don't like the herbal stuff, but I like how this smells." She held her nose over the mug and inhaled audibly. "Sweet. I'd wear this as cologne."

Zeke poked his head in. "Sheriff, we got a rollover across from the Meinrad monastery. Driver called 9-1-1 thinks he has some broken ribs, needs help getting out of the cab. I sent Diego, and—"

"We heard," Piper said. "Good job, Zeke. Keep us posted. Send Rocco as backup."

Zeke disappeared, muttering that he should have thought of the backup.

"Is that Chris Hagee's completed autopsy?" Piper nodded toward the folder.

"It is. Don't have all the tox screens yet." Dr. Neufeld gave her the professional up and down. "How are you doing? I heard you almost died. Oren told me that—"

"I'm okay."

"Okay, but not fine."

"I'll be fine in a while."

Dr. Neufeld offered a sympathetic smile, and then her face hardened. "Bebe called me this morning, said she had a run-in with you, Sheriff. Bebe said you were being unreasonable."

Piper didn't want to start something with the coroner, she liked Dr. Neufeld. She didn't offer a reply.

"But that was the lawyer in Bebe talking," the coroner went on, her face softening again. "Bebe said she thought she could get her way. Said you're young and don't have much experience, and she figured she could get her clients out of jail. Good on you that you didn't cave. Bebe can be forceful."

"So can Sheriff Blackwell," Basil supplied. "About the autopsy."

"Yeah," Dr. Neufeld said. "I was just making small talk, wasting time and hoping Oren might show up." She took a sip of the tea. "My, this is fine for something without a jolt of caffeine."

"I got it on Amazon. Grocery stores around here don't carry it."

"Organic jasmine, eh?"

"Harney and Sons organic jasmine."

"I'll look it up." Then she took on an all-business pose, opened the folder, and looked between Piper and Basil. "Like I said, I don't have the tox panels back yet. I do have a BAC; I had that before the autopsy. Took a blood sample at the scene. It was .07, so he wouldn't have been legally drunk. Chris had been drinking. He was known to be a drinker. But when he was killed, I strongly suspect he wasn't impaired."

"Go on." Basil leaned forward.

Dr. Neufeld drank more of the tea. "I called in an expert on vehicular deaths because there was one handy. He's a friend of mine. You should get a copy of his latest, interesting reading. *Bumper to Autopsy Table*, it's called, a forensics fact book, not a mystery novel. When someone is hit by a car or truck, by any vehicle really, you do a careful

169

examination from toes to forehead. It's especially important in the event the offending vehicle is unknown."

Piper felt a lecture coming on, the coroner explaining the process before she'd give them the actual results. She didn't mind. She found these sorts of things fascinating.

Dr. Neufeld tapped the papers. "We measured the size and scope of the injury sites, noted the locations on the body, and we paid attention with respect from where the bruising was relative to the distance from the top of the head to the bottom of the foot. Now, these measurements are critical in cases of hit and run, where there are no witnesses to tell you about the vehicle involved. For example, we found an outline of a headlight and fog light on Chris Hagee."

She tapped the papers again. "This report gives you the measurements of the headlight, how many inches below that the fog light sits, the bumper, and based on the shoes Mr. Hagee was wearing, how high off the ground those lights and the bumper sit. It'll be up to you to figure out the make of the vehicle from that. I know there are databases that show those types of things, right? Saw it on an episode of CSI. My numbers here might not be perfect, depending if Mr. Hagee was standing straight, or had bent over. I can't tell what his posture was when he was struck. But he'd been on his feet."

"Wow," Piper said. "Interesting."

"There's more." Dr. Neufeld seemed proud of the report. "I can tell you about the circumstances of the accident based on P.I.I. and S.I.I., which refers to primary impact injuries and secondary impact injuries. All of this is why I called in that expert. The primary is where the vehicle hit Mr. Hagee, the severity hinting at how fast it was traveling, which in this case was in the neighborhood of forty to fifty miles an hour. It clearly shows that Mr. Hagee was upright at the time of impact, and the front bumper of the vehicle got him right about knee level. The headlight hit him on the right, and we saw bruising from the radiator grille, hood, and possibly the windshield ... can't be certain on that windshield part. There were no glass fragments on the body or clothes." She paused dramatically. "We found, however, paint fragments embedded in his jeans, and those fragments have been sent to the state lab. If a vehicle has a little rust or bubbling in the paint, some of the paint can chip away in an accident. Found some small fragments on Chris Hagee's jaw, too. Light blue paint."

She stopped and drank more of the tea. In the silence, Piper heard Zeke talking to Rocco at the scene of the rollover accident.

"Injuries on Mr. Hagee were in what I call a progressive manner, going up from the initial impact with his knees. The headlight and grille showing injuries on his thigh and hip and stomach, as I mentioned, and the hood was responsible for some fractures on his chest. The fractures on his head are from the hood or windshield, depending on how he landed. The broken arm, that's from the hood most likely. I don't need to mention to Detective Meredith that the offending vehicle would show damage on its hood and grille, and possibly have a cracked windshield. Now, Mr. Hagee also had a fracture on his right leg, which my expert says meant he was in mid-step when he was hit, and that his weight was on that leg. If he'd been standing still, both legs would have fractured. And the impact was more than a glancing strike."

"Because—" Basil prompted. "You think he was airborne."

Dr. Neufeld nodded. "Mr. Hagee was propelled into the air for some distance before he struck the road and rolled. There are skin abrasions and indications on his jeans of this. My guess is he had on a light jacket or shirt over his T, and that it was removed. Maybe it had color from the vehicle, maybe it was just too torn up from the impact and the road. It was made to look like suicide, right? A torn-up jacket wouldn't have played well with the suicide bit. Anyway, the pavement was blacktop or concrete, since I found no marks from gravel, and no residual dirt. That doesn't much narrow down where he was hit, but I can tell you it wasn't on a gravel or dirt road. Nothing yet on DNA from under his fingernails."

Zeke poked his head in. "No serious injuries, Sheriff. The truck driver was treated at the scene, said he swerved to avoid hitting a pair of big dogs, and his wheels went over the edge and he flipped. A tow is on route."

Piper remembered the call that had come in earlier about dogs fighting near the monastery. Maybe the same misbehaving canines. "Thanks, Zeke." He hovered in the doorway, listening. She didn't mind; let him add to his education.

"Inside, there was the usual from an impact, ruptured and lacerated organs, torn blood vessels, some spinal cord damage. There was clear injury to his brain, and that appeared moderately significant. Given that spinal cord damage and the broken arm—even though, unlike in your own case, Sheriff, it was a simple break—there is no way he could have hung himself. He would have had to been hoisted up there like a big sack of potatoes."

Piper shuddered. "Painful. It must have been painful."

"No doubt," Dr. Neufeld said. "The impact would've hurt like hell. But Chris Hagee most certainly would have been rendered unconscious pretty fast. The pain would have been intense, but fleeting."

"Haven't been successful tracking Chris Hagee's last day, so we've no idea where he would've been hit. Yet." Basil reached over and took the folder and started scanning the report. "This is good. Should be able to find out what hit him with these headlight specs. This will give Oren a lot more to go on with the body shops. And maybe it will also hint where Chris Hagee was." A pause: "Wait. Hey—" He looked at Piper, then the coroner.

"You're a fast reader," Dr. Neufeld said. "And yes, Chris Hagee died from asphyxiation, from being hung in his garage. Not from being struck by a truck or car."

Piper nearly knocked over her coffee. "Being hit by a vehicle, all those breaks and injuries ... that didn't kill him?"

"No. I told you I needed an expert to take a second look. That's why. Mr. Hagee was alive after the impact. In a bad way, most definitely, but he was alive. Even though the injuries were severe—and the spinal and brain damage might've left permanent effects—he could have survived this."

"If someone would have called an ambulance," Basil finished.

"There wasn't a single 9-1-1 call from eight Sunday night to eight Monday morning," Piper said. She'd reviewed the records.

"Chris Hagee would've been struck well after midnight, and hung between two and four Sunday morning," Dr. Neufeld said. "Death from hanging is not a kind way to go. In this case, there either wasn't enough force from the drop to break his neck, or the knot on the makeshift noose wasn't in the correct position. He died by strangulation, and that took maybe one to eight minutes. Hopefully Mr. Hagee was not conscious during this time given the extent of his brain injury."

Basil whistled low. "This is not the sort of thing I'd expected to be investigating on a little county road."

"Not the sort of thing I'd expected to find in an autopsy." Dr. Neufeld pushed away from the table and pointed at the mug. "Organic jasmine, Harney and Sons on Amazon."

"That's right."

"I'm gonna order me some of that tonight. I'm fond of online shopping." She stopped in the doorway and looked over her shoulder. "And I'm gonna open a big bottle of wine and mute some of this awfulness. Apothic Crush Smooth Red Blend is calling my name."

CHAPTER TWENTY-THREE

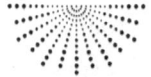

7 P.M. WEDNESDAY

Nang made pizza for dinner while Piper managed with one arm to wrap the presents for Oren and Teegan that she'd ordered from Amazon.

"That smells wonderful," she pronounced. Her arm was only mildly throbbing, and she had volunteered to cook. Nang had wisely turned her down.

It wasn't like the pizza Piper typically bought, stashed in her freezer, and that she was perfectly happy fixing after work. Her go-to was Tombstone pepperoni. Nang made his crust from scratch, applied the sauce and toppings, and was liberal with cheese. The aroma was so enticing Marmalade and Camaro hung out under the table waiting for the inevitable scraps to come their way. The dog had a small puddle of drool going.

Despite it being delicious, Piper didn't eat much; her mind was filled with everything Dr. Neufeld had presented—including stomach-churning photos from the Hagee autopsy. It seemed death was all that hovered in her mind ... Hagee, Hemi, Renegade. And Weger, the Kentucky shooter.

Afterward she basked in a hot shower before they plopped on the

174

couch, Camaro between her feet. Marmalade crept out the dog door to prowl the yard.

"I want to go back to Spaceman's cabin," she said.

"Where your friends were killed?"

"Yeah. To Jerusalem Ridge. Walk the woods. Retrace the way I went that morning. Spaceman's at Fort Campbell. He won't mind my trespassing. Of all things, he signed up for a three-month deployment to Ukraine. Normally that would be a nine-month deployment, but he only has a little more than three months left, and he's out. Civilian life, like me."

"So he wanted to see more of the world before he settles down."

"I guess," Piper replied. "He said he'd never been to Ukraine and hopes to slip in a day or two to see St. Michael's Golden-Dome or the Khotyn Fortress. I think he just wants to get far away from what happened near his cabin. When he gets back, you'll have to come to Kentucky to meet him. He's going to run a used-car business."

"I'd like that. Maybe try some paintball. I could buy a gun."

Piper grimaced. She had Hemi's fancy paintball gun, but she wasn't sure she wanted to try the sport again—at least not for quite a while. "Surprised they're sending him away, a short-timer, but he knows languages, Russian, and they speak a lot of Russian in Ukraine. I almost went to Germany, but I didn't re-up. Maybe I'll regret that. I thought I'd see a chunk of the world in the Army."

She took a breath and closed her eyes. "Anyway, I don't want to wait until Spaceman's back in Kentucky. I don't want to go through those woods in the winter. I'm going to the cabin. I just want to see everything again, the woods, get some closure. I've been dreaming about it, nightmaring actually. I desperately need to get it out of my head. The reports from the Ohio County Sheriff's Department have been helpful, but not enough. I can't drop it. I *won't* drop it. I have to *see* the place again, or I'm not going to have any peace about this. And I need to find out how Brick's doing."

"You're not supposed to drive yet."

She tipped her face and met his gaze. "I know. I figure I'll go this weekend, Saturday. It's something I have to do. My dad has the day off, and I'll talk him into taking me. He'll like the dad-daughter time. He'll probably bring Wrinkles, since the two of them are pretty inseparable. But the woods might be a tough hike for the old pug. I'll ask him tomorrow when he comes by the department for lunch."

"I'm happy you're taking the weekend off. You need to mend." He kissed her forehead and she smiled.

"I would work the weekend because of Hagee, the investigation and everything, but Oren and Basil are handling the bulk of the case. It's their case. Basil caught it, and Oren's dug in on it. They're doing a good job. I'll leave them be and go to Spaceman's woods." *I'll be the sheriff without being the boss.*

"Traipsing around in the woods? That's not a good idea. You could fall. You could—"

"I'll be careful."

"I could take you. But I can't Saturday. Sunday, I could drive you."

Piper gave a half-smile. "I haven't spent much time with my dad lately, even before I broke my arm. Oren's losing his father. Makes me think about my dad, and—"

"Good idea," Nang replied. He kissed her forehead again. "Go with your dad. But be careful. Very."

"Sure. I don't want to end up in worse shape. I just have to do this."

"I understand." Nang rocked forward. "Saturday. I have to tell you what's happening on—"

Piper saw his eyes gleam. He looked happy. "Saturday, what?"

"You know the county humane society reopened a little more than a year ago?"

She nodded. Spencer County Animal Control's shelter had closed a few years past when the director got caught euthanizing cats by shutting them in a freezer. It had made national headlines, and the offending woman was still in prison, due to get out next year. A group from Evansville helped the county to reopen a facility that was now a no-kill shelter.

"I've been calling them on and off, looking for a pug. I really enjoy your father's Wrinkles. Thought I'd like one. The smooshy face. Cute, you know. Snoring and snorting. This morning they called and said a two-year old male pug named Magoo had just been surrendered, and that I should come by Saturday to pick him up." Nang pulled his cell phone out of his shirt pocket, turned it on, and showed her a picture. The dog had a wide face and big bug eyes. "Magoo—I'll keep that name, I like it. He was being neutered today, and they said I could take him home Saturday." Nang's grin grew wider. "So, Saturday's taken for me. I've never had a dog. I bought a little bed and toys, a red leash and a collar. I've got dog food in my store. I'll have to see what kind he likes. And I'll bake him chicken. Wrinkles likes chicken. Maybe Magoo will too." He reached down and patted Camaro. "I can bring Magoo over Saturday night, and they can become friends."

"That will be lovely," Piper said. "I'll be back before dark." She liked seeing Nang so happy at the prospect of a rescue dog.

"Ice cream?"

"Oh, yes." Her stomach had settled enough. Chocolate ice cream would soothe her soul.

He hurried to the kitchen and got the carton out of the freezer, Camaro following him. The old golden retriever loved food. She watched Nang slip him a dog biscuit. Nang came back with two bowls, more ice cream in Piper's than his. It went down fast, and he took the bowls back to the kitchen, Camaro again following and getting another biscuit. She suspected Magoo would have a lot of biscuits in his future.

"You don't have to cook for me every night," she said when he returned. "I'm not complaining. Don't think I'd ever complain about that. You just don't need to go to all this trouble. I feel guilty."

He sat close and put an arm around her shoulder, gingerly. "I like to cook."

"I get that," she said. "But it feels like I'm taking advantage of you. Especially with you providing the birthday lunch for everyone tomorrow."

"You paid for the ingredients."

She laughed. "I know. But that doesn't pay for your time or—"

"I *really* like to cook."

"I get that."

"I love to cook for you."

They sat in silence for a while. No television. No talking. Just thinking—Piper about Chris Hagee's awful demise; whether they could get enough evidence against Dale Tucker to charge him with murder; if Henry Tucker also might be involved; Oren's dying father; Hemi and Renegade; how Brick was faring; and if Magoo and Camaro would get along.

"I love to eat your cooking," she said finally. "And I love having you here."

"About that," Nang started. "About my staying over so often and—"

"I know," Piper interrupted. "I'm taking advantage, really. You have a business, and you staying here instead of at your trailer, I appreciate it. But it's tough on you. You can't just run next door to the Quick Stop and—"

He gently put a finger to her lips and said, "Shhh." Then he extricated himself and stood, moved in front of her and reached in the side pocket of his jeans. "I was going to do this in a better setting, take you out to a nice restaurant, order a bottle of expensive wine and—"

"Nang, don't." Piper's eyes flew wide. She hadn't seen this coming. She loved him, adored his company and his cooking, wanted to be with him in the off-duty hours, and was most definitely serious about their relationship. But—

He took out a silvery-gray jeweler's box, little more than an inch square.

"Nang, don't—"

He opened the lid. It was clearly an engagement ring, a simple gold band with a single diamond on it. Piper didn't know much about carats, but the stone wasn't small. It was beautiful. The fingers of her good hand trembled.

"Nang, I don't—"

"It's okay," he said, edging to the side and setting the opened box on the coffee table in front of her. The stone caught the lamplight and glimmered. "I surprised you."

"Surprised isn't quite an adequate word," she said so softly she wondered if he could hear her.

"It's a big decision," he continued. "The biggest decision."

Piper stared at the ring, the diamond shimmering, filling her vision and tightening her throat. She didn't want to think about forever right now. She had Hemi to dwell on, and Renegade, and there was Brick. She had an unusual murder case to help with, evidence to collect, a suspect to scrutinize, the outline of a headlight to study, and empty cans of spray paint and size ten shoes to contemplate. And there was Jerusalem Ridge.

"I don't know," she said. Her mouth had gone sand-dry. "I don't know. I don't know. I don't—" She took a breath. "I can't process this. Not with all that's going on. I can't—"

"Just think about it," he said. "Take your time."

Piper had too much to think about.

She continued to stare at the ring.

Nang bent over and kissed her.

She didn't hear him leave.

CHAPTER TWENTY-FOUR

9 A.M. THURSDAY, SEPTEMBER 10TH

Spencer County's first courthouse burned in 1833, and while many archives went with it, marriage and deed records somehow survived. This iteration of the courthouse had always been one of Piper's favorite buildings. It was finished in 1921, Elmer Dunlap the architect, the style considered Neoclassical, and in 1999 it was put on the National Register of Historic Places. It was big and boxy, sitting on almost an acre-and-a-half bounded by Walnut, Main, and 2nd and 3rd Streets in downtown Rockport, a short walk from the sheriff's department. It was three levels, made of limestone, and the main face had Roman Doric columns. The center featured an impressive rotunda lidded by a stained glass dome, and a sweeping staircase rising to the second and third floors.

Piper always took the stairs to the courtroom. The wood bannister was smooth and warm against her good hand. She thought the veining in the stairs quite beautiful; the cost of the material must have been exorbitant even a hundred years ago. The green paint? Much of the trim in the building was a shade that was neither schoolroom nor hospital green, but something in-between. The color reminded her of sliced kiwis. It was the only thing about the building she thought gave it a poor mark.

She sat at the rear of the courtroom, had thought about assigning herself court duty for the day, but gave it to Diego, who was standing up front. The docket held only a few cases this morning, nothing especially interesting to her except the Tucker arraignment. She wanted to get back to the office. A jury would be needed for more cases coming up at the end of the month. Piper planned to put Millie on court duty then. With her online law classes, Millie would likely find the proceedings interesting.

Anthony Delaney sat in a middle row. After a moment, Piper got up and joined him.

"I'm curious, Sheriff Blackwell, about all of this," Anthony said. "And sad. I'm mostly sad. I need to shake that off. Meditate until it goes away."

"It's just an arraignment," Piper replied. "It isn't to determine guilt or innocence. Just formal charges presented, and the defendants— Henry and Dale Tucker—will enter a plea. Probably 'not guilty.' I've never seen anyone raise their hand in an arraignment and say, 'yeah, I did it.' Indiana requires arraignments even in misdemeanor cases."

Anthony wore indigo jeans and a green plaid sport shirt, the collar so stiff he must have ironed it. He had on a clunky wristwatch that Piper suspected had been his father's. His shaven head gleamed in the light coming in through the high windows.

"I know what an arraignment is. I just think all of this is so unfortunate. Sad." Anthony bowed his head. "That the Tuckers would do that to my house makes me sad. They're friends."

"Friends don't do things like that," Piper said softly.

More people shuffled in and sat toward the front. Piper didn't recognize them. They might be neighbors of the Tuckers or were here to watch another arraignment.

"No. Friends do not. They *were* friends. I hope they find peace. I hope their minds settle and all the malice that prompted this will never surface in their lives again. I am sad, but I'm not angry with them. Buddha said, 'Holding onto anger is like drinking poison and expecting the other person to die.' I will reach out to them—"

"Anthony, I—"

"But not for a while," he finished. "I am not so naïve to think everything will smooth over within a few days. There is talk that maybe they were involved with Chris Hagee's death. People along my road said maybe it wasn't a suicide. The meter reader said Mr. Hagee was murdered."

Piper was only mildly surprised at his comment. "I don't know who or what was involved with Mr. Hagee's death yet." She leaned back on the bench. "My department is working to find out."

Her office hadn't publicly released anything about Hagee's death being a murder. There might have been scanner chatter that people picked up, and Dr. Neufeld calling in a specialist for the autopsy might have leaked. Too, Oren and Basil had been asking enough questions to raise suspicions. Spencer County was a gossipy place, a never-ending game of telephone.

"I had hoped that all of this awfulness was not because of the presence of the Cultural Center ... all the damage, Mr. Hagee's death. If I would have known that opening the center—"

He stopped when DA Scales entered and Dale and Henry Tucker were brought in.

Piper lowered her voice. "Later today, would you come by the department? We've more questions, things we'd like to go over."

"Because my presence in Fulda might have triggered all this hate," Anthony whispered.

"No," Piper corrected. "Just because we have some more questions."

"I heard about your injury." He continued the hushed conversation. "It looks painful. I wish you all good health soon, Sheriff Blackwell. 'Health is the greatest gift, contentment the greatest wealth, faithfulness the best relationship.'"

Judge Vaughn entered, everyone stood, and Piper retreated to the back of the courtroom. She noticed Diego watching her. Oren and Basil were still checking body shops in the county and in nearby Vanderburgh County, which because of its size and population had many. She checked her phone: they'd not texted her any updates. Basil was also going to the DMV and compiling a list of places where Chris

Hagee regularly ventured. Piper had told them they needed to be in the break room at noon to share all the results.

She put the phone away and stared at her hands, the left still swollen, the fingers like breakfast sausages. She'd been told it would take several days for everything to settle and the bruises to fade. She needed to fixate on getting better and ignoring the omnipresent ache that ran from her shoulder to fingertips.

Last night she'd fixated on the ring. She must have sat there an hour, the dog between her feet, the diamond shining like the big light on the front of a train barreling toward her. Nang hadn't said the words, the traditional "will you marry me" that accompanied a proposal. She hadn't let him. He didn't push.

She was serious about him. But was she *that* serious?

Piper was serious about her position as sheriff, suggested to Hemi that while she was firmly entrenched in her first year, she was already thinking about a second term. A career in law enforcement in Spencer County. Was she *that* serious?

What had happened to the free spirit she'd envisioned herself as? How tight was she tying herself down? Nang hadn't said the words because she cut him off. Because she wasn't ready to hear them.

So self-absorbed, she missed the first arraignment, only vaguely aware it was a public intoxication charge. Piper snapped out of it in time to hear a court date set—the fellow pleading not guilty and asking for a jury trial.

At least she hadn't missed the Tucker case.

Focus! She buried the image of the diamond ring and concentrated on the backs of the Tuckers' heads.

DA Scales deftly—and, Piper thought, somewhat theatrically—presented the charges. He asked for a high bond, ten thousand dollars because of the hate attachment. She'd told him about the murder charge possibility, but that they lacked enough evidence at the moment. Scales said he wouldn't bring that up today. He didn't want Henry and Dale alerted.

Because malicious mischief was a misdemeanor, she couldn't keep holding them in jail awaiting trial—unless they couldn't make bail.

183

But maybe being out in the county was a good thing: her deputies could watch what they did and where they went.

"Not guilty," Henry Tucker said loud and clear. Piper couldn't see his face, but she imagined it had a defiant cast. His posture was rigid, his shoulders square.

His son, Dale, hesitated a moment, and then in a softer voice said, "Not guilty."

People lied all the time. Oren had discovered that Henry bought the cans of spray paint planted in Chris Hagee's truck. Henry's claim that he needed the paint for birdhouses? Bogus. Basil said when he was in Henry's garage, looking for damage on the vehicles, he saw more than a dozen birdhouses. All of them were glossy solid white. There also were spray cans and tins of white paint. And they had the recording of Henry admitting his guilt ... the why, when, and how of it.

Not guilty my ass.

But it was what people did in arraignments, right? Lie.

Bebe Neufeld—equally theatrical—successfully argued for the Tuckers to be released on recognizance.

Piper was the first one out the door. She returned to her office, and found Mike Hagee waiting for her.

"Had a voicemail from your detective," he said, settling into the chair across from her desk. He had Chris' build, and the family resemblance was clear. She'd met him in January when she was interviewing area residents following Conrad Delaney's murder. Mike was nearly a decade younger than Chris. "Couldn't get by here yesterday or the day before. Or the day before that. He missed me, your detective, when he came to my house. Busy with things, you know. And I'm busy helping Joan set up funeral arrangements later today."

Mike lived in Grandview, not far from Chris' farm. He was a regular at the Hagee's New Year's and Fourth of July parties. She wondered what he'd been so busy with that he couldn't stop in before now. She put a recorder on her desk so Basil could listen to the chat when he came in.

"You're going to record me?" Mike grimaced and the creases on his forehead deepened to look like old tree bark. "Not sure I like that."

"Routine," Piper said. "Just to make sure I don't miss anything. Detective Meredith is out, but he may still want to talk to you about your brother."

Mike sat straighter and his face looked hard. "Ain't no way Chris killed himself." He glared at the little recorder. "He was depressed as hell, mostly about Joan walking out. Pissed as hell about the Buddhists setting up a place right across the street. But he'd never kill himself. Joan's been talking to the coroner and some of Chris' neighbors. She says Chris might have been murdered."

"We're investigating," Piper said.

"There were a lot of people who didn't like Chris." Mike craned his neck, looking around her office, settled his gaze on her arm. "What happened to you? Looks like you lost a boxing match."

She knew the bruises on her face were still prominent. Piper opened her notebook. She had the recorder going, but Oren had taught her old school note-taking was important. "Enemies, can you name them?"

He shook his head and stared again at the recorder. "Ain't many. But my brother had a talent for riling people up, you know. Chris was a good guy, a standup guy, but he was a little too prejudiced and a lot too outspoken. He wasn't the easiest to get along with. Still, he managed to have a good number of friends. I told him to toss that damn petition. Collecting signatures wouldn't get the Buddhists to move, would just get people upset. Besides, they'd never done anything to bother him." He waited a beat. "At least, not that I'd heard."

"Other than being there," Piper put in.

"Yeah, other than that. He'd take that damn petition with him wherever he went. Grocery store, post office, bars, the gas station. Out to brunch with me at the golf course. Tried to get people there to sign it. Some manager came over and told him to either stop or leave." Mike's expression softened. "Guess I could come up with some names,

185

people he pissed off about that petition." He proceeded to list a dozen people, some that were familiar to Piper. She wrote them down.

"When was the last time you saw him?"

He shifted in the chair. "I dunno. Last week sometime. Tuesday or Wednesday. Ran into him at the grocery store. It was Tuesday."

"Did you talk to him?"

"Well, at the grocery store. He was in a pretty good mood then, had found some beer and other things on sale and had loaded his cart. He'd scored some cheap DVDs, Sylvester Stallone and Chuck Norris, some old ones. Store was getting rid of all its DVDs. Who has a DVD player anymore?"

"When did you talk to him last on the phone? How about emails? Texts?" She knew they'd have records of those, but it would be interesting to see if his recollections agreed.

He leaned forward, like he couldn't settle in any one position for more than a few minutes. "Yeah. On the phone. Friday. Yeah, Friday. Right after dinner. I remember because I asked if he wanted to come over and watch the football game Sunday. My wife hates football, has some book club to go to then. The Colts playing the Browns. He turned me down, said he was busy. I think he was going to be busy watching the neighborhood. I think he has a pair of binoculars. Bet he didn't watch the game. Hell, he didn't even make it to Labor Day. I was gonna grill some dogs and see if he wanted to come over on Labor Day. Drink a few beers."

"Do you know where he usually went on the weekend?"

He shook his head. "Maybe out for a beer and a sandwich or to get some more signatures. Joan being gone, I don't think he went out all that much. He'd already been shopping for groceries earlier in the week. Maybe he didn't go anywhere. Maybe he stayed home all day. Maybe someone came over and they argued. Maybe that someone strung him up in the garage." He cocked his head. "You should be trying to see who might have gone to his house and killed him. Ain't no way Chris killed himself. That'd be like him letting the Buddhists win, you understand."

"We're investigating," she said. "Who do you think might have gone to his house?"

He shrugged. "Dunno."

"Where were you Sunday night? Late?"

"What?" Mike made a growling sound. "You want to know where I was? I wasn't with Chris, but I should've been. He wouldn't be dead if I was over there. I would've stopped someone from killing him."

"Where were you?" she repeated.

"Hell. You're nuts if you think I had anything to do with killing Chris. He was family. You're nuts. And you don't need to know where I was. That's my business. Night? I was watching the Sunday night game. Satisfied? Are we done here?"

Piper asked him several more questions, filled a few pages with notes. "Detective Meredith will call you," she said.

"He can call all he wants, but it better not be this afternoon. I'm going to the funeral home with Joan. Finalize everything. Order some flowers. She wants Chris cremated. I suppose so she doesn't have to buy grave space and a marker. Who bothers going to cemeteries anymore anyway, huh? Going to have some sort of service though, next Tuesday she wants it. Soon as the will is all settled, she told me she's moving to Mississippi. I ought to move the hell out of this county, too."

Piper recalled that Joan promised to come by the department this afternoon to meet with Basil and Oren. She hoped Joan would be more helpful than Chris' brother had been. For some reason, she doubted that would be the case.

CHAPTER TWENTY-FIVE

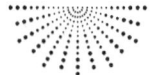

NOON THURSDAY

Paul Blackwell arrived carrying a massive bouquet of helium birthday balloons and wearing Wrinkles on his back in a dog papoose. He arranged the balloons in the break room, and then he returned to his police car and came back with a cardboard carton that looked heavy and *clinked* with each step. One of his Santa Claus police officers, a tall fortyish woman with rosy copper hair in a braid that twisted around her head, trailed him toting a large cake box. Piper watched them decorate the room, smiling when her dad took a vinyl Happy Birthday tablecloth and draped it over her whiteboard filled with facts and speculations about the Chris Hagee case. She noticed he studied the board first before covering it up.

"How are you feeling, Punkin?"

She ogled the cake without answering—beautiful, lots of purple flowers and frosting vines, an ornate scrawl with the names, Oren and Teegan. She hoped it was chocolate or red velvet; she hadn't told her father what flavor to get. *Funny,* Piper thought, she'd never been much for dessert until being elected sheriff. Maybe there was some truth to the stereotype of cops and donuts and sugar in general. Good thing she was active—or had been up until she'd fallen through the floor of the mine. Running a few miles every morning kept the syrupy calories

188

at bay. As soon as her arm and ribs mended, she'd run morning *and* evening to make up for the lost activity and the added sweets.

"I'll get the ice cream and plates," the officer said. Piper didn't know the woman, but got a glance at the nametag: S. Simonis.

"Sharon?" Piper guessed. "She's new."

"Shelly," her dad answered. "Been with me almost three weeks, picked her up from the Fort Wayne Police Department. She's sharp. Divorced, has a thirteen-year-old boy, and a twenty-year-old studying fashion design in New York. When I finally decide to retire, she'd make a great chief of police."

"Why'd she leave Fort Wayne?"

"Shelly said she was looking to live someplace less hectic. Not that Fort Wayne is all that citified." He made a humming sound. "Well, I guess it is. Got more than ten times the population of our entire county. Said she wanted someplace more rural for her son. He'd been having some trouble in school."

Santa Claus and all of Spencer County was indeed that—rural, Piper thought.

Simonis returned with two tubs of ice cream—chocolate and strawberry. The plates and bowls she stacked on the table had rainbow colors; the bag held equally colorful blue, yellow, and pink plastic eating utensils.

"Lots of color," Piper said.

"A shade for everyone," Simonis returned. "All on sale at the Dollar Store. Nice to meet you, Sheriff. Your father's told me tons about you."

An almost awkward silence followed, and then Piper made a circle of the room. "Dad, I'm going back to Jerusalem Ridge Saturday."

"I'm not working this weekend. Mind if I join you? Wrinkles, too."

"That would be lovely, and—"

"How about I drive? I barely fit into your suggestion of a car, and I don't think you should take one of your vintage autos out into the woods."

"Well, I—"

"I'd feel better if I was behind the wheel. Both of my arms work."

Piper hadn't mentioned to her father that she wasn't supposed to drive for a while. She figured Nang told him. Or he knew; he was a smart guy. "Great. How early—"

"I'll stop by around eight, eight-thirty. I'll bring donuts and coffee. We can make the day of it. Part of the day, anyway. I'm overdue for a good hike." Softer: "I want to see where all of this happened."

"I need to see the place again," Piper admitted. "I'll buy us dinner on the way back."

He grinned and pointed to the heavy-seeming carton he'd brought in. "Three dozen. One for everybody in the department—deputies, dispatchers, extras for guests who stop by. I had a hundred made because the price-point was better, got the rest of them in my office, doling them out to my officers. I might give some away for Christmas gifts." He paused. "Birthdays. Thanksgiving, Arbor Day. I've only got four officers and three reserves. Maybe I ordered too many."

Piper followed him to the counter and watched as he levered open the carton.

"You didn't answer me earlier, Punkin. How're you feeling?"

"Fine."

"I take it that you're mending," he said. "Otherwise you wouldn't be here, and certainly wouldn't be going back to Kentucky. But I can't imagine you're—"

"I'm fine. I told you already I'm fine. Really, I'm—"

He gave her a stern, sideways glance.

"Okay, I'm mending. I don't feel *bad*. Not right now. I feel frustrated."

"Frustrated is good."

"I swear I'm taking it easy. I don't want to do anything that'll screw up my arm and draw this out any longer."

"I'll make damn sure you take it easy Saturday."

Inside the box were gleaming ivory coffee mugs with wide, heavy bases, handles that looked like octave clefs, and an imprint of Wrinkles wearing a police hat.

"Had them special ordered," he said.

"I don't imagine you could just stroll into a Walmart and grab them," Piper said sarcastically. "Wherever did you find a company that would make something like this?"

"I'm on Facebook now," he returned quickly as he started setting out all the mugs, making sure they lined up precisely, the dog's face in the front. The back had the slogan: TO PROTECT, TO SERVE, AND TO BARK. "Saw one of those ads pop up on the side of the screen under my Friends list with a code for free shipping. I figured this would be fun."

"And thoughtful." *And a wholly unnecessary purchase.* But it seemed to make him happy. Piper would use one as a pen holder, wasn't about to replace her steam engine mug, which was bigger. She was saved from further conversation by Basil and a very surprised Oren arriving. Nang and Teegan showed up a handful of minutes after that.

Nang made several trips, bringing in steaming pans, setting them out on the center table, and removing the lids. Piper avoided direct eye contact with him. She hadn't let him say the words last night. She worried he might say them today, with witnesses.

"Happy Birthday!" Zeke hollered from the doorway. "Somebody dish up a plate for me." He waved and returned to his desk when the phone rang. "I'll want cake, too."

"Shrimp spring rolls, fried dumplings, and vegetarian pho," Nang said, pointing to three containers. "This one is *banh xeo*, a crepe filled with pork, shrimp, and bean sprouts. This is the sauce you dip it in. Here is *bun bo hue*, rice noodles with beef and pork, seriously extra spicy." He looked at Paul Blackwell and grinned.

Piper's dad was fond of overly spicy food.

"And these two are *ca timkho to*." He nodded to Basil. "Eggplant diced and sautéed with tomatoes, soy sauce, sugar, and peppers. And *banh goi*, which are deep-fried and filled with minced pork, three kinds of mushrooms, and vermicelli noodles."

He hurried out and came back with a stack of small Styrofoam containers. "I cooked too much, so make sure you all take home the leftovers. Happy Birthday Chief Deputy Rosenberg and Teegan." He nodded to Piper: he was so busy serving he didn't chat with her.

The next half-hour passed with conversation centered on Oren

191

and Teegan, laughter, and Nang furiously scribbling down his recipes for those who asked. He sat across from Piper, never mentioning the ring. She was grateful for that, didn't want to think about it. She'd closed the little jewelry box and placed it on the kitchen counter next to her canister set. Maybe tonight she'd hide it away in a drawer. Maybe she'd give it back Saturday night when he brought Magoo over for a meet and greet. If the ring was out of her house, she wouldn't dwell on the matter.

Oren unwrapped his gift first. It was a pair of hand-tooled black leather holsters.

"The big one is regulation," Piper said. "The one you've been wearing was looking a little grim." She was going to say "old," but managed to stop herself.

"Level three," Oren said, whistling. Most sheriff departments required a level two or level three holster, a specific design that made it difficult for someone other than the wearer to snatch the gun. The smaller holster was an ankle strap. "Thoughtful," he pronounced. "Beautiful. Thank you."

"I wanted something that would last," Piper said. "We need you staying with the department. We can't afford to have you retire." She'd heard the scuttle that Oren's wife was encouraging him to quit, and an equal amount of scuttle from the coroner that Oren didn't want to. She knew the chief deputy wasn't fond of her, but he was an asset she didn't want to lose.

Teegan cried when she opened hers: a large backpack festooned with the characters from *The Nightmare Before Christmas*. It was the most goth-looking thing Piper could find with a quick search on Amazon. Inside were pizza gift cards.

"I'd figured everyone had forgotten me," Teegan said. "Except Zeke."

"I've just been ... busy," Piper returned, finishing the last bite of the sinfully rich chocolate cake. Then she was up and collecting with one arm the used plates, her father and Nang helping.

"Gotta get back to the office," Paul said. "See you Saturday, Punkin."

When Nang started boxing up the leftovers, packing extra for Oren and Teegan, Anthony Delaney arrived. Piper grabbed the opportunity to retreat to her office with a big mug of coffee, Basil and Oren following. Piper sat back and listened.

"I know we've spoken in the past few days," Basil started, "but I've some additional questions."

"I will help in any way possible," Anthony returned.

Piper saw that Anthony had a tattoo on his left arm, an image peeking out at the edge of his shirt sleeve. She'd not noticed it before, and she suspected he'd gotten it when he lived in the county as a teen. She made out the word Rebels and booted feet above it, but the sleeve covered the design from the ankles and above. Rebels was the nickname of the high school's sports teams. Anthony had been a bit of a rebel to leave Fulda right after high school graduation for a Buddhist monastery in Thailand.

Basil began with pointed questions about the various souls who'd visited the Cultural Center this summer, especially three young men who'd been staying there for the past month and a half. He never asked Anthony where he'd been the day of Chris Hagee's death, evidence that her detective did not consider the monk a suspect. He posed a dozen questions about Henry and Dale Tucker, not coming away with much … other than Anthony still being sad they'd spray painted his house.

"I forgive them," Anthony said. "Buddha taught that it is important to forgive others, not because they deserve it, but because I deserve peace." He looked to Piper. "Sheriff Blackwell, I sincerely hope they did not kill Chris Hagee."

"Someone did," Oren put in.

"Cars and visitors." Basil changed the topic. "Chris Hagee watched your place like a hawk, he did. He filled a notebook with the comings and goings of people at your center. Even wrote down that his wife stopped by."

Anthony nodded. "Joan Hagee is a lovely woman. We helped her meditate."

"Did you reciprocate with Mr. Hagee?"

Anthony cocked his head like he didn't understand.

Basil rephrased it. "Mr. Hagee kept track of you whenever he was home. Did you keep track of him? Watch his house? Notice what was going on? Who came and went? He didn't like you, made that obvious. I'm betting that you—"

"Yes," Anthony said. "We watched Chris Hagee's house. But we didn't write our observations in a notebook."

"We're interested in who visited Mr. Hagee," Basil said. "Honestly, Mr. Delaney, we're—"

"Anthony is fine."

"Honestly, Anthony, we're trying to track Mr. Hagee's last day, and we want to talk to people who stopped by his house in the days prior."

Anthony stroked his chin, like he was losing himself in thought. The man looked so serious to her, and far more mature than his twenty-eight years. He described a middle-aged man who visited Chris Hagee usually once a week.

Mike Hagee, Piper connected. Chris Hagee's brother.

Next, he talked about a tanned man with rounded shoulders, whose description marked him as the farmer who leased the Hagee property. They'd already interviewed him and came away with nothing useful.

Finally, Anthony said: "Henry Tucker." He let out a long sigh. "I saw him bring Mr. Hagee a case of beer late one afternoon two, maybe three weeks ago. Mr. Tucker waved to me. I was cutting the grass. I'd noticed Mr. Tucker over there a few times early in the summer, but not often. I figured they were friends." Another long sigh. "Perhaps they were *good* friends. I suppose it is possible Mr. Hagee asked him to damage our house and—"

"What about cars?" Basil cut in.

Piper wondered if Henry Tucker had been so angry at Chris Hagee, why would he bring him beer? But that was well before Hagee tried to get Gretta Mueller arrested. Maybe that incident destroyed their friendship. Maybe it had started to fray when Chris Hagee tried to get the Tuckers to sign the anti-Buddhist petition.

"You mentioned cars before, Detective. Certainly no one visited

Chris Hagee's home by walking there. Always, they drove." A pause. "Except for us. We would walk across the street and reach out in fellowship."

"And that never ended well, did it?" Oren asked.

Anthony shook his head.

"Cars," Basil mentioned a third time. "Of the people you saw stop at the Hagee house—or even drive by it—were any in a vintage car?"

"A vintage car?"

"An older car. Like something from the sixties or seventies. It didn't have to look all beat up and rusty. Might have been restored, but an older model car, or a pickup. One that clearly wasn't modern and that had round headlights."

Piper sat up, remembering the autopsy photos, including the big circular bruise that the coroner had pointed out.

"A bright red Buick Skylark convertible," Anthony answered quickly. "It's a glorious-looking car."

Basil typed on his cell phone, scrolled at something. "Round headlights."

"Yes, that glorious car has round headlights. I've seen it several times. I think it belongs to Margaret Avery, the elderly woman who lives in the three-level house beyond the Saint Meinrad monastery. She has blue hair. You can see that, because she drives with the top down." Anthony raised a finger, as if something had instantly come to him. "She also drives a red Mustang convertible. I've seen her in that more often. She drives too fast. Those headlights are more rectangular, but it's a more recent car. The older Mustangs had plain, round headlights."

"Margaret Avery. That's the woman who got gas the other day at Nang's," Oren said.

Basil nodded and thumbed his phone again. "The Buick Skylark. Does it look like this?" He showed the small screen to Anthony.

"Yes, but I don't know the color of Margaret's top. I've only seen the car when the top is down and her blue hair is blowing. Once, though, I saw her with a scarf on her head. Red, it matched the car. I believe she likes red."

195

"1954," Basil said to Oren. "The car in this picture, anyway. I don't think the headlights are quite big enough, but I'll check it out."

"Any other old cars?" Piper wanted to participate. "Any blue ones?"

"Yes, a blue one," Anthony said. "Turquoise maybe. Like the color of a robin egg."

Dr. Neufeld had mentioned light blue paint chips. Piper called up the coroner's report on her laptop.

Basil leaned forward, the posture suggesting Anthony should go on.

"But it wasn't a car. It was a pickup truck," Anthony continued. "Caught my eye because it was an odd color, compared to the colors of trucks now. A delicate color. But it was quite striking, actually. It usually came down the road in front of my house in the middle of the morning. Sometimes the sun would glint off the silver trim like stars. It had big round headlights, looking old-fashioned and at the same time new. It had a white stripe along the bed. The silver trim, there was a lot of it."

"Do you know who drove it?"

Anthony shook his head again. "You couldn't see inside because the windows were tinted. Most of the cars on the road are newer. Some of the older ones that pass by often enough for me to remember are rust-buckets. Like this Chevrolet that is a cross between a car and a pickup, the rust thick on the lower panels. It goes by regularly. I should know the name of it, but—"

Basil typed in a few keys and showed the picture on his phone's screen to Anthony.

"That's it! An El Camino. The one we see once is white and rust-brown and has a big dent on the driver's side door. Don't know who it belongs to, but it's always a man driving it, and there's usually a big black dog in the passenger seat. There's a VW van that goes by, usually just on weekends. I guess you'd call it vintage. It has round headlights, too. Has a For Sale sign in one of the side windows, says 1968 and lists a phone number. I couldn't tell you the number. I'd no desire to call it. The van is olive green, but the top half is white. In real nice shape, like someone restored it. We watch American Pickers sometimes, and I see VW vans going for good money there, but they're all rusty. The one that drives by my house is not."

"You've quite the eye for cars," Oren noted.

Anthony shrugged. "Just notice them is all. When I was a kid, I'd go to car shows with my dad, and I loved to put together model cars. Still have a bunch of the kits on a shelf in one of the bedrooms. I just notice them. I spend a lot of time outdoors when the weather is nice, so I see the cars."

Zeke poked his head in. "Any of you need something to drink?"

Piper shook her head and Zeke retreated.

"Now answer a question for me," Anthony continued. "Why are vintage autos so interesting to you? Especially ones with round headlights? Apparently they are important. What do they have to do with Mr. Hagee's death? I never saw one of those old cars stop at Mr. Hagee's place. That doesn't mean one didn't. I didn't watch the house with any great purpose to record comings and goings. I just watched it because I was curious what simmered there."

"Curious about what caused Chris Hagee to be offensive," Oren said.

"Bellicose," Anthony said. "Yes. I could not stop the curiosity. Ralph Waldo Emerson said 'Curiosity is lying in wait for every secret.' Mr. Hagee did not seem to be the same man I knew as a child."

"Maybe he was," Oren said. "But your very young eyes saw him differently."

"Thank you for coming in, Anthony," Basil concluded. "You've been a great deal of help."

"Grab a piece of birthday cake," Oren suggested. "It's in the break room." After Anthony left, he added: "We need to be asking Nang about vintage cars in Fulda ... assuming Hagee was hit in Fulda. Should've said something to Nang about vintage cars when he was here. Bet Nang would have an even sharper eye than the monk."

"I'd thought about it, but Nang was busy serving us. I figure we'll talk to him over lunch tomorrow at the Quick Stop, when we can check out his video surveillance," Basil said. "It'll be my turn to buy.

197

And, no, we can't assume Chris Hagee was struck in Fulda, but it's a place to start."

Piper caught a ride home with Zeke just as Joan Hagee walked in the front door. She'd check her computer tonight to listen to that interview. She planned to keep Nang at bay this evening. She needed some quiet time for searching her soul.

CHAPTER TWENTY-SIX

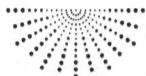

9 A.M. FRIDAY, SEPTEMBER 11TH

Chris Hagee had made two brief calls on his cell phone his final day—one to his wife early in the morning, and one to the grocer in Rockport shortly before noon, both lasting roughly five minutes. He might have stopped by the grocer, though none of the cashiers remembered him coming in. The assistant manager who'd taken his call said that Hagee had asked about the price of ground beef, Folger's coffee, and what brand of beer was on sale. Though he had a prescription sitting at the pharmacy, he hadn't gone there either. A notation in his Buddhist journal listed two unnamed visitors arriving at the Cultural Center at 1:15 p.m. and leaving twenty minutes later. He'd made no credit card purchases or debit card withdrawals that day, and he'd not stopped at G's Bar. Gretta was adamant he was not allowed on the premises, and he hadn't sent a single email.

The Sheriff's Department had been unsuccessful so far in tracking where and how Chris Hagee had spent all of his final twenty-four hours. Maybe most of them had been right here.

Basil stood at the end of Chris Hagee's driveway and watched the cars go by on the county road. Minutes stretched between the vehi-

199

cles, and most of them slowed when they neared the Hagee property, the drivers turning their heads, one of them waving to him. Some were older cars, but none what he would consider vintage. One was so new—a dark blue Toyota RAV4—it had the dealer invoice on the passenger side window, and its headlights reminded him of cat eyes. He'd soon be going door to door in tiny Fulda, trying to get a look at the residents' vehicles. He didn't need a search warrant if they simply gave their okay. He'd head over to Lincoln City, too, near the park and nature preserve, then start toward Santa Claus, see if he could spot some older cars in driveways, ones with round headlights. Oren was also out looking, a rendezvous planned at Nang's place for lunch.

It was going to be a long day ... unless he got lucky fast.

Someone had run over Chris Hagee, thought they'd killed him, and strung him up in the garage to make it look like suicide to avoid prosecution. It had started out as an accident that ended in murder because the driver didn't know Chris Hagee had survived the impact.

That was the scenario Basil operated from.

Basil believed Dale and Henry Tucker had been on a night-dark county road and literally ran into Chris Hagee. *What* road? *Where* did it happen? Could it have been right out front of Hagee's house? Which one of them was driving? And what make was the car?

Basil was confident that the father and son worked in concert somehow; but which one was behind the wheel?

The car headlights suggested by the autopsy report did not match the Tucker vehicles ... at least the vehicles that were in the Tucker garage and recorded with the DMV.

Definitely a curious case.

Last night he'd called his former sergeant in Chicago for assistance. Chicago had access to some archives normally beyond the Spencer County Sheriff's Department, like one that might better pinpoint the make and model of the vehicle that struck Chris. The resources he'd been able to employ through Indiana law enforcement sites and regular national databases had given him roughly three hundred models to pick from, based on Hagee's headlight-sized bruise and the mark from the bumper. He wanted the possibilities narrowed.

Could the Tuckers have a vintage auto not listed in the county DMV records? The Tuckers denied owning any other cars, but he'd already caught them in a lie about the spray paint. Henry had told him to "go to hell" when he'd stopped by last night.

"I guess I'm not supposed to cuss at you," Henry had said. "That's probably illegal, right? You gonna arrest me for foul language?" Henry had shut the door in Basil's face and yelled through the wood, "Talk to my attorney."

Sheriff Blackwell was working through state sources with various requests involving vintage vehicles. She'd probably come up with a more focused group of cars, but such requests typically took weeks to yield the information. Too, she was searching for vintage cars in the area via Google and other web engines, checking the county, then the state, systematically broadening the scope, including vintage car clubs and auto shows. Again, useful and necessary, but time-consuming and with no guarantees. Maybe she'd strike gold. Maybe she'd find nothing.

Or maybe his old sergeant would come through with an assist.

Find the vehicle, find the killer.

Basil was going to find the damn car—no matter how many hours he had to throw at this investigation.

He could run DMV searches for registrations on specific vehicle types … like the 1968 Volkswagen micro-bus Anthony mentioned. Sheriff Blackwell was following that up. The DMV was extremely helpful with requests about the registration of *specific* vehicles within a town, county, and state. Before the day was out, the sheriff would likely know all registered owners for 1968 Volkswagen micro-buses in Indiana.

But the DMV wouldn't help with a general search on "vintage cars." Too vague. Their system was designed to handle specific makes and models. The sheriff could, however, use the DMV to search for antique plates in the county. A lot of vintage cars carried antique plate designations: it made them cheaper to insure and exempt from state safety inspections. Indiana's Bureau of Motor Vehicles allowed any car twenty-five years or older to be plated that way. Historic plates were another option, but attached even more conditions, considered solely as collector's items and used for exhibition, car clubs, or educational purposes. It limited how far an owner could legally drive them.

All of this assumed that the car that struck Chris Hagee was registered properly. Sometimes old cars changed hands without sale records and title transfers.

Had one of the Tuckers been driving someone else's vintage car?

Or did they own the car and sell it after the accident? Had they dumped it? Could they have hidden it? He would focus on the Tuckers, but at the same time he needed to find the car. It would show damage from the impact, or evidence it had been repaired.

Find the damn car.

He swung around and went to the Hagee garage, grabbing his kit, and putting on booties and gloves. One more look, dust some more areas and objects for fingerprints, take additional photographs, and see if there he missed something on the first two walk-throughs. It wasn't like on television, where investigators made one detailed pass through a place for evidence. In real life they came back and went through it all again. He tackled the residence, too, though he nearly gagged on the mounds of stubbed-out cigarettes, dregs in beer cans, and greasy pizza boxes, the scents of which had percolated in the shut-up house. He'd opened a kitchen window on his previous visit.

Pity about this house, he thought. Nice size, beautiful wood floors, wainscoting, and crown moulding. He suspected it was well-kept when Joan Hagee lived here, imagined it smelled nice when the windows were open and a cross-breeze cut through, all the scents of summer and flowers and grass swirling. But Chris Hagee's prejudice grew so thick love couldn't fit inside the walls anymore.

He stuffed a few more filled evidence bags in his Explorer, drove down the road, and talked to Margaret Avery, who was more than happy to show him her red Mustang and Buick Skylark convertibles. He took pictures, measurements of the headlights, and noticed not a

202

scratch on either car. He doubted Chris had been struck by the Skylark.

Her husband came out with a photo album of all the cars they'd owned through the years. Basil patiently looked through the book and thanked them for their help.

"Can't you tell me, young man, why you're so interested in old cars in the county?" Margaret crooked her head to the side and the sunlight caught the blue tint in her hair. It matched the color of her eyes.

"Sorry, Mrs. Avery," Basil replied. "It's part of an on-going investigation."

"I watch some of those true crime shows on television. *Cold Justice* is my favorite. *Dateline* has too many commercials. *Forensic Files, the Ted Bundy Tapes, Swamp Murders*. Those are all good. An old car sounds like something that prosecutor on *Cold Justice* would be looking into. On-going investigation!" She grinned and shivered. "Oh, that sounds exciting."

"Tedious," Basil said. "And so far I'm striking out."

"Too bad RACE folded about twenty years ago. Rockport Area Car Enthusiasts," she said. "It was our antique car club. Called it RACE, but it was more like a crawl, none of the cars tooling around fast. Quite a big deal in the county back then. Quite a to-do in the warm months, polishing up the beauties and spreading them out on the county fairgrounds, people walking by and taking pictures, sellers swapping parts. Miss those days. Too bad fewer and fewer people kept the old cars. Interest just dried up." Margaret patted Basil's arm and pointed to the last page in the photo album that showed a yellowed flyer for the club. It had a picture of a vintage convertible. "That was our first classic convertible, a 1936 Tatra 75. They put it on the brochure that summer."

"Czechoslovakian import," Ian said. "Real comfy to ride in. Leather seats. Air-cooled boxer engine. You could get it up to fifty-five, fifty-six miles per hour if you floored it. Sweet car. Sold it ten years back for ninety thousand. I'd hoped to get more but the market had softened and I needed room in the garage for an Overland Whippet I was restoring. Hell, I'm still puttering with the Whippet."

"Sold the Tatra to some collector in Louisville," Margaret added. "He caught a look at it when we drove it to a meet down in Kentucky. Used to hold them here, like I told you, but the car club folded."

"And that wasn't twenty years ago it shut down," Ian cut in. "More like thirty, Mags. Years are like memories, you know, they sneak up on you like the mileage counter on a car. We've got a lot of mileage."

Basil estimated the Averys were in their mid-eighties.

"You could see a lot of nice, old cars at those summer meetings," Margaret said. "Old cars are the best. They were made better, not zip, zip, zip on fast assembly lines. Gotta admit, though, I like my Mustang, and it's a 2018."

"You like it because it's a convertible," Ian groused.

"I do like my convertibles. If I was younger, I'd ride motorcycles again."

"Sheriff's got a nice, old cycle," Ian mused. "Saw her on it in town a month back."

"Anyway, you're probably in a hurry, young man," Margaret said. "What with your important investigation. If you need to check out the county's old cars, go to the library. The branch in Rockport. It probably has slides of old newspapers with articles about those RACE get-togethers. I used to keep the clippings, but our daughter talked me into pitching stuff. She wants us to downsize and look at senior-living apartments in Owensboro."

"That ain't happening," Ian said softly. "Ain't giving up our home."

A thought glimmered. "Do you remember the names of other members of that car club?" Basil pulled out his notebook and frowned when Margaret and Ian shook their heads.

"Years and miles," Ian said. "Probably moved or died, all of them."

"What about the Tuckers?" Basil pressed. "Is it possible Henry Tucker was a member? He lives up the road from you." If the club ended thirty years ago, Henry would have been in his twenties. Maybe he'd been into cars as a young man.

"Tucker," Ian chuckled. "We went to Australia in 1991, and the

Aussies called lunch or dinner tucker. Breakfast was brekkies, or something like that. But the other meals were tucker. You'd hear the locals talk about where to go out for the best tucker. We got back from that trip, picked up a cat at the shelter ... that was before that woman took over and stuck the cats and kittens in the freezer to kill them, made the news, you know. That little cat was gray like fog and we named him Tucker 'cause he always wanted to eat." He took the album back from Basil. "Tucker. Tucker. Tucker. Nope. Doesn't ring a bell with the car club."

"Tucker," Margaret said. "Not Henry Tucker. But Ed Tucker was a member, Henry's father. Ed had a 1940 Dodge Luxury Liner coupe. Restored, he'd painted it a yellow-beige. Awful. Bland. Great grille on it, though. Probably some pictures of it in the library."

Basil added the library to his list of stops.

It was going to be a string of long, interesting days.

Maybe Nang would have that spinach dish on the menu for lunch.

───────

Basil settled for the stir fry vegetables over rice noodles with a side of *bánh xèo*, which he correctly pronounced as "boon say-oh." It was a pancake Nang served sizzling at the table, a liberal amount of shrimp and beansprouts heaped on top of it. Basil plucked a small bottle of orange juice out of the refrigerator.

"I thought you were a vegetarian," Oren said.

"I'm not. I just don't eat a lot of meat."

"You'll like this," Nang told him.

"I've liked everything here," Basil returned.

Oren's choice was a cup of *ga tan* soup and a plate of *banh knot*, crunchy ravioli-like pockets stuffed with shrimp, mung beans, and spring onions.

"It's good you're always changing the menu," Oren said. "But I'd like it if you repeated that spinach-stuff. That was damn tasty for something healthy."

"When I go to Owensboro shopping again, I'll get some," Nang said. He poured Oren and himself a mug of coffee, then he sat and joined them, keeping an eye on the door for customers. He pulled out his cell phone and scrolled through the pictures. He turned it so Oren could see. "This is Magoo. I'm picking him up tomorrow from the shelter."

"That's a pug," Oren said.

"I like Paul Blackwell's Wrinkles. I'm fortunate I was first on the list for this dog. He's cute, Magoo. I'm going to keep the name. Don't you think Magoo is cute?" Nang showed him another photo of the dog at the shelter.

"Cute? He's a pug," Oren repeated, his expression like he'd bitten into something sour.

"What did you want to talk to me about?" Nang put the phone away.

"Old cars," Basil said. "Old cars, Chris Hagee, Henry Tucker, and the video surveillance footage from your gas pumps."

"I love to talk about old cars," Nang replied. "Any cars, actually. I'm helping Zeke restore his. And you're welcome to my video. But I've been recording over it every twenty-four hours. Haven't seen a need to keep it."

Basil let out a long sigh and took a big slug of orange juice.

"Vintage cars," Oren said, describing the ones Anthony had mentioned.

"I've seen all of those cars since I have the only gas station around here." Nang paused. "The only Vietnamese restaurant and caterer in the county, too." He got up and refilled Oren's coffee. "I'll make you a list, connecting people to the vintage cars that have stopped at my station. It has something to do with Chris Hagee's murder, doesn't it?"

"Piper tell you what we're tracking?" Oren mused.

Nang frowned. "No, Piper doesn't tell me anything. Hardly speaks to me now." He stepped to the counter, looking distant and staring out the window as Margaret Avery pulled up in her red Mustang convertible. She put on white gloves and reached for the gas pump. "But people in Fulda gossip," he said. "This is a talky county with few secrets."

Margaret came in to pay and buy a lottery ticket. "They questioning you about old cars, too?" she asked Nang as she nodded toward Oren and Basil. "Some big case they're working on." She dropped her voice to a whisper, but it carried. "I think it has to do with Chris Hagee."

Basil finished the rest of his orange juice in one swallow.

CHAPTER TWENTY-SEVEN

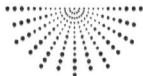

9 A.M. SATURDAY, SEPTEMBER 12TH

Hey, Tom." Piper had a dozen or so more miles before cell phone reception cut out. "I should've called before now." She listened to him. "Yeah, I'm mending. Thank you. No, I've not heard anything about Brick either, other than he's still in intensive care." She listened again. "Gonzo left the base? AWOL? I hope they find him before something bad happens."

"Who's Gonzo?" Paul asked.

A friend, Piper mouthed.

"Space, I hear you're leaving the States Monday. Short deployment. Oh, Sunday? You're leaving tomorrow. Wow. Sure, I'll come visit when you get back. No paintball for a while though. I'm calling because I have to go back to your place and walk around."

There was a crackling sound, soft, the cell phone struggling to hold a signal. The trees on either side of the road became thicker, and wooden handmade signs poked through gaps in the ground cover: MY DOG HAS A GUN AND HE REFUSES TO TAKE HIS MEDICATION; NIGHTCRAWLERS AND COFFEE TWO MILES; I'D TURN BACK IF I WAS YOU; GUNS SAVE LIVES; AFTER WHISKY DRIVING IS RISKY; APPLES WHEN IN SEASON; and FREE FILL.

"No, I can't wait until you get back. I have to see everything again

208

while it's fresh. Get some closure. Yes, I should've called you earlier. I said that. I should've called. My bout with bad manners. That's on me, sorry. I've just been real distracted with work and things. We've a case right now that's interesting. Almost there, just passing the—"

Piper had a difficult time hearing him, the connection fading. Indeed, she should have called him earlier, yesterday or before. It would've been polite. He could have met her out here today.

"No, I'm not alone. It's me and my dad. I'm not supposed to drive yet. I'll be safe, fine. Don't worry. Seriously, don't worry about me. I'm not going to sue you. I promise. Brick's family is threatening to sue? Crap. Why don't—"

The cell reception cut out again, just as it had when she drove down last week for her three-day vacation, right even with an old sign, barely legible, advertising a farmer's market that had probably closed decades ago.

"Less than an hour from Rockport," Paul noted, "and you lose a connection? Kind of primitive, like Robinson Crusoe. What the hell, Punkin? You didn't tell me that, about no cell reception. What the hell were you thinking?"

"Forgot to mention it."

"Wish I would've known about the lack of reception. If there's a problem in Santa Claus—" He held the thought a moment. "I suppose Shelly will have to deal with it."

"Sorry."

"Nice, though, this area, a good place to get away from everything. Nice getting away with you for a few hours. I don't want us out here too long, though. Should've told me about the no reception bit."

Yeah, I should have. But I should have thought of a lot of things. And maybe I should have waited until tomorrow and came down here with Nang, talk things out with him.

"Your buddy have a problem with you coming out to his cabin?" Paul had said something else, but Piper had been too tangled in her thoughts to catch it.

"He doesn't want me out here alone," Piper said, as they pulled down the dirt road, almost too narrow for a car. "Tom—Spaceman—

doesn't want me to hurt myself, knows you can't call out for help. Probably thinks he'll be liable for something if I fall. Brick's family has a lawyer, and I think he's scared. I'd never sue him, Dad. It wasn't his fault what happened."

"Litigious country," Paul said.

"I told him you were with me, and that seemed to settle him. Nice to be worried over, I guess. He was always the Mother Hen in Iraq. And two of his chicks are dead to the shooter, and one just went AWOL." She leaned back into the seat as her dad parked as close to Spaceman's cabin as possible, about fifty feet away near a line of hickory trees. "The shooting ... one of my friends had to drive like hell out of here to get reception and call for an ambulance and the sheriff."

"Like I said, nice to be with you. But I don't like being cut off from my department, weekend off or no. What were you thinking?" Paul fixed her with the sternest look she'd ever seen on his weathered face. Her dad was in his fifties, but two bouts of chemo had aged him. He could pass for someone more than a decade older than that. "Two hours at the outside, then we're out of here."

She got out of the car, grabbed her pack, and leaned in. "What was I thinking? I was thinking I have to get closure, and that you're with me so it would be okay. Nang and Basil and Oren know where we are. That's what I was thinking. And I know there's a hole in the floor of an old mine, and we're not going in it. That's what I was thinking. And I know there's a drop-off to the north. We'll stay away from that, too."

Paul waited a minute before he got out. "What the hell was *I* thinking, bringing you down here? No cell reception."

"You're thinking I *really* do need some closure." Piper gestured to the cabin. "And you said you wanted to see the place."

"A good storm could take that down."

"There was a storm last week. The old cabin is sturdier than it looks. Spaceman—Tom—is going to fix it up after he gets out. His grandfather gave it to him. I guess the land's been in his family for a long, long time."

"Make a nice fishing cabin I suppose," Paul said, his expression softening, but just a little. "If there's a place to fish around here."

"Some creeks. I got killed near one." Piper remembered the first time she was pelted by paintballs. "In the game, I got killed."

"Glad I didn't bring Wrinkles." Paul turned slowly, taking in the tall trees, the riot of late-summer wildflowers thick around the trunks, the sun spearing down in bright lances through the branches. "Lots of places for him to lift his leg. He'd be in heaven. But I wager as warm as it is deer ticks would have a party on his puggy hide."

Piper led him up the rickety steps and opened the cabin door. "No locks. Wouldn't do any good to install them, place would be easy to break into."

"Can't imagine that anyone would want to break in." Paul followed her inside, his eyes lingering on a few buckets under leaky spots in the roof. "Can't imagine anyone would know this cabin exists."

Light poured in through the windows, revealing the interior in its rustic, beaten-down glory. It was warm, in the low eighties, stuffy in here because it had been closed up, but Piper shivered. This had been such a happy place seven, eight days ago. She and Hemi, Renegade, Spaceman, and the rest eating dinner and breakfast, and talking about the Army, them asking to hear stories of her first several months as sheriff of Spencer County. She told them about the cat hoarder with the shotgun and the drunk on a tractor, leaving off the serial killer who chose his victims based on Christmas cards. They talked about bluegrass music and bucket lists, Sybil Ludington and Paul Revere, the days they'd shared together in Iraq, and the coming ones that would send them all in different directions.

She started crying and didn't try to hold it in, thankful her dad said nothing and let her drown in the memories for a little while.

"Hemi's funeral was yesterday," she said. "It wasn't *practical* to attend, but now I think I could've found a way. I didn't know any of his family. They don't know me. But him? Me and him were buds. Hell, I even basically liked Renegade."

Paul stayed quiet. She watched him walk into the kitchen and look around as if he were inspecting the place. Spaceman and Renegade

211

had cooked breakfast a week ago, eggs that tasted marvelous, plenty of bacon, and hot coffee that was passable. She'd remembered Hemi going back for seconds. Hemi was big on seconds if he liked something.

Life was so temporary.

She'd lost friends during downrange assignments, a few to mines. She'd expected to lose people during combat situations.

Not to a stranger while they were playing a game of paintball.

Her dad nodded to a paintball rifle with an R on the stock; it was propped against a kitchen cabinet. Renegade's. A case of paintballs sat on the floor near it. Next time she saw Spaceman, she'd give Hemi's paint rifle back—she decided in this instant it was not an activity to pursue ever again. The gift had been thoughtful, but it would only make Piper dwell on why she had it. She had better memories to keep of her friend.

She crossed to the table and set her pack on it. "I remembered to bring some water." She unzipped it and pulled out two bottles, one at a time. "Want to carry yours?"

He shook his head, and she put them back in the pack.

"I brought some M&Ms, too."

"The peanut kind?"

"Sorry, just plain." She reached in and pulled out the copy of the old map and laid it flat, using the pack to hold down one side. The plastic coating made it curl. "I'm still on a sugar rush from the donuts you brought, and here I stuff M&Ms to go."

"Donuts are always good," he returned. "Goes with our profession. Sugar is a good burst. The map, looks Civil War era."

"Spaceman found an old map of his land at the library and made copies for all of us so we wouldn't get lost when we played paintball. More than a hundred years old, the original, but it has more detail than something you could go out and buy now. I want to dig through the library in Rockport and see if there's an old Spencer County map something like this. Compare it to the modern one on the wall in my office."

"If I recall, that map in your office isn't all that modern. Ten, maybe twenty years old."

"Modern enough that it doesn't have Africa listed." That was a speck on the road where Piper had investigated a murder in August. She knew the older maps listed more of the county's itty bitty towns, including some places that now consisted only of a few houses or had just vanished.

"Lots of raggedy maps in the back room at the library," Paul said. "I've looked at them from time to time because of the Old Fart's Club." He looked up at her. "Yes, I know that's what you call my genealogy group."

It was what a lot of people called the county genealogy group. Her father was likely the youngest member.

"Anyway, Dad, I want to see an old map. My house in Hatfield, I'd like to see the original map for the land. Just for giggles."

"It wasn't called Hatfield originally, Punkin."

"I know. Called Fair Fight about a hundred and fifty years or so ago. I like Fair Fight better. Don't know why they changed the name."

Paul chuckled. "That's because you're not in the Old Fart's Club. Maybe you ought to join if you're curious about history around home. Would broaden your local education. Hatfield was the man who turned it into a city."

"City? Town, maybe. Dinkburg, actually."

"James Hatfield."

"Wow. He named it after himself. Fair Fight is a far more interesting name, and I've no idea why it was called that," she contended. "Anyway, I'd like to get an old map similar to this one. Or a good copy. Frame it and put it up on one of my walls at home. Hang up some history."

Paul held down the other end of the map. "A lot of history in Kentucky. A lot of it is tied to music. Can't count the number of years I went to Henderson's Blues and Barbecue Festival. Bluegrass. You went with me a couple of times when you were a kid. The music runs deep through the whole state, and around here it runs—"

213

"Blue," Piper said. "Definitely blue. Yeah, Spaceman told me all about the bluegrass festival right over the ridge. We were supposed to go." She pointed to a hashed line on the map. "Here's where his property ends along this section. Here's Jerusalem Ridge, where all the bad things happened. County owns it. On the other side, past this area where they found the shooter's car, is a little museum and gift shop, a restored homestead, and they have a lot of bluegrass during warm months. Spaceman had tickets for the bluegrass concert." Much softer: "I wish we could have used them. I suspect I would have had a good time even though it's not my flavor of country music." This time she managed to keep the tears in.

"So we're here." Paul stabbed a finger on the map. "This is where this shack is, right?"

"Pretty close."

"And you want us to go there, Jerusalem Ridge."

"Yeah. We could've stopped in the parking lot by the museum and hiked over, quite a bit longer, and probably an easier way to go, but I wanted to retrace my steps. Though we don't have cell reception, my phone's got a full charge. I want pictures. I didn't bother taking pictures when I was here last weekend." She regretted that. She would have liked a picture of Hemi, especially one with paint spattered on his clothes. "Let's get going so we can do this, then I'll buy you lunch and I'll check in with Oren and Basil on the Chris Hagee investigation, see what I can do to help—and I'll get you back home to Wrinkles."

Paul laughed again. "Millie's got him for the day. He's probably getting spoiled worse than I spoil him."

"I doubt that. You've spoiled him rotten." Piper hadn't meant to say that out loud.

"Nang's getting a pug today," Paul added. "One finally was surrendered at the animal shelter, and he'd had his name at the top of the list."

"I know."

"He's all yippy skippy happy about it. He called me two nights ago and grilled me about Wrinkles, wondered if a young pug—like he's getting—would get along with your old dog."

214

Piper studied the map again.

"Seemed to be real important to him, the dogs getting along. Are you two getting serious?"

One of us is serious.

Piper pointed to a spot at the base of Jerusalem Ridge, the faint, tiny print read Carp Mine, short for Carpenter. "This is the mine where me and Brick fell. We think the shooter was up here. He had good vantage. Don't know why the hell he started firing. Maybe alcohol. Maybe he thought we had real guns and were a threat. The sheriff is working on either one of those theories, but doesn't have a motive locked down yet. Might never have one. Honestly, I don't think he's working the case all that hard. No urgency from what I can tell. A redneck hunter with a gun out in the sticks, beer, his death tying it all up in a case-closed with a bow for the department. I certainly wouldn't vote for that sheriff come election time. Talk about a slow—"

Paul changed the subject. "What kind of mine was it?"

"Fluorite. Lot of them in Kentucky decades ago. Spaceman said his great-grandfather made quite a bit of money on that one ... before it got cheaper to import the stuff. Then the mines were shuttered."

"Should have been boarded up."

"Well, we were glad it wasn't—at least we were glad until the floor gave out. Weger couldn't shoot us while we were in there."

"Do you know much about Weger?"

"Not enough." Piper knew her deputies would have been more aggressive with the investigation. She and Oren and Basil would have gotten a lot more information about Weger. "Thirty-one. A mechanic. Had a big hunting dog in his apartment. Hey—" She took a step back from the table. "The sheriff's report mentioned he might have been out hunting, beating the deer season. You'd think he would have had his dog with him if he was hunting."

Paul shook his head. "Not if he was hunting deer. A dog would spook them. Use dogs for birds. You never wanted to go hunting with your grandad and me, or you'd know that." His finger moved two inches east of Piper's, indicating a tiny symbol of a hammer with a pointed pick in place of the claw. "Was this a fluorite mine, too?"

215

She tapped the Carp Mine. "Spaceman said he had just the one mine on his property."

"Well, it looks like he has two. Or three." Paul pointed at another symbol. "It's probably all the same mine with multiple entrances."

"Weger started firing when we were over here."

"Let's go for a hike and you show me which one you fell in. And we're not going inside it, Punkin. We're just looking for—"

"—closure," she finished. "If the local sheriff can't manage to find it, I'll get it myself."

CHAPTER TWENTY-EIGHT

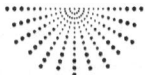

10 A.M. SATURDAY

W hen I played paintball, it was in an open field," Paul said. "And if you took a shot in the leg, you had to limp like you were really wounded. Got shot in the arm, you had to let it hang, couldn't use it. No expensive guns. No fancy rules. Just men, and paint, and a summer afternoon."

"Sounds almost primitive." Piper had meant that as a joke.

"Primitive? It was perfect. Wish I was that young again, could do it all over."

Piper had been leading her father along the small game trail that she had taken Saturday morning. She was surprised he'd played paintball.

"I remember my friend Keith, we used to go shooting with him sometimes—shooting paint. He rigged a contraption out of tennis ball cans, duct taped a bunch together, and hooked an air compressor from his auto shop to it. Tried to turn it into a paint canon, but the thing exploded. He didn't have the cans taped well enough. The paint was purple, and he was purple with bruises for a week afterward. We ended up rushing him to an ER that day."

She turned and saw him caught in the memory, smiling. She pulled the cell phone from her pocket and took his picture.

"It all turned out okay," Paul continued. "It wasn't a serious concussion. Went right back out the next weekend with us."

"You played a lot?"

"No. Well, yes. I guess it was often for a while. I loved paintball, and I got into it by using your grandfather's gun. Didn't know it's *that* old a sport, did you?"

"Honestly, no. I really didn't know much about it until Spaceman called and I did a quick Google search and bought my Splatterking. I'd had zero interest in it when they played on the base, just went last weekend to get together with some friends." *A couple of which I will never see again.* Piper felt her stomach turn, thoughts about Hemi and Renegade overwhelming her. She could have died, too, if she'd been with them. Hemi had told her to hang back, a prophetic warning.

"You know, Dad, if I hadn't joined them last weekend it all might have turned out differently. The circumstances, timing, all of it." Her friends might have lived ... or all of them might've died. Piper steadied herself. Her backpack was slung over her right shoulder, the weight uneven. That coupled with having one arm in a sling set her off balance on the patchy ground. She had poo-pooed her father's suggestion she borrow his cane—it was her arm, not her leg that was the problem—and wished now that she'd taken him up on it. The land had dried, no rain for days, leaving hard ruts and jutting roots, and the splendid scent of all the wildflowers. She had to admit it was beautiful in these woods, albeit more difficult and slow going than her previous trip. At least she remembered the way; it was easy to get lost in the woods.

Paul reached up and tugged at a branch, pulling it down and then releasing it. He spooked a long-tailed jaeger that had been higher up. They watched it fly away. Through a gap in the branches she saw a pale blue sky full of birds.

"I guess paintball is pretty much one of those extreme sports now, Punkin. Themed parties like zombie apocalypse scenarios, lots of money for high-powered guns that'll shoot paint far and more accurate than what we played with. Your grandfather's gun is still in my basement. I should check on eBay and see if it might be worth something. Very vintage, a modern antique. That gun is from before I was born, back when they started using them to mark trees and livestock."

"An *ancient* sport, eh?"

He laughed; it was a good sound to Piper.

"Some city guys—physicians, writers, stockbrokers—bought some of those livestock guns and turned it into a survival game. Really took off when *Sports Illustrated* did a feature about it in the eighties. That's when I cobbled onto that old gun in my dad's shed and took it out with Keith and some other friends. We got lost in the woods north of Spencer County, eventually found our way out. Bruised as hell from the paint. Wonder where Keith is now. Damn, we had a grand time."

Piper'd had a good time with her friends last weekend until everything went south and sour.

"I played a little into the early nineties. I guess you didn't know that."

"Before I was born, Dad. And you never mentioned it."

"I said it was an old sport." He was looking almost straight up. Piper craned her neck to see what had caught his interest, then immediately glanced down and reached for a tree, off-balance again. Maybe she should have waited a few more days before coming out here.

He stared at a whorl in a thick beech tree. "I bought a paint gun with a compressed air tank, a Spyder. It was aluminum, lightweight, cheap. Don't have it anymore, and I don't know what happened to it. I played a lot with it, only used it in one tournament, though, and joined the National Paintball Players League for all of one year ... wonder if that's still around. I did well at the tourney, I've good aim, you know. I got a trophy and a five hundred dollar gift certificate to Shula's Steakhouse in Indy. Too bad that restaurant closed up a few years back. The place was expensive, but the filets melted in your mouth."

Piper shrugged out of the backpack and retrieved the map, unrolled it and stepped on one edge to keep it flat. They were more than halfway to the ridge. She replaced it, and Paul grabbed the pack before she could put it back on.

219

"My turn for a while," he said. "I should have brought Wrinkles. I like the feel of the pug on my back. Comfortable, you know."

She didn't argue and kept going, scanning the ground for tracks from last weekend, and finding nothing but a few cracked branches. The breeze was strong and rustled the leaves, almost musical. The air felt good against her skin and moved enough to thwart the mosquitoes. People often commented how quiet the woods were compared to a city. But when Piper listened she heard lots of things—branches clicking, birds chattering, the sound of the creek to her left, and something moving to their right. She focused in that direction and saw a trio of deer. Had Weger been out here hunting? Yes. But was he hunting deer, or was he purposely hunting people?

The sounds stopped when they came to the edge of the tree line and spied the ridge. Eerie, as if the land was holding its breath.

"I saw the Holy City," Piper whispered, "the new Jerusalem, coming down out of heaven from God, prepared as a bride beautifully dressed for her husband."

"You're quoting Revelation." Paul was right behind her.

"Twenty-one, two," Piper replied. "I looked it up last night. Brick told me that a man named Buck Monroe lived around here in the eighteen hundreds and climbed to the top, claimed the view was magical, like the new Jerusalem John the Baptist saw."

"And called it Jerusalem Ridge," Paul finished.

"Yeah. Spaceman doesn't own the ridge. That's county property. In the distance on the other side is a little museum and bluegrass music. Maybe you and I can come back here when they have a concert scheduled." In spite of the warmth, Piper quivered. She took a picture with her cell phone, turned and took another one of her father.

"C'mon. Let's take a look around and then you buy me some lunch. I'll get back to Wrinkles, and you'll get home and meet Nang's new pug."

"Magoo," she said. "The dog comes with a name."

"Pugs have Magoo-eyes," Paul said.

Her feet felt heavy like cement blocks. She kept her eyes on the ridge, spotting the outcropping she believed Weger had shot from.

"Over here." She stopped behind a stand of tall sawgrass. The area was still tamped down where Renegade and Hemi had died. No trace of blood remained, but there were plenty of broken twigs, and she swore she could see the imprint of Hemi's big shoes. She took more pictures. Hemi had radioed her about going ahead and scouting the ridge, and that she should stay back. She hadn't entirely followed that directive, she had held at the tree line. Piper could have died here, too. That thought kept bouncing around in her brain.

"I should've attended his service, Dad. A broken arm was a poor excuse."

"Funerals are overrated," he returned. "It's best to spend your time with people while they're above ground."

"Brick and me, we crawled over here to get away from the shooter. I couldn't see the shooter from here, I couldn't take a shot. And it was too open for me to climb up this side to reach him." She walked toward the mine, her feet feeling even heavier. A yellow police tape fluttered near the entrance, caught on something and trying to break free. She took a few more pictures.

"Not going inside, Punkin."

"I know." She stood, right hand on her hip gripping her phone, feet spread to keep her balance. *Should have borrowed his cane. Should have done a lot of things.*

Paul took a step past her and peered into the darkness, and then he edged back and skirted around a tangle of bushes. "Those other entrances should be back around here, according to your map. Provided it's all the same mine." He dropped her pack and dug inside it, taking out a water bottle, sloshing it around, then unscrewing the cap and offering it to her.

Piper shook her head. "I'll take some of those M&Ms."

He drank half the bottle, returned it to the backpack, and passed over the candy. Then he eased out the map and looked at it while she ate a handful. "Should've brought my reading glasses. Print is small." He replaced the map, picked up the backpack and worked his way around the slope and out of her sight.

Piper popped a second handful of M&Ms in her mouth and stuffed the rest of the packet into her shirt pocket. *Not supposed to melt,* she thought, *even in this heat. We'll see if the advertising slogan is true.* Then she stared into the mine again, hearing the police tape flutter like a bird's wing, gazing into the black as if it was the maw of some great beast waiting to swallow her. It had chewed up Brick and her a week ago, spit them out. As if on cue, her arm started throbbing in time with her heart. She'd venture in, just a little way, just far enough to—

"Hey, Punkin." She barely heard her dad calling over the tape flapping and rustling of the tall grasses in the wind.

Reluctantly, she pulled back from the mine and followed his course around the slope. He was at least fifty yards ahead of her, backpack at his feet, waving his arms to get her attention. She started to jog his way and almost fell, her feet tangling in the ground cover.

"Slow down! It's not going anywhere," he hollered. Paul pulled the map out of the pack and held it in front of him, bringing it close to his face. Piper guessed by how far they'd come that they were nearing the eastern edge of Spaceman's land.

"That's county property," Piper said, gesturing at the ridge. "Spaceman only owns up to these foothills. "That's—"

"Don't know whose property," Paul said, "but I think that's another way into the old fluorite mine. Doesn't jive with the marks on the map. But this is an old, old map, and that doesn't look all that old." He whistled and pointed up. "Looks like someone's been working that recently."

A little over their heads, roughly seven feet up, the blade of a shovel poked out from a jagged slash in the stone.

"There's something inside there. See the glint?" Paul stuffed the map in the backpack, left it on the ground, and started climbing. "You stay here. I'll let you know what I find."

"Dad, this has nothing to do with Hemi's murder." Piper wanted to climb the ridge where the shooter had been, not here. "Dad, c'mon. Really?"

He disappeared inside the crevice.

It didn't look all that hard to climb, even though Piper had one arm in a sling. If she was cautious, she could manage. She went up after him, carefully placing one foot, then the other, leaning into the stone and going slow. If she could climb this, she could get up the rise where Weger had perched. She almost fell halfway up, held onto an outcropping with her right hand, ignoring the bite of the rock. If she fell, it wouldn't be all that far. What was another cracked rib or three?

Paul came back out, taking up the entire crevice, scowling when he saw her. "I said stay down there. Don't you—"

"Listen? Nope. Didn't hear you." Piper worked her way up the next few feet, gritting her teeth because her arm throbbed and her chest ached, and mentally chastising herself. She expected him to reach out a hand to help her, but apparently he was upset with her and darted back inside.

He said something she couldn't make out. Maybe she should have come out here tomorrow instead with Nang, she mused, or waited three months until Spaceman got back home. No, she had to settle this. She crawled into the crevice, her shoulders scraping the sides. It was a tight fit. The shovel head she'd seen was attached to a broken haft and looked new, the metal shiny and sharp. It took her a little effort to stand.

"How do you think you're going to get back down?" Paul said. "You're stubborn, Punkin. And one of these days that stubbornness will jump up and bite you hard." He stood a few yards inside, looming over a pair of overturned plastic milk crates that served as a table. He lit one of two Streamlight camping lanterns sitting there.

"This place has nothing to do with Hemi and the shooter," Piper said. But she came closer. Maybe it did.

Farther back there was a small wheeled cart and folded canvas sacks. On the milk crate-table in front of her was a book wrapped in plastic and another copy of Spaceman's old map. A long-handled pick and three shovels were propped against the left wall. Piper took pictures of all of it and hit the video record function.

Piper leaned over the table and read the title of the book: *The Journal of Jonathan Swift*. It was well-worn, thin, the corners were rounded and frayed, and it looked very old. The binding was a different color than the copies she'd seen in the case in Spaceman's cabin.

"What the hell, Dad? This book. Weger had one in his car. Spaceman had two." But one of Spaceman's had read John Swift, not Jonathan.

"Been a cave-in back here." Paul had ventured in deeper, taking the lantern with him. Piper lit the other one, but didn't move it. She could hold the cell phone or the lantern, not both, and she was still video-recording this. "Or maybe not a cave-in, maybe a mine in process. Looks like this section was blasted to loosen some of the rock. Maybe dynamite. Yeah, I think all of this is pretty recent. But it's a dead end."

He was right. The air felt tight, no breeze coming this far back. The day's heat seemed magnified. She wiped a trickle of sweat from her forehead.

"Let's get out of here," Paul suggested.

"With the book," Piper said, still recording. "There's something about this book."

Paul flicked off the lanterns. Piper returned to the crate, dropped the cell phone in her pocket and, reached for the journal. A rifle cracked and Piper went down as her father knocked her over. She fell, stretching out her good arm to protect herself. Two more shots followed, the bullets striking the rock beyond the entrance and spitting stone chips.

A fourth shot pinged against the rock as Paul drew his pistol and leaned up against the right side of tunnel, motioning Piper to stay down while he edged forward. He had to stoop, the ceiling too low for him. Piper scrambled to her feet and plastered her back against the opposite wall, drawing her pistol and clenching her teeth. Pain rocked through her chest and arm, sharp, dizzying, awful. She sucked in rock dust and the musty funk of the crevice.

"Who the hell's out there?" Paul hissed. "I can't see him."

Another shot, more rock spitting away. This place was so isolated Piper knew no one would hear the gunfire. No cell service, she couldn't call the sheriff's department. 9-1-1 wasn't going to happen.

Her phone was still videoing images of the blackness of her pocket, but it was recording the sounds too.

A few more shots, nothing coming close, though it was enough of a threat to keep them plastered against the walls. The shooter couldn't see back in the crevice with the lanterns off. She holstered her gun and picked up the journal.

It was about this book, right? Somehow the book had triggered this. Spaceman had two copies in his cabin, one here, another one found in Weger's car.

"Throw out your guns, Christmas! Throw them all out and we'll talk about this. Nobody else needs to die."

CHAPTER TWENTY-NINE

10 A.M. SATURDAY

Oren took the side of the booth where he could both look out the window and see the front door. Basil slid in across from him, opened the menu, and made a face.

"My kids would like this," Basil said. "Me? I'm thinking *oh hell no.*"

Basil had picked Oren up from the memory care center parking lot and asked him to name a spot for breakfast. Oren's breakfast choice had started as an IHOP, but when it turned into Pearl's Pancake Palace a few years ago the interior had been transformed into an explosion of pinks and purples with splashes of orange. A variety of castles, knights, dragons, and exquisitely-dressed princesses filled the gaps between framed posters displaying stacks of castle-shaped pancakes that showed syrup spilling out the drawbridges and filling moats.

"If you look past the fairytale names and ignore the pictures and all the pink, you'll see some good options." Oren ran a finger down the right-hand side of the menu. "I want the Dragon Slayer Special, no onions in the potatoes, and a half-size order of Camelot Cakes with blueberry syrup." He handed the menu to the waitress. "A large glass of apple juice, too. I've got to cut back on the coffee."

Basil pointed to something. "How's this?"

"Prince Charming's Omelet. A lot of folks order that," the waitress

226

said. "Three or four eggs? And you have your choice of ham or bacon crumbles, cheddar, provolone or—"

"Three eggs, cheddar, bacon. No, skip the bacon. Make it cheddar *and* provolone. And give me a side of Princess Polly's Peaches and herbal tea."

"Don't have herbal tea."

"Just water then."

The waitress grinned and strode away.

"You said I could pick the restaurant." Oren stared out the window. Another Owensboro diner sat across the road, this with a baseball theme. Batter Up! was essentially a greasy spoon, and the lone time he'd been there it smelled bad. "I wanted something warm, and something I'd had before that I knew wouldn't give me a gut ache." He paused. "Ate here a month back, digging into the murder of that comic shop owner. Liked it then, despite the circumstances and all the pastel decorations."

"I guess we could make this a tradition, work a murder case and come to Pearl's Pancake Palace for breakfast." Basil took out his notebook and started flipping pages. He and Oren normally would have today off, but not with the Chris Hagee case ongoing.

Oren had thought about spending the day with his dad, but for the past two nights he'd stayed in the care center, his dad hadn't stirred. The nurses said he was sleeping all the time; and they'd stopped trying to rouse him to eat or drink. Oren read aloud those nights, thinking some part of his dad might hear him. He read the local newspaper, his notes from the Hagee case, and he talked about his various theories regarding the murder. Oren agreed with Basil: someone struck Chris Hagee by accident, thought they'd killed him, and strung him up in the barn to make it look like suicide.

"They probably got scared," Oren said. "After they hit Hagee, didn't want to call the sheriff's department because they feared getting charged with murder."

"We had a lot of hit and run cases in Chicago where the driver freaked and kept going. If they'd stopped and called the police, they might not have been charged, or at least not gotten jail time. Acci-

227

dents happen. But fleeing from the scene of an accident makes it all worse, turns it into a Class Three felony adding up to five years."

"I'd just like to know who fled from the scene and took Chris Hagee with them, all the way to his garage and up the ladder."

"The Tuckers."

Oren nodded. "No doubt." *Fingerprints and boot prints pointed that way*, he thought. And Henry Tucker was too belligerent and outright lied at first about the spray paint. "Yeah, the Tuckers. Which one was driving?"

"And where's the damn car? Really need to find the car."

The waitress returned and moved into Basil's line of vision. She tapped Basil on the shoulder with her order pad. "Boss says we have some citron green or cherry blossom teas with no caffeine. Whatcha think?"

"I'll try the citron green. Thanks."

"Gotcha." She spun away. "I didn't figure you for cherry blossoms."

Oren leaned back into the booth, the vinyl making a crinkling sound. Conversations from other tables drifted toward them. A pair of women in their thirties, wearing shorts and oversized t-shirts, chatted about their grocery lists. A middle-aged man at the adjacent table held a conversation with someone on the other end of his cell phone, talking about childcare options and dog-sitters. Two young mothers with two infants in booster seats gabbed loudly about the price of diapers and Gerber baby food. The middle-aged man waved at them and shushed them. Muted behind everything, Oren heard piped-in music, Noel Harrison singing *The Windmills of Your Mind*. He empathized with the singer—sometimes he felt like a carousel spinning around the moon.

"Chevrolet C10 pickup," Basil said. "The headlight size, height of the bumper from the ground, assuming standard tires, manufactured between 1960 and 1967. The year after that there were some design changes, and those later years don't match the bruises and marks on Chris Hagee. They stopped making it in 1987. It's all Colorado and Silverado now."

"That's pretty damn specific. How'd you come up with that?" Oren cut off a chunk of pancake and ran it around in the syrup. Delicious. It was almost good enough to take his mind of his dad and to stop thinking of himself as a carousel circling the moon.

"I reached out to a buddy in Chicago and asked him to run our specs through his database. The department there has so many research tools. I just took advantage. I'd say I'll have to return the favor sometime, but we don't have resources they'd find useful."

"Wow," Oren said, going for another chunk of pancake. *If heaven was breakfast*, he thought, *it would be buttermilk pancakes*. "Sure it's a Chevy pickup? And sure of the years? Like I said, that's specific."

"Nothing's a hundred percent," Basil cut back. "Nothing ever. But that's his best guess, and so I think we should go with it. Funny, you think, Chris Hagee drove nothing but Chevrolets, and here he got run over by one. Spent all of yesterday trying to find the damn car. Up and down roads, riding, walking, looking for something vintage with round headlights. I found most of those vehicles Anthony Delaney mentioned to us, and none of them fit the measurements close enough. Didn't see a single Chevy C10."

"Yeah, I couldn't find anything with round headlights that fit either. Struck out." Oren looked across to Batter Up! as he said that. Oren had volunteered for the library search since he was familiar with their microfiche reader and remembered the old car club. "Nothing that came close to matching anyway. Nothing worthwhile. Sheriff Blackwell struck out, too. Said she found some old books in her basement about vintage cars and spent the night going through them. Finding the car ... pickup ... is key. I mean, we can try to charge at least Dale Tucker because of the fingerprints, but it isn't going to be enough for DA Scales. He'll toss it right back at us."

"We hit the car lots here," Basil said. "Soon as we finish eating."

"Evansville and Henderson, too. More chance we'll come across it over there."

"Because you don't think we'll find it here? This is closer to Spencer County."

Oren shook his head. He'd already stopped at the body shops in Owensboro and in Spencer County; none of them reported any

229

vintage vehicles brought in during the past few days with front-end damage.

"Nope. I think the Tuckers either dumped it or sold it ... or hid it so well we'll never find it. I'm betting on them selling it. Henry Tucker's not someone to toss out anything that has some value to it. We drive around and see if anyone sold, maybe traded in, a Chevy C10 with the years you mentioned. Round headlights, definitely makes it an older vehicle. We throw in those years and our search is real damn specific. And I'm guessing Evansville because there are more options, might get a better price."

"I'm skeptical. I'd lean toward the truck's been hidden. Not smart to sell it. Can be found that way." Basil drained the last of his tea and pushed his empty plate away.

"Who's saying the Tuckers are smart?" Oren was only halfway through his plate, and he wasn't about to hurry. The eggs and pancakes were good, worth savoring. The potatoes should have been crispier. The apple juice was so sweet he asked for a refill. Oren posed a few more questions so Basil would talk long enough that he could finish the breakfast at a comfortable speed.

"Joan Hagee is the sole beneficiary. She gets all the money, the property, the vehicles, everything. Money's not the motive, and we know where she was during the time it happened. Nothing else in the safe deposit box other than the will." He thumped his fingers against the edge of the table. "And nothing at the DMV. But when I was there, I didn't have the particulars on the C10. I just got that in an email this morning. Diego's going to the DMV today to have them run records for the C10 pickups. But we're talking eight years' worth of trucks, so Diego likely will be a while and have them broaden to statewide. I don't want to wait for the results. I want to actually put my hands on the vehicle. But if it's hidden, then—"

"Sold it. Henry would have sold it. Blue," Oren said, as he speared the last of the potatoes. "A light blue Chevy C10."

"Blue," Basil echoed. "Anthony Delaney mentioned a blue pickup with silver trim, regularly going down the road. That, I could not find in all my driving around. Not sitting out in anyone's driveway, not cruising up and down any county road. Not out in the open."

"And we certainly can't get a search warrant for everyone's garage." Oren pushed his empty plate away, sated. The carousel image still hung in his head. "It's a big haystack. But it's a pretty big needle." He raised a hand to the waitress. "I'm stuffed. Let's go find your blue truck."

CHAPTER THIRTY

11 A.M. SATURDAY

C hristmas! I said throw the guns out! Do it now!"

"You know this guy?" Paul squinted, looking out the crevice, and then drawing back when another bullet splintered stone. "You know this son of a bitch?"

"It's Spaceman," Piper answered in disbelief. "My friend, Tom Carpenter."

"Friend? The guy who owns the cabin?"

"Owns the cabin, all these acres, and multiple copies of this journal." She edged forward and hurled the book as far as she could, watched it sail out and over and land below in the tall grass. Spaceman was somewhere in those bushes, careful not to give away his position; he didn't take the bait and show himself to go after the book. She couldn't catch a glint off his gun. "Well, that was stupid, Dad. Act before thinking. Stupid. Stupid." It was an old book, probably valuable, and it tickled in the back of her mind that it had something to do with Hemi's and Renegade's deaths. "Stupid. I shouldn't have tossed it out there. I thought he'd go get it. So friggin—"

"I don't want to kill you or your dad, Christmas!"

"Then why the hell are you shooting?" Piper hollered. "*You* drop the gun, Spaceman. *You* throw it out where we can see it." She and her

232

dad had the height, a little better vantage and position ... but her former friend, though not far away, was too well hidden. She couldn't lay prone at the opening, not with the sling. Maybe she could crouch low enough, or lay on her side. She eased to her knees and crawled even with her dad.

"Not happening! And here's the thing, Christmas, I've got dynamite, and I will use it if I have to. I can lob a stick up there and end your pretty little ass. But I'd rather not do that."

"Because it would mess with your digging operation?"

"Ha! I gave up on that one, Christmas. There's nothing there. I told you not to come out here. You're trespassing!"

Piper realized he must have sped away from the Fort Campbell base after she'd called and told him she was going to his land to look around. The timing fit. He could have made it here in an hour or so, spent another half hour working his way through the woods to find them.

"I want all of us to walk away happy from this. Throw out the guns and let's talk. Don't be an idiot, Christmas."

"Shit," Piper muttered. "Can't see him, Dad. Even if I could, I don't want to shoot him. Can't shoot him. Can't do it."

She wouldn't get answers if she killed him, and she needed answers to settle her soul. Against the wall, in the shadows, she knew Spaceman couldn't see her either. She reached down and unstrapped her ankle holster, took it off and hid the gun. "He's my friend, Dad." *Used to be my good friend.*

"Some friend. Well, I can shoot the son of a bitch. He's not my friend," Paul said. "But you're right. He's hunkered down. All I see is green." Paul fired then, three times in a spread. "Maybe get him to move, show himself."

"That's it! Last chance, Christmas! I've got dynamite."

"Shit." Piper stood and stepped forward and hurled her service pistol, watching it arc and come down in a patch of tall sawgrass. "There you go, Spaceman! Happy? There's my gun. Let's talk."

"What are you doing?" Paul's tone was ice.

"Saving us *and* him, I hope," Piper whispered. "If he really wanted to kill us, he would have waited until we left this hole and climbed down the rocks. He would have waited and killed us then."

"All the guns, Christmas!"

"Stay here, Dad. Please. Please. Please. Don't argue with me. I really don't think he's going to shoot to kill." Paul grabbed at her good arm. She shook it off and stepped past the opening, her shoulders brushing the sides. Louder: "I'm coming down, Spaceman. I'll be an easy target. I'm not moving so fast right now." She counted on him not shooting; they used to be good friends, right? No one else needed to die; he'd said that.

"Piper! Don't do this." Paul made another grab for her, but she was already heading down the rock face.

"I have to do this. Stay up there," she begged him. "Stay sharp, Dad."

"All the guns!" Spaceman called. "Your ankle gun, Christmas. I know you have one."

"No ankle gun!" She was halfway down and balanced herself against the stone, carefully bent and raised her pantleg. She was wearing jeans and had to tug to get the material up to her knee, the action setting her off balance. She held her breath, grabbed the rock, and righted herself. "See? No gun."

"The other leg!"

It was more difficult to reach across and pull up the left pantleg, but she accommodated him. "Good enough, Spaceman?"

"Your dad's guns, too!"

"We're starting with mine," Piper returned. "Let's talk Spaceman. Just like you suggested. Me and you. It's between me and you." She reached the bottom of the hill, raised her right hand and spread her fingers so he could see she wasn't armed. She guessed, at best, he was a dozen yards away. "Can't raise the other arm, but you can see that."

"You come forward. Good. A little more. Stop. You stop right there."

Piper could tell where he was now, crouched behind a tight weave of chokeberry bushes. Her dad couldn't get a shot at him there. She saw the rifle barrel, aimed at her.

"Tell me about Jonathan Swift," she encouraged. "And Charles Weger and why Hemi and Renegade had to die."

"They shouldn't've died," Spaceman said. She had to strain to hear him over the *shush* of branches in the breeze. He was talking softly. "All a misunderstanding."

"Was it a misunderstanding, you shooting at me and my dad?"

"Just warning shots, getting your attention. You know that. Don't want to kill you, Christmas. If I wanted that, I could have waited until you climbed out. I just want you off my property. Shouldn't've come out here. Should've listened to me. Don't need to kill you."

"Could've fooled me," she said. "You're aiming a gun at me right now."

The barrel lowered a few inches, and his voice came out as a hiss. "You don't listen, Christmas. So bullheaded. I *told* you, I *insisted* you not come out here. Hell, I shouldn't have had you out last weekend. Shouldn't have had any of you here."

"But you did."

"There was a misunderstanding," he repeated.

"Tell me about it, Tom. What's this about? This misunderstanding?"

The barrel inched up again. Piper risked a glance over her shoulder; she could barely see her father in the crevice. Only a good marksman would be able to take a shot at him, and Spaceman was a very good shot.

"Buried treasure," Spaceman said after a few moments. "Misunderstanding and buried treasure."

"Follow the money," Piper said in a low voice. "Lennie Briscoe said you always follow the money."

"Who's Briscoe?"

"Who's Jonathan Swift and Charles Weger to you, Spaceman? Why the fascination with *Gulliver's Travels*?"

The wind teased the leaves and tiny branches of the chokeberry bushes. From somewhere overhead a hawk cried. Piper kept her eyes on the gun barrel.

"*Gulliver's Travels.* Shit, when you were ogling those old books in

235

my cabin you didn't know what you were looking at. Wrong Jonathan Swift. Should've hid those books, I should have. You shouldn't've seen them. Never should have invited you here."

Piper's throat tightened. She'd been pretty sure when she came down the slope that Spaceman wouldn't shoot and that this could end peacefully. Doubting that now, queasiness took root.

Drop the gun. Drop the gun, Spaceman.

"So tell me about the right Jonathan Swift." Piper slowly lowered her right arm.

The barrel didn't waver. She spotted Spaceman's eyes and the bridge of his nose. There was a tree directly behind him.

"Can I come closer?" She gave him a few beats to answer and then inched forward. "Can I come in there?"

Still no answer. Still the gun didn't move.

She walked forward until she was right against the chokeberry and saw where she could work through the bushes.

"I gotta see you, Space." Piper sucked in a breath, the air filled with the scents of wildflowers and her sweat. She hoped her dad was staying put, at least until she could distract Spaceman. She turned sideways and pressed between the branches that grabbed at her clothes and scraped the skin of her right arm.

"Stop right there."

She did, midway through the greenery, the bushes almost as high as her shoulders.

"Okay, a little closer. A little. There. Stop there."

Piper was through the bushes, and Spaceman growled, his gaze shifting from her to the crevice. He wore jeans and a camouflage-patterned t-shirt, sweat stains heavy under his armpits, beads of sweat on his forehead.

"About Jonathan Swift?"

"The only Jonathan Swift that matters."

"Please put the gun down, Space."

Spaceman leaned back against the trunk, slid down it with a grating sound, pieces of bark fell away. He laid the rifle across his knees and looked up at her. "Old Swift."

She swore his eyes were glossy, like he was fighting off tears. "Please, tell me about old Swift."

"My grandfather said one of his ancestors knew Swift, that he'd been on this property, lived here, hiding out for a while."

"And what does that have to do with treasure and a misunderstanding?" Piper edged closer and Spaceman raised the gun off his knees. From where he sat now, he couldn't see the crevice where she'd left her father.

"Sometime in the mid-seventeen hundreds Jonathan Swift—not the writer—was said to have buried ore and silver bars worth a hundred and fifty thousand dollars, and my grandfather said it's somewhere on this land. Gramps could never find it. I promised I'd split it with the old man when I found it, and with my buddy who helped me look."

"Weger. Your buddy Weger." Piper's voice was flat. "I figured out that you knew him. He was a year older than you, but he'd been held back in school. Found the yearbook online, saw you graduated in the same class. Did some digging and discovered he was a mechanic for your grandfather's used car lot."

"Sharp, Christmas. Always thought you were sharp. He tried to join the Army when I did," Spaceman said. "Charlie couldn't have passed the drug test. Too, he had asthma pretty bad back then. Cleared up some, the asthma, days you wouldn't know there was a thing wrong with him, but he still had lung trouble sometimes. Days he couldn't come out here, he was wheezing so bad. Never kept him from hunting, though."

"But he wasn't out here to hunt last weekend, was he?"

"Don't think so, no. Why'd you have to come back here, Christmas? Local sheriff, he's not going to pursue this. It's a closed case as far as he's concerned. Why'd you have to come back?"

Because it was festering, Spaceman. Because I couldn't let it drop.

"I saw his yearbook pictures, tall, thin," Piper said. "I remember that you asked me if I'd seen the shooter. If he was tall, thin. I thought you might've been talking about Gonzo. But you weren't. You knew then the shooter was Weger, didn't you? When I radioed you about Hemi being dead, and Renegade, you knew it was Weger."

Spaceman drummed the fingers of his left hand on the stock. "I didn't want to shoot Charlie. I really didn't. I'm really broke up about that. He was a good friend, a partner."

"In your treasure hunt."

"I'd never shot a civilian before. I didn't want to shoot him."

"What was he doing out here? Why did he kill Hemi and Renegade? You know, don't you? You know *why* he was shooting. You know all of it. What the hell, Space? Was it all—"

"Hell, Christmas, Charlie didn't know I was having my Army buds out here for paintball. I told him a few weeks ago, but he said he forgot. That's on me. I should've reminded him. I should've called. He just forgot, that's all of it. He saw Hemi, big, with his paint rifle. Charlie said he was pretty sure you all were *really* armed and were out here looking for the silver. He hadn't seen me when he started shooting. Just saw Hemi and Renegade at first. Then he saw you and Brick. If he would've seen me, things would've been different. He wouldn't've fired."

"How'd he get out here, Space?"

"Charlie'd come in from the parking lot on the other side of the ridge, the way he usually came, so he didn't have to trek through the trees. Asthma, you know. Safer route for him, more level until you get to the ridge. Longer, but easier to walk it. He saw the guns and the backpacks, didn't know it was paint, had forgotten all about my paintball weekend. He figured you were out to steal the treasure, which I'd promised him a share of. He said it was a mistake. He said he was sorry."

"Treasure." Piper spat the word. "Treasure. Silver in the backwoods. What the hell were you—"

"Smoking? I was smoking a little pot for sure." Spaceman offered her a sad smile. "There really is treasure out here, Christmas, on my land. The silver's real."

"Bullshit," Piper said. There was death, though, Hemi and Renegade and Weger. That was real.

"No, seriously. Silver in the ground. My grandfather knew it, had never been able to find it when his back was good. Jonathan Swift's treasure."

"No treasure is worth Hemi's and Renegade's lives!" Piper yelled.

"Well, I agree with you there," Spaceman said. "I'm not the one who killed Hemi. Or Renegade. And I didn't make Brick a cripple and I didn't break your arm. Damn shame this happened. If there was a do-over in life, I wouldn't have had the paintball here last weekend. I'd had them before, and Charlie'd not been out here those times, knew to stay away. Hadn't forgotten those times. There's no way our game would have messed with my treasure hunt. Hadn't before. Wasn't supposed to last weekend. No digging involved, no scenario objective would've sent anyone underground or into one of the mines. It should've been safe, the secret safe. But Charlie said he forgot. Just forgot."

"Jonathan Swift, eh? All of this pain and grief for some man who didn't write *Gulliver's Travels* but supposedly buried a treasure on your property. It's bull—"

"No, it's real." Spaceman's eyes were wide, unblinking, and bored into Piper. "Old Swift, he was a British sailor. Him and a few others, including a man named George Mundy, who'd been a captive of the Shawnee in Kentucky, mined silver from along a large, rocky creek. They had some trouble with the Indians, so they buried several loads of their gain. That's the short version of the story. In one of the spots —in 1769—Swift and Mundy planted about thirty thousand English crowns and marked the area by carving their initials on a beech tree. Well, me and my friend Charlie, we found that old, old tree, and after a lot of digging found the crowns. They're all nice and tucked away in some safe deposit boxes in town. They're real, the silver. But they're only worth about a half a million. I want the rest of what Swift buried on my land. I just haven't found his other hidey-holes yet." Spaceman stood again, raising the rifle, pointing it at her. "But I will find them." Louder: "You, old man Blackwell. Drop your gun or I shoot your daughter."

Piper looked over her shoulder, seeing above the bushes. Her father had been approaching.

"Don't think I won't kill her! Hold up the gun. There, that's it. Now drop it. I'm a good shot, old man. I won't miss." He drew in a short breath. "The one at your ankle, too. Now!" Spaceman pointed the barrel at Piper's head. "There, that's a good police chief. Now you back up. Farther. Farther. All the way to the rocks."

"That's a lot of money, half a million," Piper said, trying to hold his attention. "And now you won't have to share it with Weger."

"Half a mil is nothing next to the motherlode. I did some research, Christmas, spent some time with a coin collector at Fort Campbell. Figured out just how much silver would have been involved back in 1760, based on what Swift said he buried. Following me, Christmas?"

Piper didn't answer.

"Eighteen million. Except I'd told Charlie it was only a million. I never told him about the other seventeen."

"Maybe there is no more to find. Maybe Swift came back and got the rest."

"Nope. Nope. Nope." Spaceman twisted his heels into the ground, looking to steady himself. Piper tensed, mulling her options. "Swift ended up back in England. Oh, he had plans to return to Kentucky and retrieve his treasure, but he was arrested for supporting the rebellious natives of Williamsburg and Boston, so says one of the journals I have."

"What ... three copies of it? Four?"

"And they're all a little different," Spaceman said. "But they all have the same thread about the treasure. The different versions are just making it a little tougher to figure out where it is. Some say he mined silver for nine years in Kentucky, finding the veins in a cave where he'd chased a wounded bear. In one version, Swift's pal Mundy found the silver when he'd been held by the Shawnee."

"Did he write them? All the different versions? Or maybe they're just tall tales like *Gulliver's Travels*."

"He wrote things when he was in prison." Spaceman seemed to enjoy talking about Swift. His shoulders relaxed just a little, but he didn't lower the gun. "Swift was in prison all through the Revolution, and by the time he got back to America, he was practically blind. He couldn't find his original journal and the map he'd drawn. He spent his last years in Bean Station, Tennessee. One of these journals supposedly came from his caretaker, the widow Renfro, the book you tossed into the grass. Shouldn't've done that. Pissed me off. The treasure's real, Christmas. I'm going to have more money than I'll ever be able to spend in one lifetime. Told my grandfather I'd split it with him. But he thinks the treasure is only a mil. I told him and Charlie the same."

"How about you let me and my dad leave?" Piper asked. "We'll go back home, leave you to the treasure, and—"

"I'm gonna be gone for the next three months," Spaceman said. "Deployment. How am I gonna keep you from coming back out here while I'm away?"

"It's your land. Your treasure."

"But you know about it."

Piper also knew that Spaceman *murdered* Charles Weger. Spaceman had said that Weger thought Hemi and Renegade had real weapons, and that they were out here looking for the silver. And for Spaceman to know that, he had to have talked to Weger before he shot him. That hadn't been self-defense. *But Charlie said he forgot*—that's what Spaceman had told her minutes ago. *Charlie said.* Spaceman figured Weger was a liability, would be grilled by deputies over the shootings, and he couldn't risk that. Spaceman killed his friend.

"I know you, Sheriff Christmas. You aren't going to walk away. I'm sorry."

Me too.

Piper dropped and thrust her right hand inside the sling that held her broken arm, where she'd stashed the small pistol that had been in her ankle holster. In the same motion, she pulled it out, cocked and fired, striking Spaceman high on the left side of his chest, firing a second time at his left arm that held the rifle.

Pain shimmied through her arm and chest. Her throat tightened in response and she fought for breath as she stood and plowed forward, not waiting to see if he was going to drop, ramming her good shoulder into him and knocking the rifle from his hands. The back of his head cracked against the tree and he toppled. She followed through, kicked the rifle away, and straddled him at the waist, fighting the throbbing from her broken arm and aiming the pistol at his face.

"Don't move," she barked. "Don't twitch. Don't do a damn thing."

Blood oozed from the chest wound and darkened his t-shirt. More blood pulsed from his arm. She heard her father crash through the bushes.

"Don't want him to die, Dad!"

Paul stripped off his shirt, balled it up, and pressed it against the chest wound with his right hand. With his left, he reached into his jeans pocket and pulled out the car keys, tossed them to her.

"That's my girl. You're not supposed to drive," Paul said, putting both hands on the wound now. "But I'd get lost trying to find my way back to the car. Be careful. Be very, very careful. And hurry."

CHAPTER THIRTY-ONE

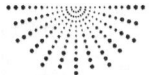

2 P.M. SATURDAY

Basil drove with Oren riding shotgun to three car lots in Owensboro, a small one thirteen miles away in Curdsville, another one twenty miles past that in Spottsville, and then reached the strip between Henderson, Kentucky, and Evansville where a trio of large dealerships sprawled. His eyes were getting blurry looking at cars and trucks and chrome. They stopped for a quick lunch at Bangie's Café, feasting on stuffed peppers, macaroni salad, and two overlarge sodas to go, one without caffeine.

Evansville would have even more car lots, and they might not get through it all today. But in the end, Basil didn't have to worry about searching there.

They found the blue pickup at their second stop north of Henderson and before they reached the bridge. They were about forty miles from Rockport and the sheriff's department.

The mechanics hadn't started on it yet. The baby blue Chevy C10 was behind the main building among a string of vehicles that eventually would be repaired, polished, and displayed on the used car side of the dealership.

Basil radioed Diego to get a search warrant and bring it to the lot. The truck wasn't going anywhere, but Basil was staying with it nevertheless, not taking his eyes off it. Oren got the dealership's permission to search it and collect evidence. Still, Basil wanted the search warrant to be safe and official, and before the afternoon was over they'd move the truck back to Spencer County. He contacted the Henderson County Sheriff's Department to let them know about the Fulda homicide and the truck as evidence; there would be no problem taking the Chevy back to Indiana.

Since the dealer was the new owner, Basil knew there was no longer an expectation of privacy on behalf of the previous owner. He took video and stills, elated they'd discovered the truck and that it hadn't been hidden. Oren had been right; the owner had wanted some money for the vintage pickup.

"Doesn't need a whole lot of work," the head mechanic explained. "Not going to cost all that much. Just need to replace one headlight and the grille, fix the hood and bumper and left front panel. Little bit of rust and chipped paint near this spot on the hood, but that's all relatively easy. Touch up some paint. Interior's spotless. It was loved."

It was a 1965 Chevrolet C10 short bed Fleetside with a rare big rear window and a V8 automatic transmission. Tinted windows and vents, new bed wood with several coats of polyurethane, and a first-class Bluetooth stereo.

"You can tell the interior dash was updated recently. I'd say in the past year or two. Leather seat covers installed, better carpet, twenty-two inch wheels," the mechanic said. "A beautiful vintage pickup. One of our salesmen is interested in it. Probably will sell it without ever putting it out on the lot. Provided you tell us we can sell it."

"Eventually," Basil said.

The warrant and Diego arrived an hour later.

Oren and Basil got out their evidence kits and went to work while the mechanic copied the paperwork for them. They'd go over the truck a second time at the department. The former owner had brought the truck in Tuesday morning and traded it in on a new dark blue Toyota RAV4. Basil thought it might have been the one he'd spotted driving past Chris Hagee's house the other morning, the sticker still on the window.

"The owner said she hated to part with it, but figured rather than pay for repairs it would be better to get something brand new, with good mileage and easier to steer," the mechanic said.

The previous owner was Gretta Mueller.

"Next stop, G's Bar," Basil said.

"The next stop for you," Oren told him. The chief deputy had been on his cell phone and stared out across the sea of cars. "Please take me back to Owensboro. My dad's gone."

CHAPTER THIRTY-TWO

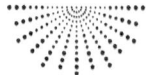

6 P.M. SATURDAY

Piper sat behind her desk, exhausted, aching, abysmally down, and yet strangely placated that she'd gotten some resolution about the deaths of Hemi and Renegade ... and Charles Weger. Spaceman—Tom Carpenter—was under arrest for murder, two counts of attempted murder, and a variety of lesser charges, and was being held in the hospital in Hartford, KY.

She'd turned her cell phone over to the Ohio County sheriff. It had kept recording while in her pocket, caught the entire exchange between Spaceman and her. That confession, plus testimony from her and her father, would send her once-friend to prison for twenty-five years to life. Kentucky had the death penalty, but she suspected Spaceman could dodge that. Maybe he'd resume the hunt for Jonathan Swift's silver when, or if, he got out.

Brick was out of intensive care. She'd go visit him in a few days and tell him about the paintball weekend aftermath. He'd never walk again, but at least he'd have use of his arms.

She was patched up—her left hand wholly bandaged, which a paramedic managed in spite of her sling; a cut on her right arm stitched; and her left ankle wrapped. Somehow she'd managed to sprain it.

She'd called Nang a few moments ago, gave him an abbreviated report on her day's adventure, and invited him and Magoo over tomorrow night instead; she had an ample supply of Tombstone pepperoni pizza and a twelve-pack of Mountain Dew. She still had some work to do tonight, and tomorrow afternoon was the funeral for Oren's father. Observant Jewish, he was being buried within twenty-four hours of his death.

Piper shuddered and closed her laptop.

There'd been way the hell too much death in the passing of a week.

"Ready?" Basil stood in the doorway. "Sure you want to come with me?"

"Yeah," she said. "Hell, yeah. I want in on this. I've never been to G's Bar."

"It's a rocking place." Basil's voice was heavy with sarcasm.

He'd radioed dispatch after dropping Oren off at the memory care center in Owensboro an hour ago. Piper had just come in and told him she wanted to go to Fulda, Diego, too, in a separate Explorer. She clipped her body cam to her shirt, saw Basil do the same, and settled in the passenger seat to take in the scenery on the road to the bitty-burg.

Piper could have driven, had managed it on Spaceman's property, out on a county road until cell reception kicked in and she could dial 9-1-1. But Basil was driving now; this was his case. He'd found Hagee's body. She was just shotgun tonight. And that was fine.

The Nitty Gritty Dirt Band was singing *Fishin' in the Dark* on the jukebox when they entered. Four young women surrounded one of the pool tables at the front of the bar, and roughly two dozen patrons spread out among the tables, most of them with beer glasses on coasters and an assortment of sandwiches. It was a sizeable crowd for the tiny town.

Henry and Dale Tucker sat at the end of the bar.

"Doesn't get more convenient than this," Basil said. "God is smiling on us."

Gretta scowled in Piper's direction and balled up the towel she'd been wiping the bar with.

247

"They don't look happy to see us." Diego held back behind Piper and Basil, posted himself near the door like a sentry.

Piper turned on her camera. "I'm just going to watch," she told Basil. She caught his slight grin.

The detective walked to the bar, standing directly in front of Gretta Mueller. Gunther hurried out of the kitchen and took up a spot near the cash register, eyes locked on Basil. The place had gone silent, save for the Dirt Band. Everyone was intent on Basil and Gretta.

"Found your pickup," Basil told her. "The vintage ride, the pretty blue one."

"I don't have a pickup" Gretta returned. Her voice had a sharp edge. Piper watched the woman rub her palms on her apron. "I drive a RAV4. I needed something newer, better mileage."

"Saw it, the RAV4" Basil said. "Shiny blue, several shades darker than the pickup you owned. You hadn't taken the sticker off the window when you passed me at Chris Hagee's house."

"What's this about?" Gunther raised his voice and stepped next to his sister. They stood shoulder-to-shoulder. Piper noted the similarities in their builds and features.

Basil looked from Gretta to Gunther. "Gretta hit Chris Hagee with her pickup. Ran him over. Hit him so hard she damaged the truck, then dumped it at a dealer in Henderson."

"I did no such—"

"Figured she'd get rid of it to hide the evidence, the broken headlight, grille, damage to the hood and the bumper. Quite an impact. She sent Chris Hagee flying."

Gretta's face colored. "I did no such thing!"

"We've got the truck back at the department. Pictures. Plenty of evidence. Chris Hagee was struck with that truck. It was your truck. Are you saying you weren't driving it?"

"Does she need an attorney?" This came from Henry Tucker.

Piper saw that Dale had started to sweat, his face beaded up, his fingers twitching.

"That's up to her," Basil said.

Piper prayed Gretta would make this easy and keep talking. A request for an attorney would end the questions to her.

"I don't need a damn lawyer. I didn't do anything wrong," Gretta growled. "You get out of my bar. All of you."

Basil didn't move. The Dirt Band stopped singing and another tune started, Willie Nelson crooning about *Whiskey River*.

"Was someone else driving your truck?" Basil persisted. His voice was as smooth as glass. "Did someone else run over Chris Hagee?"

"Don't say anything Gretta," Henry warned. "They're just out here fishing. Chris Hagee hung himself. Everyone in the county knows Hagee was messed up in the head. His wife left him. He hung himself in the garage."

"He couldn't have hung himself," Basil said. "He wasn't conscious, was he? And he had a broken arm. He couldn't have done it."

Piper was surprised Basil revealed that, but maybe it was a tactic to get them to talk.

"Chris Hagee looked like he was dead, didn't he?" Basil's voice was a purr. "Run over, bloody. Unconscious. He didn't string himself up, did he?"

Gretta slammed her fist against the polished bar, the glasses jumping. "That son of a bitch," she spat. "Hagee was an asshole, and you know it."

Henry was on his feet. "Gretta, stop. She needs an attorney. Sheriff, stop this."

"Everyone knew it, that he was an asshole," she ranted. "Blustering. Coming in here, waving his petition. Demanding *I* be arrested. Me! Claimed I'd broken the law 'cause I gave Henry a few beers. That asshole—"

Gunther placed a hand on his sister's arm. "Calm down. Don't say anything else. We can—"

Gretta shook off his hold.

"Gretta," Henry cautioned a little louder. "You need an attorney. Don't say—"

"It was an accident, Henry, and you're well aware of that. An accident. I hit that asshole by accident."

"Lawyer," Henry said, the word soft. He looked defeated. Behind him, Dale slipped off the stool and started to edge toward the door. Piper interposed herself.

"Go on," Basil encouraged. "I know you hitting him was an accident. You didn't run him over on purpose."

"Gretta, shut up," Gunther said. "You don't need to—"

"I just didn't see him walking across the road to the parking lot. I didn't know he was out there, that son of a bitch." She lowered her voice. There was a meanness to it now, and her face looked venomous. "He'd come here so late that night, strolling in. I was just closing. I told him to leave. I didn't know he'd stayed around outside. I'd told him to leave. An accident. I didn't mean to hit him, didn't mean to kill him."

Piper knew the state's murder statute and figured Gretta wouldn't qualify. An accident, Gretta had thought Chris Hagee was dead. Vehicular manslaughter maybe, though he didn't die from being struck. Manslaughter likely, or involuntary manslaughter. Maybe she'd get five years or more. Maybe the Tuckers, too.

"Dale and Henry helped you," Basil speculated. "You asked their help in covering it up, making it look like Chris Hagee had committed suicide."

Gretta glared. Patrons' whispered conversations became a susurrus that competed with the fading notes of Nelson's tune.

"They tossed Mr. Hagee in the back of your truck, and you drove to his house. They hauled his body up the ladder in his garage and put a rope around his neck, staged a suicide. That would leave you blameless, if it worked." Basil looked between Gretta and Gunther. "Did your brother help, too? Or was it just you and Dale? And Henry? I can put Henry and Dale in that garage."

"Lawyer," Henry said. "I want a lawyer."

"He's not talking to you, Mr. Tucker," Piper warned.

"I want a lawyer," Henry repeated.

"Gunther helped!" Dale blurted. "Not just me and Dad. Gunther helped, too."

"Shit." Gunther's eyes were daggers aimed at the Tuckers.

"We weren't there when it happened," Dale continued. He ignored his father jostling him. "Gunther called us, told us Hagee got hit, said he'd loaded him on the truck and needed help."

"Piss," Gunther said. Then resignation overcame his face.

"Lawyer," Henry whispered.

"Yeah, *I* helped her," Gunther said. "*I* put that asshole in the truck. I called Henry and told him to meet us at Hagee's. I've got a bad back. I needed someone to help me hoist him up the ladder. Hard enough on me to get him in the truck. Henry and his son came over. But they didn't do anything wrong. They didn't hit that asshole. I didn't hit that asshole either."

They just helped Gretta try to cover it up, Piper thought.

"So you and Gretta drove Chris Hagee home," Basil said. "And you met the Tuckers there."

The whispers crescendoed. Some patrons pulled out cell phones and started taking pictures, recording video.

"Lawyer," Henry repeated. "Lawyer. Lawyer. Lawyer."

Piper knew they were all right at the moment if they didn't talk to Henry. Gretta and Gunther had not asked for an attorney, neither had Dale.

Gunther continued. "Hagee wasn't moving all that much when I picked him off the road, just moaning a little and twitching."

Piper's eyes widened. They'd *known* Chris Hagee was still alive after Gretta had struck him! "Moaning and twitching" was evidence of life.

"I knew he was gonna be dead soon," Gunther said. "I knew he couldn't survive that accident. He'd been thrown a good ten, twelve feet. I knew he was on his way out of this world. Hell, when Dale and Henry hooked the rope to him, he was barely breathing. He was gonna die anyway."

Barely breathing.

But he wasn't dead yet, not when they hung him. The coroner

251

thought he could have survived if he'd had help. Hanging Chris Hagee killed him.

"Kidnapping," Basil said. "Murder."

"It was an accident," Gretta maintained.

"You all have the right to remain silent," Basil told them.

It was going to be a long night to tie up all the ends.

From the jukebox, Deana Carter started singing *Strawberry Wine*.

CHAPTER THIRTY-THREE

6 P.M. SUNDAY, SEPTEMBER 13TH

Piper wore a pair of faded sweatpants and the big comfy t-shirt Nang had bought her at August's county fair. The shirt was sky blue, like the pickup that had struck Chris Hagee, and read: *Sic Me Another*, advertising Clint Holster's big country hit. It was casual attire that she managed to put on with her arm in the sling, and much more comfortable than the dress she'd worn to the funeral.

She opened the door to see Nang standing there, his dog on a leash.

"That doesn't look like the picture of Magoo you showed me."

He grinned sheepishly.

The dog was singular, ugly, *butt ugly*, Piper thought. It was big, probably close to a hundred pounds, maybe more, and it appeared to be a mix of shepherd, pointer, some flavor of retriever, and maybe a touch of Great Dane.

The fur was patchy and shades of black, gray, and off-white, with an egg-shaped brown spot on the top of its head. Its front feet pointed outward, the legs slightly bowed. It had one eye, the left removed and sewn shut, leaving a depression, and part of its left ear was missing. The dog had a pronounced underbite, the lower jaw protruding beyond the upper, the visible teeth large and crooked.

It was worse than butt ugly.

It looked like Dr. Frankenstein had assembled the dog from discarded spare parts.

She stared at it, wholly at a loss for words.

"Can we come in? The shelter says Tater is housebroken, never messes in his kennel. He's very friendly."

"Tater?" Piper waved them in and closed the door, still staring at the dog.

"They've been calling him Tater. I figured he was used to the name and I should keep it. Suits him, don't you think?"

Camaro raised his head and regarded the visitors with suspicion. Marmalade left his perch on the coffee table, hissed, and retreated to the kitchen.

"What happened to Magoo, the pug you wanted?"

Nang stroked Tater's head. The dog wagged his tail, sending a breeze Piper's way. His tongue lolled and a line of drool appeared and stretched to the floor.

"There were fifteen people on the list hoping to adopt Magoo. My name was at the top. I could've brought him home. I almost did. Cute dog, and I *really* wanted a pug. I got to pet him while I was there. Sweet dog."

"But—"

"But nobody wanted Tater. He'd been at the shelter for more than a year. They thought he was maybe two or three years old. Has Cushing's Disease." Nang quickly added: "It's not contagious. I have to give him a special diet and some medicine once in a while. They said maybe he'll live another three years, four if I'm lucky and he's lucky. I didn't want to leave him there, so I left Magoo to one of the other people on the list. What do you think of Tater?"

Piper just stood there, unblinking.

"Say something," Nang encouraged. "What do you think? Say something, please."

Her left hand was still bandaged from yesterday's ordeal, and her arm still in the sling. She met Nang's gaze and held out her right hand. It had the engagement ring on it.

"I say yes," Piper said.

THE END

ACKNOWLEDGMENTS

Many thanks to Robert Scales for his legal eyes; Bill Gilsdorf for teaching Piper how it's properly done; Dr. Carla Rafferty for helping with my wounded sheriff; Brian A. Hopkins for arming my shooter; Mike Black for his military touches; Jody Flener of the Ohio County Tourism Office for her help with the real Jerusalem Ridge; Ohio County librarians for their maps and shared knowledge; Mary Hadley, the owner of The Gold Nugget, for valuing my treasure; Vicki Steger, Donald J. Bingle, Janet Deaver-Pack, and Christine Verstraete for their reviews; Mindy Mymudes for her promotion and encouragement; and Missy, Hunny, and Fable for keeping my feet toasty warm and my heart happy.

SPENCER COUNTY, INDIANA

It's a real place, about as far south in Indiana as you can go. The towns, roads, and some of the businesses I reference in this novel exist. There really is a Santa Claus—it's nestled between the Ohio River and Interstate 64. On my visit to the Christmas store there I picked up some walnut fudge and a Boston terrier ornament that I had personalized with Missy's name. Rockport is about twenty miles away from Santa Claus, and is where the real Sheriff's Department sits. I've fictionalized the county, taking considerable liberties. I used to live in Indiana—Evansville, during my newspaper reporter days. Spencer County isn't far from there. The place is a good home for Piper Blackwell and company. I also took some liberties with Jerusalem Ridge and Horse Branch, KY, real places thick with bluegrass music and mosquitoes and lacking cell phone service.

ABOUT THE AUTHOR

I write…a lot.

And I write with dogs wrapped around my feet. I get to wear sandals or bedroom slippers to work, and old, comfortable clothes. When the weather is fine I get to write on my back porch. I love summer. I started getting published when I was twelve, studied journalism at Northern Illinois University, and then went to work as a news reporter...eventually for Scripps Howard, where I managed their Western Kentucky bureau. Getting itchy feet, I moved to Wisconsin and went to work for TSR, Inc., the then-producers of the Dungeons & Dragons game. I wrote Dragonlance tales for several years and reached the *USA Today's* Bestseller list with a few of them.

I've written forty novels (along with a couple of ghosted projects), more than a hundred short stories, and I've edited more magazines and anthologies than I care to count. Right now it's all about mysteries...thrillers, suspense, and uncozy-cozies.

My novel, *The Bone Shroud*, won the 2019 Soon To Be Famous Illinois Author Project competition, voted on by librarian judges across the state. I was presented the award in the Adult Fiction category at the Illinois Library Association annual conference.

I attend game conventions—I am a geek about boardgames and rpgs, visit interesting and quirky museums, and at every reasonably good opportunity I toss tennis balls for my cadre of dogs. Wrinkles is named for my black pug.

Visit me at jeanrabe.com

OTHER BOONE STREET PRESS NOVELS BY JEAN RABE

The Dead of Winter

The Dead of Night

The Dead of Summer

The Bone Shroud

Fenzig's Fortune

The Finest Creation

The Finest Choice

The Finest Challenge